Far Away Home

The Knowing

J. T. Conners

Copyright © 2022 J. T. Conners
All rights reserved
First Edition

PAGE PUBLISHING, INC.
Conneaut Lake, PA

First originally published by Page Publishing 2022

ISBN 978-1-6624-7364-7 (pbk)
ISBN 978-1-6624-7363-0 (digital)

Printed in the United States of America

To Brian Conners, my rock.
Best roomy award goes to Chris Watson.
And finally, to life, for throwing me so many
curve balls; so far, I have hit them all.

Acknowledgments

I would like to thank Page Publishing for giving me this exciting opportunity and believing in my manuscript. A huge thank you also goes out to my literary agent, Robert Deluise, who called me every day to make sure I had all my questions and concerns taken care of. I also would like to acknowledge Jordyn Trisket, my publication coordinator, as well as the entire editing staff for being fast, friendly, efficient, and amazing at editing my manuscript to be the best that it could become. My gratitude goes to Mason Dodds (gvphotoart@mac.com) for such a wonderful author's photo and for making me feel beautiful. Last but not least, I want to thank my family for putting up with me shutting everyone out as I typed at my computer, immersing myself in my own little world of make believe.

Chapter 1

Sheye felt her shoulders instantly begin to relax as she turned onto the long dirt driveway leading up to the family cabin. She had been mentally strained the entire six-hour drive. Her muscles were tight with tension, but now she felt like she was home. It had been far too long since she had been to her family cabin since the death of her father a few years earlier. This had always been their place to get away from the drudgery of the world together. It was a place to hide away from their busy lives. It was their own private piece of heaven. The cabin lay in the middle of the woods with no other cabins or people nearby. The nearest hamlet with a small store was a two-hour drive from their remote cabin. One made sure they had absolutely everything they needed for an extended stay, as there was no leaving for a casual trip to town to pick up supplies. It had been far too long since Sheye had allowed herself to return. There were too many memories of her father here. She needed to grieve and overcome the loss of her father before she was able to face their sanctuary without him. Sheye's dad had been her only remaining family as well as her best friend. The cabin was a place of happiness and peace for them both. Sheye had convinced herself that she was finally ready to enjoy the cabin without her dad.

The driveway was long, unkempt, and bumpy from the last couple years of neglect. Sheye slowed her speed to make sure her horses, Onyx and Big Red, were not getting jostled around in the trailer as well as her best friend, Mandy, that was beside her in the passenger seat. Sheye giggled as she glanced at Mandy. She was being bounced and knocked about in her seat. Mandy was holding on for dear life with one hand on the side council and the other hand on, what her dad used to call "the holy shit handle," just above the window.

As Mandy was being treated like a bobblehead in her seat, she stated, "Wow, Sheye! When you said this was out in the boondocks, you were not kidding. You neglected to mention, however, about the four-by-four ride till your insides are on the outsides though."

Sheye giggled again but had to pay attention to the road as she came up on a slightly washed-out part of the driveway because of it being partially eroded down by the overflowing creek. It was slow going, but they all managed to make it through safely. They were soon pulling up in front of the coziest little cabin with a small barn and corral off to the side. The cabin was surrounded by lush green forest and a small creek flowing off to the side and down the edge of the driveway.

"Oh, my goodness!"—Mandy sat straight up in the seat and slid forward—"this is the most picturesque place that I have ever seen. Oh, Sheye, I could just die! I can't wait to see the inside. I hope it is as homey as it appears."

The two women exited the truck and stretched out their fatigued driving legs. It had been a prolonged drive, but now they were here. It had all been worth it. Sheye inhaled a deep breath of fresh mountain air and smiled at Mandy.

"Don't hold your breath, Mandy. I haven't been here in over two years. The inside is going to need a lot of maintenance before it will be back to the way it once was. Before we go in though, we need to remove the horses from the trailer. They can graze on all the tall grass in the corral. I will pump some water from the well out back for them."

Mandy pouted somewhat but did as she was told. Soon, the horses were corralled, watered, and contently munched on fresh wild grass within the overgrown corral.

Sheye and Mandy grabbed their bags, coolers, and packs and dragged everything up onto the porch. When they went toward the front door, Sheye faltered a little before unlocking and opening the door. She was anxious about how well the inside of the cabin held up as the outside was surprisingly in excellent condition. With an intake of breath, she unlocked the door and swung it open stepping inside. Everything was shrouded in a layer of dust, but it was exactly as her dad and herself had left the cabin the last time that they were here together. Suddenly tears welled up in Sheye's eyes. It was just as she remembered as she looked around. To the left was a small but pleasant living room with two rocking chairs, a small round coffee table with a throw rug underneath of it. There was an old worn but comfortable couch with a checkered quilt thrown over the back of it and a large soft lounge chair by the fireplace. The fireplace was on the side wall of the living room, with a large, mounted elk head looming on the wall above. There were some unlit candles and an old oil lantern on the mantel with a picture of herself and her dad when she was a young girl back when times were happy and carefree. The dining room table seated four and was made of solid oak her dad had made when he first purchased the cabin with matching chairs. The place mats were still on the table as well as a vase of antiquated flowers.

The minuscule yet fully functional kitchen was behind the table with a tall island. Two could sit and have coffee on the stools that were placed before it. There was a modest fridge, stove, and sink that had a window above it to look out into the trees as one washed the dishes. The side window by the dining room table was large, and the late afternoon sun was streaming through, revealing all the dust particles they had disturbed sifting in the air when they entered. Behind the kitchen was a small operational bathroom. Opposite the bathroom was a set of stairs leading to two small but quaint bedrooms. Each bedroom had a door exiting onto a shared balcony in the back. Sheye reminisced all the nights how her father and herself would go onto the balcony with cups of hot coco and watch the stars together. It was good to be back. She had missed being here so much.

"Sheye, this is the most perfect little cabin I have ever seen. It is rustic, simple but so snug and homey. This is going to be the finest three weeks of my entire year. I can just feel it. Thank you so much for the invitation. This is precisely what I required to get away."

Sheye chuckled at Mandy and turned back toward the porch to go back to the truck to move it away from the cabin.

"You won't say that after I tell you we need to unpack and then tidy up the cabin before the sun goes down."

Mandy groaned in the direction of her best friend. "Man, you are such a slave driver, all work and no play. Fine, but when we are done, I am going to kick your booty at a few games of Sequence, deal?"

Sheye smiled and headed down the steps and back to the truck and threw the comment, "Deal," over her shoulder as she exited the cabin.

By the time the sun descended below the mountain, the two women were exhausted. They relaxed by enjoying hot mugs of coco, munching on cheese and crackers, playing the game that Mandy mentioned earlier in that afternoon. Mandy was right; she was kicking Sheye's booty. Sheye looked at Mandy over her cards and smiled at her friend as she squealed out, "Sequence," yet again.

Mandy was a tiny four-foot-nine-inch ball of spitfire. They met each other at Mandy's job not long after Sheye's father had passed away. Mandy was the aerobics instructor at the local gym that Sheye had decided to join, to get her mind off the loss of her father. The two soon became fast friends. Mandy was a little drill sergeant in her class as she fired out orders to "move faster, stop whining, pick up those feet, and put some more pep in the steps." She was the Energizer bunny on steroids, with such an aggressive workout that Sheye all but forgot about her sorrow of losing her father when she was in Mandy's class.

Sheye had never sweat so considerably in her life. Even with all her martial arts training she had completed over her life to obtain her third-degree black belt, she had never worked so hard in any exercise class. Her martial arts training was nothing compared to Mandy's hour and a half class of hell every Monday, Wednesday, and Friday evenings. After the first couple of classes Sheye had attended, Mandy finally approached Sheye and introduced herself. Mandy welcomed her to the class and complimented on her being able to keep up with her being new to the classes. They soon found themselves going out for a smoothie after the third class, and they had been joined at the hip ever since. When Mandy found out that Sheye was the owner and operator of a horse stable that offered riding lessons, Mandy weaseled a deal from Sheye. Mandy would get free riding lessons in exchange for Sheye getting free aerobics classes. It was a bargain. Mandy was getting the better end of the deal from Sheye, but she had liked Mandy so much that it did not seem like a loss on her end either. This enabled her to spend more time with Mandy, and that was what mattered. Sheye did not have much time for friends. She was far too busy with her business, and that was okay until she met Mandy. Sheye was happy with her life, her business, and now with Mandy added to her life, and knowing that they were now the best of friends was all she needed in her life.

The two women could not be more opposite in appearance and personality if one had intended it to be. Mandy was petite, standing at only four foot, nine inches. She was loud and assertive with a short blonde pixie haircut. She had piercing blue eyes and was built like a tiny brick powerhouse.

Sheye, on the other hand, was tall, standing at six feet. She was quiet and introspective with long, thick, wavy dark-auburn hair. She had bright emerald-green eyes. She was very lean from all her experience horseback riding and martial arts training. She towered over Mandy. The height difference between the two was almost comical. They made quite the pair when they went out on the town. Men were attracted but very intimidated by them both. They were complete opposites in every sense of the word. Mandy was brass, loud, and performed everything with intense gusto for anything and everything she wanted. Sheye was a tall, stunning beauty that was the owner of a successful stable. Her stable raised some very renowned quarter horses for racing and breeding. The two women together were a powerhouse couple of ladies. This daunted every man who even tried to approach the two when they were out together, which was always.

If Mandy was not at the fitness center working, she was at the stables with Sheye. If Sheye was not at the stables at work, then she was with Mandy at the center in Mandy's class, or they were hanging out together. Mandy pretty much moved in with Sheye as well, especially after her terrible departure from her boyfriend. Mandy started helping Sheye at the stable when she was not teaching her class. Mandy loved the stables, as it also included riding lessons and boarding options on the side. This enabled Mandy access to some beautiful horses to assist and take care of. Sheye operated the business that had been her father's before he suddenly passed. He constructed the stables to be extremely successful over his lifetime. When he passed, Sheye inherited the business. Sheye knew all the ins and outs of the business because her father taught her everything that he knew over the years as she grew up.

As late spring was approaching, Sheye decided it was time to visit her neglected cabin. She invited Mandy to come and stay with her for three weeks to get away from the world for a while. This way, Sheye would have some support with her to go to the cabin since the passing of her father. She could spend quality time with her best friend in her favorite place in the world. Mandy also needed a getaway for a while. Her recent break up with her bodybuilding meathead of a boyfriend was not going well. This would hopefully enable Mandy the time to find peace and joy in nature. Mandy needed to get away from the lug nut that would not leave her alone.

Mandy jumped at the chance to leave for a while to let things cool off. Her ex-meathead did not believe that they had broken up as the truth. He kept coming around the gym bothering Mandy and was disrupting her business. He even started to cause trouble at the stables and blamed Sheye for Mandy leaving him. Stupid man. Mandy telling him over and over that "we are done and over with forever" obviously did not sink into that pea-sized brain of his. To many steroids had gone to the idiot's head was obvious to Sheye. Three weeks away was the best thing for them both.

"Sequence!" Mandy shouted again and laughed. "Wow, Sheye, you suck at this game. I don't mind though because I win again!" Mandy sure loved winning.

The two women laughed together, enjoying each other's company. Then Mandy let out a yawn loud enough for the horses to hear outside.

"Well, I don't know about you, darlin', I just hate beating you so much. It is no fun when you are not even trying. I need to get me some beauty sleep. All this perfection takes a lot of effort. The work you just put me through earlier, getting this place up to snuff, has done wore me out. I am off to bed. See you in the morning, sunshine." Mandy removed herself from the table, and Sheye followed suit. They both climbed the stairs and stopped at their bedroom doors.

"Good night, Mandy. Sleep well. Oh, I have a surprise for you. I will show you tomorrow. Get some good zzz's because it will take a bit of riding to get there."

Mandy clapped her hands excitingly and jumped up and down a couple of times. "Woohoo, I finally get to try out my riding lessons for real? Oh, Sheye, I can't wait. It sounds so adventurous and so what I need right now." The two entered their bedrooms and were both asleep so fast that their heads barely touched the pillows.

*****

After a few hours or so, Mandy awoke. A sound outside aroused her out of her slumber. Mandy rubbed her tired eyes. *Probably just the horses,* she thought. She yawned and slipped out of her cozy, warm bed. She padded out of her room and down the stairs to use the facilities. Mandy then decided to make herself a hot chocolate. For some reason, she was wide awake now. After she had a cup of steaming hot cocoa in her hands, she snuck quietly back up the stairs, into her bedroom, then out the back door in her bedroom, to have a seat on the balcony to watch the stars. Mandy breathed in a deep breath and exhaled slowly. It was so damn beautiful out here. No noise or hustle of the city. No sirens, traffic, or streetlights. All she could hear was the sound of crickets chirping and frogs croaking by the creek. She sagged in the chair and just listened for a while. It was almost meditative. The darkness amazed Mandy. She could barely see her hands in front of her face. The night sky was so filled with stars that the more you investigate the sky, the more stars upon stars could be seen. The sky looked almost cluttered with so many stars. Mandy had never seen the sky in such unpolluted beauty before. She had certainly not dreamed it could be so breathtaking. She did not want this night to end.

Mandy was about to take a sip of her cocoa when suddenly all the frogs and crickets became silent. She thought she heard a rustling noise coming not far from the cabin, a bit away from the balcony toward the woods. As she listened, she could not hear anything. The silence was deafening. Her hair stood up on the back of her neck, and her ears literally felt as if they perked forward to hear better. Again, she heard it. There was a rustle in the trees below, but this time, it was a little closer. Mandy's heart began to pound, and the blood rushed in her ears. She scoffed at herself.

"Stop letting your imagination freak you out, girl," Mandy said to herself. "The cabin is out in the middle of the forest. Of course, there are wild animals roaming around out there in the dark, you silly chit."

This time, when she heard the rustling, it was even closer to the balcony, and Mandy had to suppress a squeal bubbling up in her throat.

Oh god, Mandy thought, *what if it is a black bear, or worse, what if it's a grizzly bear? Can grizzly bears climb up balconies?* Mandy's mind was thinking of all the worst scenarios that could happen if a grizzly could climb when she stomped down her fear once again.

She giggled to herself for being so silly. Before she could stop herself, she quietly put her hot chocolate down, silently stood up, and went over to the railing. She convinced herself that she was safe up on the balcony from any predators, or so she hoped. Maybe, she would be able to see a real live grizzly without having to go to the zoo.

Wouldn't that be exciting, Mandy thought.

Mandy squinted to see better in the direction of where she heard the rustling. Her eyes were becoming a little more adjusted to the darkness, and to her surprise, she saw a dark figure of something looming in the trees. She leaned over the railing a little more to get a better look, and then she froze. This was no grizzly bear. Yes, it was an exceptionally large figure, but it was not moving like an animal. It was squatting and then moved into a standing position.

"Maybe it is standing up on its back legs and scratching its back on a tree." Mandy tried to persuade herself that it was a bear, but deep down, she knew that this was no bear. She leaned in closer to the railing and stared hard at the image. Suddenly, Mandy could hear Onyx and Big Red start to snort, whinny, and stomp around the corral at the side of the house.

Without hesitation, Mandy stepped back from the railing and exhaled, "Oh lord!" Mandy very quietly snuck back into the cabin with her heart pounding and her breath stuck in her chest. She stealthily locked the door and then proceeded to lock her windows in her bedroom. She then went throughout the rest of the cabin staying low and out of sight, which was not hard with her tiny stature. She locked all the windows and doors on the main floor, and then without hesitation, she bolted back up the stairs and entered Sheye's room and climbed on her bed.

Without a second thought, Mandy shook Sheye awake. "Sheye, honey, wake up. There is something or someone outside the cabin. Wake up, Sheye. I am scared."

Sheye moaned and rolled over to see Mandy looming close to her face, and she let out a slight yelp, but Mandy covered her mouth with her tiny hand and said, "*Ssshhh*, they may hear you."

Sheye sat up in bed and removed Mandy's hand from her mouth but quietly whispered, "What the hell, Mandy! Who will hear me? We are in the middle of nowhere, and it is the middle of the night."

Mandy leaned into Sheye's side and explained quickly what it was she had seen. When Mandy was finished with her quick explanation, Sheye promptly and silently slid out of bed and went down to the living room. Sheye could hear the horses making a ruckus outside as well, which put her on even more alert. She opened a cabinet close to the fireplace and took out a shotgun, quickly found the shells for the gun, and loaded it. Mandy was staying remarkably close behind Sheye and was in fact, holding on to the back of her pajama top. The two crept around to the side window by the dining room table. Sheye stood to the side of the window and peeked out. She could not see anything, so she crept to the kitchen window with Mandy still holding on to her pj's. Nothing was there either that Sheye could see, so she led Mandy up the stairs and checked out both bedroom windows. Again, she could not see anything. Sheye opened the window in her room to see if she could hear anything. She could not detect anything. Even the horses had calmed down. With a sigh, she triggered the safety on her gun and placed the gun on the end of her bed. She turned to Mandy, who was still gripping the back of her shirt.

"Mandy, let go of my shirt, hun. I can't see or hear anything. No one is out there, at least not anymore. Are you sure it was a bigfoot or a large man you saw? It could have been just the shadows looking like it was. The dark out here can sure play tricks with the mind and make you see things that are not there. I am only saying this because it used to happen to me all the time. My dad would always go and check out everything. Sometimes it would be a deer or an elk or a bear, but sometimes, it was nothing at all. We are so far out in the middle of nowhere. I am so sorry that you were scared, hun, but I am going back to bed." Sheye looked at Mandy, who did not appear appeased, so she stated. "Okay! Come on then! You can sleep with me!"

Mandy looked so relieved that she squealed a little, then gave Sheye a hug. They both crawled in and snuggled into Sheye's soft, warm bed. A restful sleep did not come to either of them though as each pop, creek, or snap of the cabin had them both spooked.

Chapter 2

The morning came too soon for both women as they had certainly not slept well after Mandy's middle-of-the-night panic fest. They survived the night though, with no one trying to break in, to both women's relief. Mandy slid out of bed, and when Sheye sat up and yawned, Mandy spoke. "I am so sorry about last night, Sheye. I was so damn sure it was a either a bigfoot or an exceptionally large man standing in the trees. My fear of the dark forest just got the best of me, I guess. I am such a city sissy, I know! I promise I won't let that happen again." Sheye sleepily smiled at Mandy.

"No worries, girl. It happens to the best of us. What an adventure for our first night alone in this lonely, spooky cabin, hey?"

Mandy picked up a pillow and tossed it at Sheye's head with a laugh.

"You darn right it was an adventure. There is so much more where that came from. You know me, Sheye, I am never boring."

Sheye crawled out of the bed and threw the pillow back at Mandy and hit her square in the head. "That's for keeping me up half the night thinking we were being invaded by a crazy mountain man." Soon, the two women were throwing pillows at each other in a good old-fashioned pillow fight laughing the whole while.

After Sheye and Mandy finished their pillow fight, they both separated and completed their morning routines. Then they met up in the kitchen for breakfast. They had oatmeal, some apple slices, and hot Earl Grey tea as they sat watching the beautiful morning out the large dining room window in silence until Mandy could not wait any longer.

"So what is this big surprise that you have for me today, Sheye? Don't keep me in suspense any longer. You now better than anyone that I have absolutely no patience in the slightest."

Sheye just smiled and shook her finger back and forth at Mandy as she stood up and started cleaning up the breakfast dishes. "It won't be a surprise if I tell you, silly! You are just going to have to learn to be patient as I won't cave to your demands. If I tell you, it won't have the same effect as you will be by seeing it for yourself."

Mandy stood up and stomped her foot but smiled surreptitiously. "All right then, suit yourself, but it better be spectacular whatever it is, or I will hold this against you. Mark my words."

Sheye had no doubt that Mandy would pretend to hold it against her. She knew that as soon as Mandy sees the surprise, she will forget all about holding the so-called grudge.

The two women cleaned up after breakfast and then packed a lunch. It was quite warm out already, so they both wore simple jeans and T-shirts with their riding boots and only brought a light jacket in case the weather changes to the cooler side. When they were done preparing for the day, they both went out to the corral and saddled the horses and packed up the saddlebags. Sheye helped Mandy with her saddle as she was much too short to get up onto Big Red herself. Big Red was sixteen-hands high and towered over poor little Mandy. Even though Red was a dark-red, large American Quarter horse, he was well suited for Mandy. He was gelded and calm with a cooperative temperament.

Mandy had trained with Red for over a year, and they knew each other well. Red had never thrown anyone and never spooked. He was a perfect fit with Mandy, and they worked very well together. Big Red followed Onyx anywhere he went, so controlling Big Red was not difficult when they rode together. Onyx, on the other hand, had a fiery personality. He was a heavy draft black Percheron that they used as war horses in France back in the old days. He was a tall seventeen-and-one-half-hand high with extreme intelligence and was very athletic. Sheye's dad purchased Onyx for Sheye when she was much younger. He wanted her to have a strong horse with high endurance for all their riding in the forest trails. Onyx would only let

Sheye ride him. Anyone else who ever tried to get on him was thrown instantly. When Sheye rode Onyx, it was like they were one being. Sheye's dad had given Onyx to her on her tenth birthday when he was just a two-year-old colt. Sheye had a hand in breaking him with her father, and now they trusted each other like best friends. Today, Sheye was twenty-four years old, and Onyx had been her trusted steed for fourteen years.

The horses could feel the excitement of the women and were just as ready for the day's ride as the women were. The ladies were finally situated. Both mounted their horses, and with a quick deep breath and excitement in her voice, Sheye looked back at Mandy. "Ready?"

Mandy gave Sheye a huge smile and replied, "I am so ready. Lead the way, girl. Lead the way." Sheye did not give Mandy a chance for a calm ride at first and spurred Onyx into a fast gallop as she turned him to the trail that headed away from the cabin and toward the mountains. Mandy was caught a little off guard at the speed of Sheye's galloping departure and grinned wickedly.

"So it's going to be like that, is it! Come on, Red! We can't let those two shows us up, can we?" At that, she did not need to convince Red to be on his way, as he was already beginning to gallop to catch up to his buddy that was tearing up the trail ahead of them.

The morning was breathtaking. The weather was perfect with a slight breeze, and the warm sun was not overly hot currently as it was only late spring. The duo invigoratingly galloped for a while and then slowed to a canter to enjoy the view as they rode. Both women were enjoying themselves so much that they almost missed the strange oval spot, flattened in the field as they rode by. Sheye only caught it out of the side of her eye as they were about to enter some trees again. She slowed Onyx a bit to look and then turned him around back to the small meadow. She stopped Onyx and slid off him and let his reins dangle. She knew he would not go anywhere when she dropped his reins. Onyx had been trained well, and then she entered the center of the strange oval burned site.

Mandy rode up beside Onyx but did not dismount.

"What the devil is this, Sheye?"

Sheye just shook her head and shrugged her shoulders. "I am not sure!" She bent down and examined the soil that was bare in the area she was standing on. The ground had been scorched somehow but only at the surface of the soil. All the grass had been charred in a perfect oval, and the area was about twelve or so feet in size. The tall grass was in perfect condition just outside of the scorched oval.

"Can you feel that, Mandy?" Sheye asked as she stood back up. "It's like a soft buzzing going through my entire body."

Mandy frowned at Sheye. "I don't feel anything."

Sheye rolled her eyes at Mandy and motioned for her to get off Red and join her in the circle.

Mandy said, sighing, "I am not sure if I want to stand in there. Something does not feel right, Sheye. What if it is radioactive or something?"

Sheye looked at Mandy and tsk'ed at her. "Just get down here, please. It is the weirdest feeling. I want to know if you feel it too or if I am just buzzing from the exhilarating ride."

Mandy let out a huge sigh but threw her short leg over Red, slid down as she mumbled how Sheye better help her get back up on Red when they decided to continue. Mandy entered the strange burned space.

"Oh my god, what the hell is that? I feel it too. It somewhat tickles the insides, doesn't it?"

Sheye and Mandy just stared at each other for a moment, and then Sheye shook her head. She headed over to Red and motioned to help Mandy get back on.

"I have an idea, Mandy. Let us get a better look up there on the hill and see this patch from up above."

The two women rode to the top of the hill ledge that was close by. When they looked down above the patch, they both gasped. The oval was dead center in the middle of the small meadow, and it was pitch-black. It was like someone had placed a black stamp on the grass. They were looking at a perfect oval scarred into the center of the meadow. Mandy pulled Red up beside Onyx and Sheye.

"What do you think could have achieved that, Sheye? Have you ever seen something like this up here before? Is this the damn surprise? If it is, I must tell you, it is the worst surprise, ever!"

"Oh, for heaven sake's, Mandy, this isn't the damn surprise! And no, I have never seen anything like this before, here or anywhere. It sure is strange though. No tracks in or out. It is just there like it appeared out of nowhere. Maybe someone is doing soil testing, or maybe it is some new thing the forestry is doing to check tree growth or something."

Mandy snickered. "Well, if you ask me, its spooky, and I don't like it. Can we just go? I don't even care about the surprise anymore. I just want to get away from this area. It feels amiss."

Sheye agreed wholeheartedly with Mandy but stated that she was still taking her to see the surprise. The surprise would defiantly cheer up their mood and make them forget about the weird scorched oval patch in the meadow. Sheye directed Onyx to the east, and they again headed off toward the mountainside.

After another twenty minutes of riding, the two women rounded a bend in the trees. There before them nestled in the opening of the trees backed by a mountain was the most beautiful lake. It even had a small waterfall at one end of the lake, by some low cliffs to the right of them. It cascaded cool, crisp water into the lake from a small river that fed the falls from the mountain runoff. It was like a hidden oasis in the middle of the forest. Mandy gasped as she pulled up alongside Sheye. She stared at the beauty of Mother Nature before her. It was the most beautiful place she had ever seen.

"Well, what are you waiting for? The last one in is a rotten egg." Sheye slid quickly off Onyx and was running toward the small outcropping of rocks, stripping her clothes off as she ran. Within minutes, Sheye was naked. With a barbaric yell, she jumped off the rocks and splashed into the cool water. Mandy whooped with joy as she watched her friend cannonball off the low rock shelf into the lake in her birthday suit and quickly slid from her saddle and followed suit.

Soon, the two were splashing, swimming, laughing, and having an amazing time enjoying the crystal clear blue water.

Sheye swam over to Mandy and said, "Swim with me. I have something else to show you." They swam toward the small waterfall, and suddenly Sheye dove below the water, but she did not come back up. Mandy began to panic. She was just about to call out when she heard Sheye calling to her from the other side of the waterfall.

"What are you waiting for Mandy? Swim your tiny, cute butt in here. Swim directly under the falls. Don't worry, it only takes a few seconds."

Mandy hesitated. "Oh, girl, this better be amazing. I have never swum under a waterfall before. "Okay, darlin', you can do this." Mandy plugged her nose with her left hand, and with a deep breath, she dove under the falls. Mandy came up from under the water gasping for breath. "I did it, woo-hoo! I did it!" Mandy was in awe when she cleared her eyes from the water. She saw that it was a small beautiful little hidden cave. Life could not get any better than this. She felt like she was in a scene from the movie *The Goonies*. Sheye was up on a flat rock shelf. Sheye reached down and helped Mandy exit the water as she climbed up the low rock shelf. "This is amazing, Sheye. It is dry up here too. How in the world did you ever find this remarkable gem?"

"My dad found it the year he had purchased the cabin. We went riding one day, and we came across this lake. It was hot out, so my dad suggested we go for a swim. I always wanted to play in a waterfall, so then we both swam over. My dad dove under and scared me to death when he did not come back up. I thought he had drowned. Then I heard him call out to me. He told me to do the exact same thing I had just did to you. He told me to swim under the waterfall. Ever since then, this has been our special secret spot. Every year after, we would always come here for a swim and visit our little cave. Isn't it cool? I wanted to share this with my best friend since my dad is gone, and he can't be here with me anymore. Now this can be our secret spot."

Mandy sat beside Sheye and gave her a hug. "This is the best surprise ever. You are off the hook. Thank you for not telling me before we came here. You were right. It is so much better experiencing this beauty firsthand than being told about it first."

The two naked women started to shiver, so they entered the lake again to swim for a while more.

When they both had enough of the water, they climbed up on the rocks and lay on the small outcropping of a rock shelf, still in the buff to dry off in the warm afternoon sun. Mandy giggled as they lay there. "Who would have thought skinny-dipping would be so much fun without any men around. It is so freeing to be here naked as Mother Nature intended, just soaking up the sun." Mandy sat up and turned to Sheye. "I know I have said this a lot lately, but again, thank you for inviting me, Sheye. Thank you for this breathtaking surprise."

Sheye did not feel it was necessary to respond with words, so she only smiled and nodded. Soon, both girls snoozed in the warmth of the sun on the rocks, peacefully thinking they were the only two people in the world at that very moment. It felt so wonderful.

Chapter 3

Two-hour-distance away from Sheye's cabin, in a small hamlet from where Sheye and Mandy lay sunning themselves, a pretty brunette was putting in her earbuds. She pushed play on her iPod for her jog down the familiar path that she took every afternoon for the last two years. After a few minutes into her jog, she was deep in the forest path. The small town was out of sight now. She jogged deeper into the forest with her music blaring in her ears. As she was getting into what was quite straight and even-grounded trail, she had a nice, steady jog. Suddenly, several deer darted out in front of her. The deer bolted past the jogger and into the trees on the other side of the path. The brunette was startled so much that she skidded on the gravel path landing hard on her bottom. Her right wrist twisted painfully as she came down with a heavy thud. With her heart pounding, she sat on the path for a minute catching her breath. She cursed out loud as she slowly stood up and brushed herself off. She looked down at herself, making sure that she was not hurt, bleeding, or had any torn or dirty clothing. "Stupid, crazy deer!" She had jogged up upon deer before but never had she had them dart out right in front of her, causing her to tumble.

Other than a sore wrist and some dirt on her shorts, she was none the worse for wear. Other than wounded pride she felt toward herself for falling and feeling like a fool, she collected herself and was about to get back to jogging when she noticed two very tall large figures standing a way down the path. They were both dressed in all black. The hair on the back of her neck rose, and her inner voice screamed *danger*. Being a victim of abuse before, she never even hesitated. She quickly spun on her heels and began to head back in the direction that she had come, only this time she was running now instead of jogging. Maybe they were just men in black jogging suits and hoodies. Maybe they just happened to be resting and talking together on the path, and she was just overreacting. She did not think so though as she always listened to her "Spidey senses;" they had never steered her wrong before. Besides, if she could believe her eyes, she could have sworn that they had helmets or head coverings on that covered their faces. If she could trust what she saw, that was super weird. The brunette rounded a bend in the path; she quickly glanced back to see if the men were following her. To her relief, she could not see them, and they were not coming up behind her.

She slowed a bit but decided to end her jog for the day. It was turning out to be a little too strange of a day for her. To her utter horror, when she was rounding the last bend in the trail just before she could see the parking lot, she ran right into the two large figures in black that were now situated right on the path in front of her. She bounced off the closest figure and screamed as she fell on the gravel path again. She found herself back on her butt with her wrist twisting painfully again on the path as she went down. She knew she had really sprained her wrist as she landed on the ground. Before she was able to get herself back up and run into the trees from the two strange, terrifying people, they were on her, grabbing at her. She screamed and kicked like a wild woman as one of them picked her up as if she weighed no more than a doll and tossed her over his shoulder. She saw the other figure reach out toward her head and soon felt something cold on her neck. A distinct buzzing sensation ran through her entire body, and then she instantly blacked out.

*****

Seventy-five miles north of the jogger, an attractive sandy-blond-haired waitress ended her shift and exited the restaurant out the back entrance. She unlocked her bicycle for her ride over to her boyfriend's house. It was much quicker to cut through the woods and past the cemetery. It would save her about ten minutes to get to her boyfriend's house than it was to take the sidewalk and streets. She did not want to be late. They had a raid to play with their guild for the computer game World of Warcraft, which they were both very addicted to. She was sure to be early so she could sneak in a few kisses and then grab a drink. This way was on a dark and scary path that went beside a cemetery, but it was worth the saved time for her. With the decision to take the scary shortcut made, she mounted her bike and took off toward the wooded path to her boyfriend's house. Just as she was about to enter the back side of the cemetery path, she noticed in the distance two large men dressed in all black just standing on the trail.

She slowed a bit thinking that it may be some cemetery employees, but they also had full masks on, covering their entire faces, and they were just standing there facing her. Suddenly she got the chills. This just did not feel right. She slowly turned down a different path going into the cemetery. She hoped that there were a few visitors visiting their loved one's grave within this part of the cemetery so she would feel safe. To her disappointment, no one was in the back of the cemetery today. She looked back just to make sure that the strangers were not following her when suddenly she felt her bike jerk to a stop. As she snapped her head back around, she found that the two large men were now right in front of her, grabbing and holding her bike. Before she could even scream, she was lifted off her bike by one man, and the other man had a rod of some sort in his hand that he placed on her neck. She felt a strange buzzing feeling through her entire body, then quickly passed out.

*****

A black-haired beauty entered her vehicle after her work out at the local gym thirty miles west from the sandy-haired waitress. She decided to go on a drive to visit her parents on their family farm on the outskirts of the small town. She had nothing better to do that evening. She had not seen her parents for a few weeks, so today was as good as any for a visit. She drove down the pavement and was soon turning off onto the familiar, quiet gravel road that led her to her family home. The road was tucked in a forest with trees on both sides of the gravel road she traveled on. It was like being in the middle of a beautiful tree tunnel. She was thinking about how beautiful the trees looked with all the fresh spring greens and sunlight filtering through as if from heaven. As she was daydreaming, she almost missed seeing the two large men dressed in black just standing in the middle of the road. She had to slam on the brakes in order not to collide into them. Her car skidded sideways and slid to a hard stop just before the men with the car half in the ditch.

For a moment, she just sat there catching her breath, stunned. She sat staring at the two figures just beyond the passenger side of the car in total shock. She was confused about what had just happened. Why were they just standing there? She was breathing heavily, and her blood drained from her face. When she calmed down a little, she became angry. She was about to get out of her car to give these idiots what for, but she stopped herself. A foreboding feeling washed over her screaming for her to not get out of her car. She took a closer look at the men just standing beside her car. They had not moved. Both were dressed in some type of flexible black armor, and they had sleek black helmets covering their faces. For a split second, the movie *Deadpool* flashed in her mind to come up with comparison for the armor on these men. Were they filming a movie in the area that she had not heard about? Her brain was trying to make sense of the scenario before her.

The two large men began to move and split to either side of the car. She quickly locked her doors. The men jiggled the handles on either side. She was about to put her car that was still running in reverse to speed away when her car, for no reason, stalled. She slammed her steering wheel in frustration, and then she frantically tried to start it again. The huge man on her side of the car took out some sort of tool from a belt around his waist. With a light tap of the tool on her window, it instantly shattered. With a scream, she struggled to get her seat belt off and awkwardly scrambled to the passenger side of the car, but that window was shattered as well. She quickly yet clumsily, clambered over the passenger seat to get to the back. She had never been more terrified in her life. What did they want from her? What the hell was happening? Both men unlocked the doors from the now smashed windows. They were entering the car. Before she could open the back door and jump out to escape, the men had a hold of her legs. They pulled her back to the front and then out of the passenger side of the car. She felt something cold on her neck, and an electrical buzz spread through her body. She slumped unconscious beside the car. The armored men picked her up, walking in the opposite direction, leaving it half in the ditch with the doors wide open and two front windows shattered with glass scattered on the seats and in the ditch surrounding the vehicle.

*****

Sheye roused from her lazy slumber on the rocks and sat up a little dizzy from her hour in the sun. When her slight disorientation went away, she nudged Mandy. They both decided to go for one more quick dip to cool off. Then they got dressed, had a quick lunch, then head back to the cabin. As the girls mounted up and started off toward the direction of the cabin, Mandy pulled Red up beside her best friend and suggested, saying, "I have a brilliant idea, Sheye. When we get back to the cabin, why not pack up some stuff and camp at the lake for a few days? Wouldn't that be fun?"

Sheye turned to Mandy and smiled. "Why, Mandy, I think you have yourself one heck of a brilliant idea. That sounds amazing. Let's do it."

With their new camping adventure decided, the ladies made it back to the cabin, settled, and fed the horses. They went into the cabin and started getting things ready for the next day's escapade. They fell asleep that night with nothing disturbing their slumber. They woke up early, refreshed, and excited for the new day. They packed their saddlebags with a few days' worth of food, bedrolls, blankets, clothing, tarps, and some survival equipment for starting fires and cutting wood and rope. Sheye also brought her rifle and a box of ammunition just in case they encountered a bear that may want to bother them or try to steal their food. Not to be outdone, Mandy decided to bring a machete that she found in the barn. Sheye grinned and arched her brow in the direction of Mandy as she stuffed the large knife into the side of her pack. Mandy just grinned and shrugged her shoulders with her arms thrown up in the air as if saying "What? If you have something to protect yourself, then why not me too!" When the ladies were all packed and ready, they mounted up and headed off once again toward the lake with an air of excited freedom.

Chapter 4

Across the provinces of Canada, radio, news broadcasts, and law officials were exploding with reports and investigations of missing women from across the country from all over smaller and remote areas. The reports were flooding in faster than they could be kept track of. There was panic everywhere. All the missing reports were of young women in the early to midtwenties who had not yet bore any children. They were unmarried with small or not much family. All the women were in good health and physical condition without any history of drugs or alcohol abuse or any restraining orders or complaints about an abusive relationship. None of the women were a flight risk or had any reason to disappear, yet they had all vanished without a trace. No one heard or saw anything untoward in the areas of the missing women. No one knew who took them or why they disappeared. There was no evidence left in the areas of the disappearances, except for the vehicles or bikes the women had used that were left abandoned in the areas they were abducted from. Over five hundred women had been reported missing across the country in the last few days. The police were advising all young women in remote areas to not be alone when they had to leave their homes or jobs for any reason until they could find out what was going on. Everyone was on high alert, and all the small towns and remote officials were overloaded with phone calls and investigations of the missing women. Even the Canadian National Police Force had been called in for the overwhelming number of sudden disappearances to help with the investigations. Everyone involved with the investigations were completely mystified as to what happened to all these young women. Not one of the women had been found yet nor where there any bodies discovered.

*****

Oblivious to all the disappearances going on in many of the remote areas of the country, the two ladies continued their way to the lake for their camping trip. When they passed the area with the burnt oval, they both ignored it. Neither of the two ladies wanted anything to disturb their exuberance for their camping trip. When they reached the lake, they picked out a lovely space in the trees with the lake directly to the west of them on a small grassy area. They decided to break ground for their camp on that spot. The ladies tied the horses on some trees near the camp within a grassy area after they led them to water. Sheye then laid a tarp down on the ground and proceeded to tie another tarp above the bottom tarp in case it rained. Then she laid out the bedrolls in the middle of the bottom tarp. Mandy collected rocks and built a nice firepit and started collecting wood so they could make a fire. When they were both satisfied with the set up of the camp, they decided to go swimming again. The women were so wrapped up in their own pleasure of nature they were oblivious to what was about to happen that would drastically change both their lives.

*****

Several large well-built men dressed up in black armor were getting ready to head out to collect a few more last specimens before they departed. Another immense figure came through a sliding door and approached the men who were donning their armor.

"Mind if I join you all in the last of the collections?"

All the other men hooted and slapped the newly entered intimidating man on the back with nods of appreciation.

"Jodar! What brings you away from your duties today of all days? I haven't seen hide nor hair of you since we arrived."

Jodar smiled at the man who questioned him and grabbed him by his head and placed his forehead gently against his bonded friend as a greeting.

When they were done with the quick greeting, Jodar responded, "The supreme commander gave me a few days rest. Chanlon is taking this time to make sure everyone has reached their quotas, and then he can prepare all to head back home."

Tannor looked at his bonded friend and laughed. "This is what you call a day off, my brother, helping with collection work? Well, I won't turn you away. We can always use a man with your skills to collect with us. This also enables us to work together like old times until you must return to your duties. You are welcome to accompany me any time, my brother."

The men boarded the vehicle and departed the bay as they headed off to a very remote part of the countryside. Jodar sighed as he watched the scenery of the area come closer. It was so beautiful and lush. It was so remote in this area with no visible signs of human life. Jodar frowned and turned to Tannor.

"Where are we headed, my friend? There is nothing to collect here."

Tannor smiled and turned to Jodar. "Since you are helping us on a day off, I have decided since we are close to collection quotas, I figured that the other crews could bring in the remaining collections. We are all going to have a well-deserved day off. We came here a few days ago to view the area, and it is beautiful here. I have a place that will be to your liking, so you can actually relax for a bit before we head back."

Jodar smiled and nodded. He anticipated a nice day with the men to just take it easy for a while. Being the sole protector of the supreme commander was a very heavy task indeed. The job did not give one a whole lot of time to relax. Jodar sat back with a smile on his face and patted Tannor on the shoulder. "Thank you, my friend. I can always count on you to come up with a clever idea."

The vehicle positioned itself on the same spot it did a few days previous, and the men exited. They unloaded smaller quad-like vehicles and boarded them and headed west of their location. Within a few minutes, they could see a beautiful body of water in the distance, and the men stopped and parked the vehicles on top of a bluff above the lake. They all began to dismount when Jodar stopped them with a warning by holding up his hand and signaling them to all stay quiet and still. All the men froze. Jodar stepped forward and strategically placed himself flat on a rock so that he could scan the lake for trouble and still not be seen. He was behind some smaller pine saplings and searched for the sound that he had heard. Jodar soon found what had been making the sounds that had him on alert and ready for battle.

Not so far below the bluff that hid Jodar from sight were two women happily swimming and splashing around as they enjoyed themselves in the water. Jodar could not believe his eyes as he watched the most beautiful female he had ever encountered rise her glorious self out of the water. She pulled herself onto the shelf of rocks on the edge of the lake. To Jodar's utter and pleasant surprise, she was completely naked. She seemed to not have a care in the world at that moment. She was so enchanting he could not remove his gaze from her, even if he had wanted to. He drank in the sight that was before him. He gasped as he watched her take her long, wet hair and twist out the water and let it splash onto the stones she stood on. He observed her perfect body as the water from the lake trickled off her tall, lustrous, sun-kissed frame.

Jodar had to shift himself so he could be comfortable. The midsection of his body was beginning to become quite uncomfortable and bothersome as he watched this beauty while lying on his stomach. Never had he been so aroused by just the sight of a woman before. Tannor came forward slowly and lay out beside Jodar, and he, too, gasped. They both just watched this female in silent awe as she lay her long perfect form out to tan in the sun. Jodar signaled the other men to stay back as they all started to wonder what the two men were gawking at and were starting to come forward. Jodar became instantly possessive toward this beautiful woman sunning on the rocks. He was even upset that his bonded friend was witnessing this beauty in all her naked splendor. He did not want any of the other men to ogle her as they were. He signaled his hand for them to keep back.

It was Tannor's turn to gasped as the other woman that was with the tall beauty exited the water and lay herself out beside the taller woman. Tannor snickered toward Jodar. "Look how tiny the second one is. At first, I thought her a child, and yet that is no child laying in the sun in all her magnificence. I think I am in love, my brother."

Jodar turned toward his friend and stated, "You had better be talking about the little one, my friend. The tall one is spoken for, by me."

Tannor huffed a little and raised his brow at Jodar. Never in all their years had he ever heard such possessiveness come from his friend. Jodar was very much sought after by all females who met him. They all hoped that he would end up having the "knowing," an inseparable bond that occurs between two people that are meant to be together forever, between themselves and Jodar. Their wishes however had never come to pass. He had never shared his bed for more than a night or two with any one woman at any given time.

Jodar was stuck to the old dying ways of their kind. The knowing never happened much anymore, especially since the devastation that caused them to come here to do this collection in the first place. The last time Tannor even remembered the knowing happening was with supreme Commander Chanlon, with his life mate. Tannor backed up slowly toward the other men as Jodar continued to drink in the sight of the woman below. He almost did not even see the tiny one lying beside her as she did not matter to him. Jodar felt something inside himself that he had long lost hope of feeling. He just knew that this female was different, that she was meant to be here on this very day—this very day that he had decided to come down with Tannor and that he would be the one to collect her.

It is fate you could say, Jodar thought. Now he had to collect her and find out if she was what his heart desired her to be.

Jodar stood at a staggering six feet, nine inches in height. He was not the tallest of their kind, but he had extremely well-built muscle from years of hard training to be the best bodyguard of his class. He had dark-brown wavy hair that cascaded just below the tops of his shoulders. He had bright amber-colored eyes that were so amber they were almost yellow in intensity. His eyes had dark-black rings that encircled his irises to make them even more penetrating when he turned his gaze onto you. With his strong jawline, cleft chin, straight nose, and broad cheekbones, all the ladies swooned at the sight of him and his intense eyes, especially in the bedchamber. But for the men stupid enough to challenge him felt like they were going to be ripped apart by a lion by just one look of those same eyes.

Jodar was so remarkable in his abilities and skills of combat that he had saved the life of the supreme commander not once, but twice in battle even before he completed his training. The supreme commander had allotted Jodar to be his personal guard the day he had saved his life the second time. Jodar had been at the supreme commander's side since. Not one man yet could beat Jodar in hand-to-hand or hand weapons combat, not even the supreme commander's own son, Broud. Sadly, Broud developed a deep jealousy and obsessive hatred toward Jodar. Broud tried to nip at Jodar's heels any chance he could. The feeling was mutual though. Jodar respected the supreme commander like a father but had no love loss for his son, Broud.

"Well, men, so much for a relaxing day," Tannor stated to the other men hanging back by the vehicles. "Looks like we are collecting like we were supposed to after all. Helmets on, and rods out. Do your best not to harm these specimens as Jodar seems very particular to the tall one, and well, to tell you the truth, I feel the tiny one may just be my flavor as well."

All the men smiled and joked quietly together as they readied themselves for the collection. They were all very curious to see what kind of specimen had grabbed Jodar's interest. They all knew how he had never settled on any one woman. This female would have to be exceptional to snag mighty Jodar's attention. They all were interested to see this specimen.

*****

Sheye and Mandy languished in the sun for a few minutes. When Sheye was dry, she stood up. "I am famished. Do you want a sandwich, Mandy?"

Mandy rolled herself onto her stomach and put her arms under her head to support her chin as she looked at Sheye. "Ooh, a sandwich sounds delicious. Can you bring out the fruit salad as well, please? It's in the large red bag you hung up on the tree to keep away from the bears, and I can't reach that high." Sheye giggled as she went over to get dressed. As she slipped on her clothes and shoes, she flipped back at Mandy. "I think you are just being lazy. Why not just admit that this is the best vacation you have ever had and don't want to get up to help? I did not tie it up that high. Okay then, lazy bones, lunch is coming right up." Sheye busied herself getting out the tuna sandwiches and the salad as Mandy finally got up and got dressed. She came over as she was starting to feel hunger pangs as well.

The two women sat on the grass by the makeshift tarp tent and happily ate their meal. Mandy said, sighing, "I could stay here forever, Sheye. I never knew of such peace and bliss even existed. I love it here. I think my life has changed for the better just being out here with you and getting away from, as you like to call him, my ex-meathead."

Sheye was about to respond to Mandy's comment, but unexpectedly the horses started to snort angrily and pull on their tethers with their ears laying flat onto the backs of their heads. Sheye jumped up and immediately went over to where she placed the rifle and picked it up. Sheye also grabbed a few more shells and stuffed them into her shorts pocket. She then went over to calm down Onyx and Big Red. "Hey, boys, what is it? Do you smell a bear?" Onyx really began to become upset, so Sheye placed her hand on his neck. "Hey, hey, buddy, it's okay!" Just to be on the safe side, Sheye moved and untied the two horses. If it were a bear and they had to mount in a hurry to get away from a charging bear, it would be that much easier. Mandy began to get nervous and went to grab her knife she placed by the tent when the horses did not calm down with Sheye's soothing voice.

"Do you think it's a bear, Sheye?" Sheye looked all around but shook her head.

"I don't think it's a bear. The horses are acting strangely." She looked back at Onyx who was keeping close to Sheye but pawing his hooves at the ground. Big Red was sidestepping back and forth, tossing his head up and down, up and down. "The horses had been around some bears before. Onyx here knows he could kick up a good fight if it comes close. They sense something else I think."

Mandy started to back up away from the horses, afraid that her small stature would get trampled if the horses did decide to run. She backed up toward a large spruce tree when suddenly she screamed and dropped her knife.

Sheye spun around to face where Mandy was. To her horror, she could see Mandy was being grabbed by a large man. Sheye assumed it was a man. The sheer size of him was staggering, and he was dressed in black armor with a black helmet of some kind. Maybe this was a robot. For a moment too long, Sheye hesitated, but luckily, Mandy managed to slip away from the man or robot thing that had tried to grab her from behind. The being had not been ready for Mandy to be so flexible and fast. With Mandy out of the way, this was all that Sheye needed. Sheye raised the shotgun and aimed. With a loud blast, Sheye shot the stranger right in the middle of his chest. The figure fell backward and a little behind the tree. Mandy stumbled forward only to scream again. Sheye turned to see two other immense figures dressed the same as the first one, coming up to them fast from the other direction. Sheye aimed and shot one of them in the shoulder. He staggered to his knee's but did not go down. Mandy and Sheye stood back-to-back to each other; to both their dismay, the first figure that Sheye had shot was standing back up and coming back around the tree. Sheye panicked a little and realized that she had to reload her gun. Her hands were sweating badly she almost dropped the shotgun when she opened the barrel. Then when she pulled two more shells out of her pocket, she almost dropped them as well but managed to jam them into the barrel.

The first man stepped out from behind the spruce tree and was slowly coming back toward them. The man who had been shot in the shoulder and was down on his knees was beginning to rise back up as well. The third man was getting uncomfortably close to them. Sheye snapped the gun back together and aimed at the closest one. This time, she shot this one in the head. The man went down flat on his back and did not move. The other two men were again coming forward. A few more men came up behind the first man from out of the trees. Onyx was having nothing to do with this disturbance of the new men coming toward his beloved owner, so he charged in, rearing up, slashing his hooves toward the men blocking them from getting to the women.

One of the men stepped away from Onyx. He was holding a long metal rod of some kind and raised it toward the large horse. Sheye screamed at the man as she thought it was a weapon and he was about to shoot her cherished companion. He turned toward Sheye when she yelled at him. Without hesitation, Sheye aimed her rifle and pulled the trigger, but her gun jammed. Immediately without thought, Sheye cursed loudly, dropped her gun, and charged at the man holding the rod weapon. With all her weight, she jumped in the air with a spinning kick and connected her foot to his head. This was no easy feat since the man was about six feet eight inches in height. The man's helmet cracked a little, and he staggered back. Again, Mandy screamed as two men approached her, only this time, she was angrier than scared, so she charged at them screaming like a wild banshee the whole way.

Mandy attacked like a wild boar and fought them as hard as she could, but with her small stature, she was no match for them. Mandy was overtaken within a few heartbeats. Sheye noted when Mandy went down and realized if she did not flee, she would be next. With the grace of a ballet dancer and the fear of a desperate woman not wanting to die, she was on Onyx's bare back in what seemed like one fluid movement. She spun Onyx around knocking two of the men down in the process and charged in the direction away from the lake. Big Red was right behind them as they galloped at full speed down the trail back toward the cabin's direction.

The five men gathered themselves around the unconscious Mandy, and they all took off their helmets. They looked at one another, and they all began laughing together.

"Well, I never expected that. You were right to want that one, Jodar! She is amazing. How is your head by the way?"

They all laughed again as Jodar looked at the crack on the side of his helmet. He shook his head somewhat shocked as he stated, "My head's fine, but I don't know about my heart."

Tannor nodded toward their catch. "For such a little thing, she can fight like a beast. If she were as tall as the other, I think we would have to be chasing both women down instead of one. Did you see that kick? I have never seen anything like that before with any of our collections and with the strength to crack our armor! That alone was impressive. Her weapon never pierced our armor, but her kick cracked your helmet." All the men examined the helmet in awe.

Jodar turned toward Cranon and Brastin. "Both of you, take this one back to the ship and wait for us. We will be back with the other female soon. Have the ship ready for departure."

The two men looked a little deflated. They, too, wanted to come with the other three men to collect the other wonderful specimen. When they all saw the tall woman with the astonishingly beautiful red hair, they were stunned at her perfection as they snuck up on the unsuspecting women. No wonder Jodar was smitten. They all were. All, except Tannor, who seemed to have his eye on the tiny blonde. The other three men secretly hoped that they would be able to be worthy of Jodar's find when the time came to apply for mates. Even with Jodar wanting this one, if Jodar was unable to have her, they would all apply for her. They all coveted her for their own.

Jodar, Tannor, and Fallon mounted the small gliders that resembled tireless quads, which they had hidden behind some bushes and headed off in the direction the woman had taken. Tannor knew that she was headed toward the small shelter that they had been to when they were checking it out a few nights before. He thought that the shelter had been empty and unoccupied. He would have inspected the inside of it and was about to had the beast that the woman rode on, not attacked the other man he had with him. Since it had been just the two of them, they had to retreat to the ship to get him to the "Blue Cloaks," who were scientists, doctors, inventors, engineers, and holy men all rolled into one, as his leg had been broken by the large black beast. They hoped to get there before she did. They were not quite sure how fast her beast was for they really had not studied up on these particular beasts from this planet. They had studied up on other wildlife as well as human languages, weaponry, and military forces before they came here to collect. With undue haste, they sped toward the shelter of the female.

*****

Sheye was at her wits' end. She was terrified and not thinking straight. *Is Mandy dead? Oh god, I sure hope not,* Sheye thought. Tears stung at her eyes as she urged Onyx on toward the cabin. Suddenly Sheye realized something. *The other night when Mandy had feared she had seen a bigfoot in the woods by the cabin, could she have been right? Could it have been these men?* Sheye slowed Onyx down and then quickly guided him off the regular path to a smaller trail more concealed in the trees. Sheye's brain was in survival mode now. She was thinking at a fast pace. "So if it was them, then they know where I am headed. They will show up there at the cabin too! I dropped my gun and have no way to protect myself. I can't go back." Sheye was talking out loud, and Onyx snorted at her wanting to get moving faster. "No, Onyx, we are not going back to the cabin. We must hide for a bit—somewhere they can't find me." Sheye turned Onyx around and whistled. Big Red turned with them, and she took a different way through a new trail that was much more concealed and headed back to the lake.

*****

When the men reached the cabin, they realized that they had made it there before the female had. They hid their vehicles and lay in wait to ambush her when she showed up. Jodar was insistent that he be the one to collect her. He did not want anyone else to touch her now. He already considered her his. He placed himself by the front door and activated his stealth shield in his armor, and he suddenly disappeared. Tannor and Fallon cloaked themselves in other places they figured she would come and waited as well. After quite a bit of time passed, Jodar uncloaked and walked out into the open.

"Tannor! Fallon! She is not coming. She has outsmarted us. I think she knew we would be here waiting for her to come back. I have a feeling she is smarter than we have given her credit for. Tannor, you come with me. Fallon, you wait here just in case she does come back. There is nowhere to go other than here. Is that right, Tannor? There are no other human shelters around?" Tannor shook his head toward Jodar. "I was shocked when we came onto this place. There were no human readings other than some wildlife the day before we came down to hunt the area. I happened to stumble on the shelter when we were on the hunt for food to fill the reserves before we leave for the trip home. This area is so ripe with wildlife. We just happened to stumble on the shelter that night, and that is when Shainor was trampled by the woman's black beast."

Jodar nodded and smiled. "Then I have a feeling I know where she is headed back to."

*****

Sheye made it back to the lake and slid off Onyx and slapped his rump. Onyx and Big Red trotted away. Sheye made sure there was no one around. She quickly but silently slid into the lake without taking off her clothes and swam toward the waterfall. Soon, she was hidden in her little dry cave, but she shivered with fear. She was sure that she was safe in her secret spot, but the fear and adrenaline she had experienced made her jumpy and doubting her choice of hiding spots. Sheye curled her legs up to her chest, and she hugged them for dear life. She let herself silently cry as she rocked back and forth in the small cave. After about twenty minutes or so, as she was self-pitying herself, she was disturbed by some voices above the waterfall. They seemed like they were coming closer. *Oh god,* Sheye thought. It was male voices she could hear. The closer they came, the more she could start to hear their words though she could not understand what they were saying. They were speaking a foreign language that she had never heard before. Sheye held her breath.

Slinking as far back to the wall of the cave as she could, she hugged her legs even closer. Sheye could not stop herself from shaking. She was freezing in the cave, but she would not dare leave it. It was also getting dark out. She stayed tight in a ball so she could keep some of her body warmth, and she listened intently. She no longer could hear the voices but still sat very silent and still. After about an hour, her limbs ached from her violent shaking, but somehow, she manages to lapse into several hours of unrestful sleep as her body was overcome with exhaustion from the fear of the day. Just before dawn, Sheye was awoken by the angry neighing and commotion by Onyx and Big Red. She had forgotten about the horses. "Damn it!" Sheye cursed to herself. They would know she was around here somewhere because she had forgotten about the horses. Angry with herself and scared for her horses' well-being, she had to do something.

Painfully she released her stiff legs. With a stifled moan, she stretched out a bit before she lowered herself back into the now very cold, dark water. Sheye slowly swam around the edge of the lake, keeping to the rocks and the reeds of cattails on the side of the banks. It was a full moon thank goodness, so she could see quite well in the dark. She hoisted herself up painfully to look over the ledge of the rocks where they had set up camp earlier, toward the open grassy area. Her muscles screamed at her from the hours of freezing on the rock ledge in the cave. As she peered over the ledge ignoring her painful muscles, she saw Onyx rearing up on his legs, trying to keep two large men away from him. She could see that Big Red was lying sprawled on the grass, and Onyx was trying to keep the men away from Big Red's body. Sheye felt bile rise in her throat at the sight of her poor horse lying dead on the grass. Onyx was fighting so desperately and squealing in anger. The sound pulled Sheye out of her shock at seeing Big Red dead on the grass. Her anger welled up in her throat, and she hauled herself from the ledge and snuck around the trees, closing the gap between her and the scene before her.

She was not thinking straight, nor was she thinking about her safety anymore. All she could think about was she had lost her father, Big Red, and Mandy, and there was no way in hell she was going to lose Onyx too. When she was close enough to the men, she hid behind a tree trying to think about what she was going to do next to try to get to mount Onyx and charge out of there. Suddenly one of the two men lunged in and jammed a long metal rod into Onyx's neck. He fell to the ground motionless in a large heap. His long legs just gave out, and he collapsed. Intense, hot rage burst out of Sheye. Blinded with rage, she screamed a brutal growl as she charged out from behind the tree she was hiding behind.

Sheye managed to startle the man closest to her. He was not prepared for her kick to his knee as he spun around. As his knee collapsed from under him from her precise kick, he went down on that knee. Sheye proceeded to direct another bone-crunching kick to his other knee. With a moan, the man went down flat. All the years of martial arts training had finally paid off. Without hesitation, she proceeded to lunge at the other large man, who had spun around to witness the feral, possessed woman take down his friend.

As she lunged in the air toward the second man with a cracked helmet, she could swear she heard him laughing just as she noticed a metal rod being held out toward her body. The large man braced himself against her flying weight, and with one arm, he caught her out of midair and turned her around so that she landed with her back hard against his chest, and one large strong arm held her around her torso. He leaned into her, and just before he touched the rod to her neck, she heard him say, "You are the one." Then there was an intense buzzing sensation, and she was out cold.

Chapter 5

Tannor had to be carried back onto their craft and groaned as he was sat down beside Jodar. They had to wait a bit for Fallon to get back from the females' shelter. Jodar was staring intently at the unconscious burgundy-haired beauty in one of the pods lined against the opposite wall. Beside that pod held the tiny unconscious blonde she had been with. Tannor rubbed his knees as they throbbed painfully. He would have to go see the Blue Cloaks and get seen in the medbay as soon as they returned to the main ship for repair of his knees. He knew his one knee was positively blown out. His other knee was close if not blown as well. They had been trained well to ignore pain, but the woman had taken him down with ease. This astonished and mortified him. She was fast. They had never seen the moves that she had produced against them before. It was a fighting technique that was very foreign to them.

Tannor groaned again, and this snapped Jodar out of his focus from staring at the woman. Tannor looked at Jodar and stated, "I heard you laugh right after she took me down. Just so you know, she caught me unawares as I was focused on the black beast that was about to trample us."

Jodar laughed again and stated, "My friend, she would have taken me down if I was her first target too. The way she has been taught to fight is unknown to us. This will be one of the first things I'll get her to teach me when we are bonded."

Tannor sucked in his breath and turned fully to Jodar, groaning at the tight twinging in his knees. "Jodar, I have to tell you that I am worried about your attachment to this female. She is magnificent for sure. There is no argument about that, but I have been thinking—"

Jodar sighed and stopped Tannor from continuing by holding up his hand.

"I know what you are thinking, Tannor. He…will…never…get her. He…will…never…touch…her. You can't go against the knowing, not even if you are the son of the supreme commander. It is the law. I know that as soon as she looks at me, she will "know" me. The knowing will happen. I can feel it as if it has already occurred. I don't know how to explain this to you, Tannor. I just know."

Tannor sighed and looked away from his bonded friend. He prayed to the fifth star of Prantus that this would be so. He had never seen Jodar like this, and it worried him. He knew that this certain female would catch Broud's eye, knowing or not, and this worried him. Broud was in a position of power. He was cruel, and soon, he would take over his father's position as supreme commander. The competition between Jodar and Broud had always been fierce. Now with this female in the mix, Tannor knew nothing good would come of it.

As Jodar and the other men were down on the surface, a pretty female with soft fur for hair that covered her head, the back of her arms, and a strip down her back scurried out of a bedchamber with a sheet wrapped around her naked body. She had blood flowing from a cut on her brow and from her nose as well. She had been bedded and then beaten by Broud in his personal chamber on the main ship. She scampered away even faster when he yelled again behind her, "Get out!" Broud paced around his bedchamber angered at the female who had just left his room. Sure, she had pleased him in bed, but as he looked at her when he was finished with her, she disgusted him. His appetite for females was always insatiable. He would take a woman at least two to three times a day. He had a dream woman constantly stirring around in his head. He would never be satisfied until he found her. Woman always came out of his bedchamber with wounds, cuts, bruises, and tears. Some more than others. The more a woman looked like his ideal woman he had in his mind, the less chance he would beat her as savagely. Some of them even graced his bed more than once, and they would exit his bed with not as many welts or wounds on them.

Broud walked over to his hologram screen and touched a few tabs that made the base of the hologram port light up. The lifelike figure of his perfect woman that he had created on his hologram unit flashed before him. He placed his hands on the clear screen of the control panel and punched in a command to have the hologram slowly and continuously turn around so he could view her entirety. Broud gazed wishfully at his creation from all angles. The hologram looked so real yet was so unobtainable. It was of a female that was tall with long slender, shapely legs, and a flat stomach. She had perfect-shaped perky breasts. She had a sleek arms and rounded hips, with feminine curves in all the right places. She also had long flowing auburn hair, full lips, high cheekbones. She had a slim nose with bright, sparkling large almond-shaped emerald-green eyes. He reached out for her. His hand passed right through the hologram's midsection. Broud sighed and then picked up a goblet of Jusberg wine and threw it right through the hologram. It bounced off the wall and splashed all over the wall and the floor. Instantly an automated cleaner popped out of the wall and immediately began to clean the mess. Broud ignored the cleaner and ran a large strong hand through his long black hair and again sighed heavily before one last look at his ideal hologram before he angrily shut it off.

After Broud had shut off the hologram, he was fully aroused again. He stomped over to the communication system by his bed and pressed the button. Without waiting, he spoke into it. "Send up another. This time, she better be more to my taste, or one of you Blue Cloaks will pay dearly for the error."

Within minutes, a tall, pretty red-haired woman was escorted into Broud's chamber by a couple of Blue Cloaks. They took her to the bed and forced her to lay down on it and tethered her to the bed before they left her there. The Blue Cloaks slunk back in shame at what they did for Broud but still bowed toward him as they exited the room. Broud immediately crawled onto the redhead, and with no concern for her in anyway, he proceeded to rip off her clothing. He mounted the woman and roughly penetrated her before she was even ready. A scream was ripped from her throat as he pumped in and out from on top of her forcefully. Broud thought only of his needs, without a care for the woman beneath him in the least.

*****

Jodar and Tannor exited their transport shuttle after it docked in the bay of their mother ship. Jodar was carrying Tannor and placed him on a transport cart. There were many other collection shuttles already landed or about to land in the landing bay. The landed shuttles were all unloading their collections. The shuttle crews would go over to inspect other crews' collections and boast or bet on who had the best specimens. When Jodar saw all this, he became very uneasy and turned to Tannor.

"I don't want all these men ogling over my woman. Can we lock the shuttle doors, or can we get her off the shuttle another time or somewhere else?"

Tannor shook his head sadly toward his friend. "The only way to unload collections is here in the docks. All the specimens are taken through the scanning section so the Blue Cloaks can code them and see if they are worthy and healthy. Then they immediately go to the hibernation chambers for the journey home, Jodar. Don't worry, my brother, we will just try to slip by quietly. We won't stop and see other shuttles' collections. We will have my little blondie go first. Maybe no one will notice your lady's pod as we just slip through."

Jodar frowned for he knew the minute they unloaded the pods, someone would be bound to see their collections. No sooner did Jodar think this to himself when he heard his name called out by someone at another shuttle across the bay. Then they were running up along the shuttle to greet Jodar.

"What are you doing down here with us lowlife collectors, Jodar? Why aren't you at your established post with the commander?" The man was teasing Jodar as he slapped him hard on the back. "We have missed you, old man! It is good to see you. It has been a long time."

Before Jodar could even try to step in the man's line of sight, to the women in the pods on the shuttle wall, he spied them and immediately entered the shuttle with his mouth agape.

"What in Prantus's stars do you have here, Jodar? Where did you find such a divine specimen? Svanus and Ranolt have got to see her. She is definitely going to attract the interest of the commander's son."

Jodar growled loudly and was about to stop the man from exiting the shuttle, but instead of exiting, he just shouted for his friends to come over directly, which, of course, to Jodar's acute anger, they did.

Soon, the whole bay was over at Jodar's shuttle, and they were all trying to get a glimpse at Jodar and Tannor's magnificent collection. Tannor found this quite humorous even though his best friend was in a state of barely controlled rage now. Tannor just shrugged his shoulders and shook his head at Jodar when he noticed his glowering was directed toward him. Jodar would have to get used to this female bringing in a lot of attention wherever she went, no matter if they were eventually bonded or not. She was just that beautiful.

All the commotion at Jodar's shuttle had caught a few of the Blue Cloaks' attention as the line for coding and scanning had all but stopped. The two short men draped in long blue cloaks with their faces completely covered slowly entered the center of all the men. When the large group of men noticed the Blue Cloaks, they all stepped back to let them move into the shuttle, so they, too, could see what it was that all the men had been so interested in. When the Blue Cloaks saw the specimen in the pod, they looked at one another with immense excitement. They immediately demanded that all the men back away. They were considered ones who knew it all. They only expressed and followed the ideologies of the supreme commander and the laws. When they spoke, most listened without hesitation as they were considered incredibly wise and the second hand of the commander himself. As the Blue Cloaks had the shuttle doors cleared of all the men, they then sealed the shuttle doors, and no one was allowed in.

Jodar was bubbling with fury now, as he, too, was forced out of the cargo bay of the shuttle with all the others. The female who was causing all this fuss was his, in his mind already. He was so sure that they would experience the knowing as soon as they were able to look into each other's eyes, that he just never thought about anything else. Jodar was angry at himself as he began to feel afraid for her. He never realized what a frenzy she would cause. He should have thought more clearly about this. He had just become so blinded and so obsessed about her he never thought that possibly everyone else would see and feel the exact same when they saw her also. Suddenly he realized maybe Tannor had been correct in his thinking. Would she be ranked to be in the trials of acceptance for Broud? If she were ranked this way, then he would lose her if they did not experience the knowing. Jodar realized that he did not even care about them experiencing the knowing anymore. He still wanted to be bonded with her forever no matter what.

Jodar clenched his jaw and then his fists. Then without a word, he stormed away from the shuttle bay in frustration. He had to keep believing that he would meet up with this female soon, and they would immediately experience the knowing. Then no matter what she was ranked, they would be together and bonded forever as the law had always been. Tannor had the transfer cart follow his friend to make sure he did not do anything stupid. Tannor knew he would see his little blonde again. He was very sure that he would be able to ask for her when the time came. He would probably not have any problems with being granted this female. This would not be likely for Jodar though. Tannor knew where Jodar was storming off to. Jodar was headed to the Nightery to get very inebriated. Tannor just could not let Jodar drink alone, especially when he was this angry. Jodar would possibly end up doing something he would regret, so Tannor followed close behind. He pulled the transport chair by Jodar's table and joined Jodar without a word and ordered his own beverage. He would end up regretting this the next day, but for now, one thing good came out of pounding drinks back with Jodar. Tannor's knees went completely numb by the fifth round, and he was no longer in pain.

*****

In the shuttle, the two Blue Cloaks could not believe their eyes. Standing in the pod before them was the very image, most of them had seen on Broud's hologram screen more than once. It was as if she had just walked off the hologram base and had come to life. They immediately looked at the pod's readings and found her to be in perfect health—no underlying genetic diseases, no mental instabilities, and her reproductive attributes were in harmony. So far, she was perfect. They whispered between each other, both convinced that if they scanned her incorrectly, they would be banished or, worse, put to death. Incorrect ranking was unforgivable. They did not want to make this huge decision on their own. They had yet to rank a female from all the collections the supreme rank for possible commanding inspection. This specimen could be the one that could receive this status. They needed all their brothers to help on this ruling. This was not to be taken lightly.

With the choice made, the Blue Cloaks released the pod of the tall female from the hold in the shuttle. They punched coordinates into the pod's control panel and then walked beside it as it hovered and moved on its own. They followed the pod as it silently glided directly to the Blue Cloaks' scanning station but then turned and entered an elevator that led them to a large medical chamber where many more Blue Cloaks were working. Here they could conduct more tests for analysis before they delved into the possibility of giving her the "supreme" scan. When the pod exited the elevator, all the other Blue Cloaks looked up at the entering pod. They all stared and whispered to one another as pods never came up to the medical chamber straight from the scanning bay. They were curious. They began to gather in the center of the room where the pod had stopped. For a few minutes, they all just stood and stared at the contents of the pod without a word. Then suddenly they all started talking at once. Within seconds, they had the pod locked into a large computer that did a full and complete scan of the woman within. The Blue Cloaks read all the evaluations that popped out, and they all nodded in unison.

She was flawless. They all agreed that she could be ranked Supreme. Now she would have to pass the other tribunals. First, they had to tell the supreme commander that they may have found a possible mate for Broud. Second, they would waken her and prepare her for the commander, who would have to find her acceptable. If he did, then she would go to the next stage. Third, she would have to be placed in a room with many other women. Broud would then have to pick her out from all the other women in the room. They all hoped that the knowing would occur in which they would be bonded immediately. If it did not, they would see if he did not pick her, then she would be considered an unfit match, and she would be coded with the next lower rank, which was of the Soldier rank. If he did pick her, even without the knowing, then she would be sent to the preparation chamber and hibernated in a royal pod for the long travel home beside the commander's family. Then she would be readied for the bonding ceremony to Broud as soon as they reach their home world.

Chapter 6

Jodar awoke with one of the worst headaches he had ever experienced in his lifetime. *So be it,* he thought, as he lifted himself into a sitting position on his bed. He deserved to feel this poorly considering how irresponsible he was with not being prepared at how the Blue Cloaks would take his woman. He scoffed at himself for not clearly thinking the minute he laid eyes on his female. He had trained his whole life as a soldier for his planet. He was so good at what he did that he was now the supreme commander's personal soldier. This was the most coveted position of all combatants. Jodar held on to his head as he moved to the side of the bed and rose to relieve himself. "Ugh," he groaned aloud. A medibot materialized out of a wall as soon as Jodar groaned and zoomed up to him with a glass of glowing liquid. He took it and drank it down immediately. Within moments of finishing the contents of the glass, his headache was gone completely, and the medibot whisked away, back into its spot in the wall.

Jodar stepped into his cleaning unit and closed the door. A quiet humming sound lasted in the unit for a few moments, and then the doors silently slide open. Jodar stepped out clean, dry, and fully groomed. His armor popped out of the wall beside the personal cleaning unit, and he put it on. Just as he was about to order his breakfast meal into his console, his intercom chimed with the voice of the supreme commander's commissioner. The commissioner's voice resounded throughout the small room. "The commander needs you to accompany him this evening to deal with an important matter. Meet him at the medical level, section 4, bay 1, promptly at nightfall." Without a goodbye or a need for a reply, the intercom shut off.

Jodar glared at the contraption but nodded. He figured he would be called back to duty this day anyways. He still had time in the day to try to find out what happened to his woman before he had to restart his duties. He was grateful for that. Now he just had to find Tannor so he could help him. He was most likely still sleeping off their night of drinking. Jodar smiled to himself. Tannor could never keep up to the amount of drink Jodar could consume, but he always tried.

*****

Sheye shifted her body in her sleep and groaned. She slowly awoke with a headache, and her muscles were still screaming at her from the cold cave floor she had endured. Abruptly she sat up but groaned for the effort as every muscle in her body shrieked with painful protest. She looked around and was very confused. Was she in a hospital? If she was in a hospital, then it was the strangest and barest hospital room she had ever been in. As she looked around the room, her memory suddenly flooded back into full working order. When she had first awoken, she expected herself to be lying on the grass beside her precious horses. "Oh my god! Onyx! Red!" Sheye looked at her surroundings again. She was not lying outside on any grass. She was in a white room with nothing else in it but the platform she was lying on in the center. She could not see where the walls ended or where the ceiling started. There were no windows or doors that she could see. It seemed as if she were in a large white bubble for all she could tell.

"Where the hell am I?" Sheye slid her legs off the side of the platform and sat there with her head in her hands. "Think, think!" Sheye said aloud to herself. Everything slammed into her brain at once again. She remembered the large men in black armor and what had happened at their camp. She remembered Mandy being taken down by two men as they fought for their lives. She remembered fighting to get away to save herself. She remembered the terrifying and freezing time she had in her hiding spot under the waterfall. She remembered hearing her horses in distress and trying save them.

She remembered seeing Big Red lying dead on the grass with Onyx fighting for his life. Sheye began to rock back and forth and moan as the pain of losing her prized horses rushed back to her. Tears flooded her eyes and ran down her cheek. "I am so sorry, my poor friends. I could not save you." Sheye sat with her head hanging for some time as she just let herself cry out her grief in great gulps and sobs. *What? Where? When? Why?* All these questions popped into her head at once. The why stood out the most. *What did we do to deserve what had happened to us?*

With a sudden swishing sound, a space opened on one side of the bubble, and a man in a long orange cloak with a hood over his face entered her space. In front of him was a trolley that appeared to be floating just above the ground. There seemed to be food and drink on the tray. The door in the wall whooshed shut again, and the man came closer with the trolley. Sheye leaped off the bed and placed herself behind it with the bed between herself and the stranger. He did not speak or even look up at her. He continued to ignore her as he opened the lids on the trays to display the different colorful foreign foods and poured out a liquid that had a purple glow to it into a tall, sleek glass. Sheye frowned at him as she wiped away her tears. She cautiously watched him for a few moments for any sign of him faking it to try an attack. When she felt, he was not going to attack her, she spoke to him. "Where am I?" When the man did not respond, acknowledge, or even look at her, she became irritated. Sheye spoke with a little more force in her words. "What do you want from me, and where is my friend, Mandy?" Still no response from the man. *Is he deaf and dumb?*

With a quick frustrated shake of her head, Sheye was not going to be treated this way by anyone, especially one connected to her kidnapping, so with a very quick decision, she attacked the man in the orange cloak. He did not even see her sail over the bed as she launch herself at him in the air with a kick to the head. She landed on her feet with him between her legs lying on the floor out cold. Sheye was panting from her sudden viciousness. She had no remorse though as she looked down at him lying unconscious on the floor. He was involved in her kidnapping or whatever this was. She had to escape.

Without much thought, she moved the young man onto the bed platform. She removed his cloak, thanking God, as she was delighted to find he had a tight bodysuit on under the cloak and was not naked. Sheye quickly donned the cloak. She covered the young man with the thin sheet she had woke up under and then walked over to the part of the wall that she thought he had come in through and tapped on the wall. She hoped that whoever opened the door on the other side would just assume that she was the man who delivered the food and the person on the slab in the room under the blanket was her. With a soft whoosh, the door opened a little to her left, and she exited. She tried to stay calm as she noticed that there were two large men in that black armor standing outside on each side of the door.

Sheye's heart began to pound as she adjusted the cloak so her face was hidden. She tucked in her hair and hunched over a bit with her head hanging down. She took a deep breath, crossed her fingers under the long sleeves of the cloak, and exited the room. As she passed the two large men in the black armor, one of them spoke to her in different language. She panicked a bit. She stopped, turned a little, and then decided to just nod. The guard must have liked her action to his words as he laughed and pushed her away from the door down the hall. She stumbled a bit, which made both armored men laugh again. She then just kept her head down and walked at a normal gait straight ahead until she came to a split in the hallway. She turned to her left and exited out of view of the two armored men.

When she was out of sight and knew she was alone, Sheye stopped, leaned against the wall, and let out a large exhale of breath she had not even realized she had been holding in.

Okay, Sheye thought, *that wasn't too difficult.* Now she had to figure out where to go and how to get out of this building they were keeping her in. There were corridors everywhere. One of these hallways had to lead to an elevator or a stairwell. All the doors she passed had strange electronic locks of some kind on them. None of the doors she tried would open for her, so she just kept her head down and walked. Panic started to creep into her thoughts again as she tried to figure out how to get off this floor. The next turn down yet another corridor found her almost face-to-face with a couple other persons dressed as she was in long flowing cloaks. She stepped aside quickly, and they passed her with not even a second glance. They opened a door to her right and entered. With a quick turn, she followed them into the doorway as they did not seem to be suspicious of her at all. They just assumed she was one of them.

The cloaked men had entered an extremely large room that was filled with large tubelike containers hanging row upon row down below the walkway. They were all suspended by a single thin pipe from the ceiling. Sheye had to stop and look over the railing. The sheer size of this room was baffling. The number of these tubes had to be in the hundreds as she scanned across the massive room. The room was sectioned off with different lighting. Each section of the room had a different color. The tubes' buttons and electronics in each section matched the colored lights of the section they were in. There was white, yellow, orange, red, blue, green, and every other color in different sections throughout the immense room. Sheye's curiosity got the better of her. She may as well see what these things were. Somewhere in this room may be an exit as well. These tubes may also give her insight as to why she was here and what they were doing. The other cloaked men had gone down the rafter to another door and exited the room. Sheye turned back to the massive room and looked around to find a way down to the floor the tubes were at. She spied a ladder, so she directed herself to it and proceeded to make her way down.

First, she entered the gray zone where all the tube colors and keys were gray. As she went to the front of the first row, she noted that they all had a small oval window near the top. Sheye had to stand on her tiptoes to see what was inside. When she did, she was so shocked at what she saw; she gagged and staggered back. In doing so, she bumped into another tube that was hanging behind her. The tube she banged into swayed enough that it bumped into another tube and made a loud metal ringing noise like you would hear with a large bell being rung. Sheye sucked in her breath. She cursed at herself for being so stupid and went over to steady the swaying tubes. Sheye held her breath to see if the noise she caused had grabbed someone's attention and would come to see what had produced it. Thankfully, no one seemed to have heard or noticed the disturbance she had caused. Still, she hid between two tubes just in case for a few more minutes. When she was sure no one was coming, she exited her hiding spot and looked in the tube again.

There in the tube was a woman floating in a liquid with tubes connected to her chest and arms. Her eyes were closed, and according to the control panel at the front of the tube, she was indeed still alive. Sheye assumed that it was a life monitor for vitals. It was a panel she had never seen before, but she got the gist of it.

"What in god's name is going on in this place?"

Sheye was very confused and extremely frightened. Curiosity roused again, and she continued to look in all the tubes as she went down the rows. All of them where full of young women around the same age as herself. Sheye did notice that the color changes with the tubes were also related to the women getting more attractive as she went farther in. The women in the black tubes looked a little less appealing compared to the women who were in the white tubes and so on. All the women were attractive just that the more she went into the room, the colors changed with the pods, and the woman were more and more attractive. Sheye also noted that the farther she progressed into the room, the less tubes there were in each section.

Sheye finally entered the green section and noted that the women in this section were incredibly beautiful and very physically fit. She looked at a few more tubes, and suddenly she gasped. There in the next green tube was her best friend, Mandy.

"Oh no, oh god, no!" Sheye placed her hands on the tube and stared at her best friend's beautiful face as she floated in a dormant state in the liquid. A few emotions flickered through Sheye as she looked at Mandy. One, she was so happy finding her friend alive she almost cried; the other was anger that her friend was in this position, and the last was, how the hell was she going to get her out of there?

Sheye looked at the control panel frantically. She had to stop herself for a few moments and just take a few deep breaths and think. She looked around at all the tubes again and observed that all the tabs on the side of the containers were colored tabs, but they were not lit up. Sheye took one more deep breath and hit the green tab that was the color of Mandy's tube. Sheye stood back and crossed her fingers. The tab glowed a light green, and within a few moments, she could here a suctioning. She could see that the liquid was draining up into the suspending pipe, into the ceiling by way of the pipe the container was hanging from. When all the liquid was gone, the door slid open. Mandy was released from the tubing connected to her arms and chest. Sheye leaped forward as naked Mandy began to fall out of the tube. As gentle as she could manage, she laid Mandy out onto the cold floor half on her lap with Mandy's head supported on her abdomen. Sheye just sat there not sure what to do next. Rapidly Mandy began to cough and choke. Sheye rolled her into a recovery position, and Mandy began vomiting loads of the liquid that she had been suspended in out of her lungs.

When all the liquid seemed to have been expelled, Mandy began to gasp in huge lungfuls of air, coughing and gagging in between each ragged breath. Mandy was grabbing at her throat, and then she groaned.

To the delight of Sheye, Mandy croaked out, "What in the devil? My throat is so dry. Why do my lungs hurt so much?"

Sheye sobbed out a laugh and just grabbed slimy, naked Mandy into a huge hug. "I got you, hun. We're going to be okay. I got you."

Mandy struggled to sit up as she was so slippery and wet. Sheye let her use the sleeve of the cloak she was wearing to get all the sticky liquid off her face and out of her eyes. Mandy was disoriented for a bit and turned to her rescuer. "Is that you, Sheye? Where the hell are we?"

Before Sheye could answer, Mandy looked down at herself and noticed that she had nothing on but her birthday suit. "Why the hell am I buck naked and lying on a damn cold floor?"

Sheye immediately stood up and took off the cloak she had stolen and gave it to Mandy so she could put it on. She was just so happy to have her friend back alive that after Mandy had put on the cloak, she had to laugh. Poor tiny Mandy. The cloak swallowed her like she was wearing a tent. It was far too long, and the sleeves went down past her knees. Sheye took it upon herself to roll up the sleeves and tried her best to tie the bottom of the cloak up so at least Mandy could walk without tripping. With that done, she stood back for a moment to view her handiwork. It was not perfect, but it would have to do.

Sheye grabbed Mandy by both her arms, and in her most serious tone, she stated, "Mandy, you have to listen to me and please be quiet while I try to explain what I know to you." The seriousness and fear in Sheye's voice had Mandy's full attention. "We have both been abducted as well as all these other women in this room." Sheye swept her hand around them when she said this. Mandy looked around her but could not see up to the windows of the tubes and looked back at Sheye extremely confused. Sighing, Sheye grabbed Mandy and lifted her up just enough so she could have a look. She knew Mandy could see the contents of the tube when she let out a loud, shocked gasp. When Mandy was standing back on the floor, she went over to look at the now empty pod beside them.

"You are telling me...that I...was in...one of these things? Shit! That is just so wrong on so many levels. How the hell did I breathe in there?"

Sheye shook her head but added, "It must be liquid oxygen that keeps you in a suspended state. For what, I don't know."

Mandy was peering inside the container that she had been in with the look of shock and disgust on her face. As she investigated the inside of the tube, she uttered, "Remember that movie about the weird water creature that was in the big underwater machine mining thing? Did they not have to use liquid oxygen to go down deeper into the depths of the ocean so they would not implode?" After Mandy had uttered her thoughts, she suddenly turned from the pod she was inspecting and put her hands up to her mouth, horrified. Mandy looked at Sheye in dread. "Oh my god, Sheye! Are we deep underwater? Are we going to implode?"

Sheye shook her head and placed her hand on Mandy's arm. "I really hope not, Mandy. All I know is, whoever abducted us are doing some kind of experiments on women. We have to find out where we are and then get the hell out of here."

Mandy shivered violently but nodded with Sheye.

Right after Sheye had made that statement, all the lights dimmed. A loud alarm began to wail throughout the vast room. A male voice came over the intercom again in a foreign language that the two girls could not make heads or tails of. Sheye grabbed onto Mandy and tried to decide where to hide. "Shit, I think our escape has been noticed!"

Out of nowhere Mandy stated, "By the way, Sheye, who let you out of your tube?"

Sheye frowned at Mandy before pulling her toward what she hoped was an exit. As the two headed toward the door to the back of the room, Sheye hissed, "I wasn't in a pod, Mandy. I woke up in a white bubble room. I escaped when a man in the cloak you are now wearing came in to give me food. I clobbered him and was able to get out. I was trying to find a way out of this building and found this room by chance. As I looked in these pods, I happened upon you. I thought you were dead, Mandy."

To Sheye's surprise, Mandy stopped and stared hard at Sheye. "Well, damn, that sure ain't fair!"

Sheye just shook her head in frustration with Mandy. Maybe the liquid in the tubes addled her brain a little, or this was how Mandy dealt with stress, so she had to give her the benefit of the doubt and just proceeded to push Mandy forward toward the door.

"Right now, we have bigger fish to fry than what is fair and what is not fair, like finding a way out of this mess."

Mandy shrugged her shoulders but fell silent. When Sheye pushed herself past Mandy, Mandy snagged on to Sheye's T-shirt just like she did the first night in the cabin as she followed her quickly toward the door. To the girls utter disappointment, the door they were headed toward flew open, and large men in black armor started to enter. When they spotted the women, they pointed and yelled. Both women skidded to a stop. Sheye instantly turned down one of the rows of pods and ran like hell with Mandy clinging for dear life to her shirt trying to keep up with the much longer strides of Sheye's.

They weaved in and out of the pods to try to not be predictable by running in a straight line in order to try to lose the men who were following them. Suddenly, Sheye had an idea. Without delay, she began punching the color tabs on the sides of each of the tubes that they were passing. Behind them, all they could hear was the sound of suctioning coming from dozens of tubes. Mandy quickly got the hint.

"Tell me what to do so I can help."

Sheye yelled over her shoulder, "Green containers, green tab. Yellow containers, yellow tab. Got it?"

Mandy got it all right and began doing the same thing to the tubes on the other side of the rows they were running past as they went.

The men in armor were not as fast as the women. They had to make sure the women were not hiding between some of the pods. When they heard all the suction noises start, they all stopped and looked around.

"Damn it!" the head trooper bellowed as he turned to all the other men, "they are releasing the hyperpods. Split up, find them fast before they do any more damage."

Before the men were able to split up, naked screaming women came at them from every direction. Some were running blind as the slimy liquid was in their eyes, and they could not see. Other women were running and slipping everywhere extremely confused and bewildered. Some of the women were even attacking the soldiers who were trying to look for the two escapees. It was a comical naked mayhem.

The head trooper swore a fine line of curses as he turned to head in the direction, he last saw the two women, only to see them both climbing the ladder back up to the walkway rafters at the front of the room. There on the top of the rafters were a bunch of cloaked figures of all colors gathered and gawking down from the walking rafters to see what was taking place. None of the cloaked men were paying attention to the door to the outer room as it was propped wide open. The head trooper watched as the two women slipped unnoticed by the men in cloaks out that very door. He swore out loud again and pressed his com button. He gave the coordinates to some other soldiers on the ship. He decided to stop pursuing them since they had nowhere to escape to other than run around and maybe get lost for a while on the ship. Besides, they had one hell of a mess here to clean up and to try to get all the other women gathered up, drugged, put back into their containers, and rehibernated for the journey home. The head trooper shook his head; this was going to take a long time to accomplish.

*****

Sheye and Mandy turned right when they exited the pod room. Sheye did not want to go the left way as that was where she escaped from the room that she had been held in earlier. All she could think about was to find a damn staircase that they could take to get the hell off this floor and maybe get outside. Thank God the two of them were in amazing shape and were able to keep up a good pace. All the doors that they came upon were locked. The alarm was still blaring everywhere that they turned. Sooner or later, they would come upon someone whom they did not want to see. They had to find a place to hide and fast. Just in front of them, a door slid open. A small man in a blue cloak exited the room only to be accosted and pushed back in by Sheye with Mandy close behind. Without a second thought, Sheye smashed her fist into the face of the man cloaked in blue, and he none to gently fell to the floor. Just for good measure, Mandy kicked him in the stomach hard while he was down. Unfortunately, the ladies realized too late that the room was full of other blue-cloaked men, and they all froze in place for a few seconds. Both sides were analyzing what to do next. Then they all moved at once.

Blue Cloaks charged at the ladies, and the ladies were letting their fists and feet fly. Blue Cloaks were going down as fast as they were coming at the women. Mandy was screaming bloody murder as she kicked, bit, smacked, pulled their cloaks up over their heads so they could not see, and slammed anything into them that she could find and get her hands on. Sheye had a bit more finesse as she quickly was able to do simple moves to take out the Blue Cloaks coming for her. There was only two Blue Cloaks left, and they were at a stand-off. The last two Blue Cloaks did not want to take on the two crazy females. They thanked the fifth star of Prantus when four soldiers entered the room behind the women. Sheye spun around just in time to see one of the soldiers approach Mandy quickly and hit her in the neck with one of the rods. Mandy went down in the arms of the guard. Sheye was so disappointed in herself. She had failed Mandy, and she had failed to escape. She would not go down without a fight though. At least she had found out her best friend was still alive. That was comforting for a whole second. Three men in armor approached Sheye and started to surround her.

They all had their metal rods out, and she knew if one touched her, she would be in the same state as Mandy. When one of the armored men lunged in to get her with his rod, she ducked and slid to the ground, landing and kicking hard on his ankle. He stumbled into a medical tray and bounced off the countertop beside it as his ankle gave out beneath him. Another guard took the opportunity to try to swoop in with his rod, but Sheye was quick and full of adrenaline. She came up off the floor, grabbed the guy she had just kicked in the ankle, and used his momentum of unbalance to shove him hard in the direction of the other guard. They both stumbled backward giving her the space she needed to flee out the door. The third guard was not far behind her. With the speed of a gazelle, Sheye flew down the hallway only to run smack tab into what felt like a hard wall. She realized that it was another armored man. This one though did not have his helmet on, and he was just coming out of another room. When Sheye slammed into him, they both grunted. Sheye was not small, and she was running fast. She had hit him hard. Stunned, the guard only held on to her for a minute. Then he looked down at her. His grip was extremely firm though. Sheye was in a hold she could not get out of, and this frustrated her. She glared at the guard that held her, and to her dismay and abhorrence, he was smiling. The more she struggled, the larger his smile became.

"So we meet again, rider of the black beast."

Tannor was shocked to find Jodar's woman run smack dab into him as he exited one of the medbays, having just had the Blue Cloaks fix his knees to be good as new. Tannor was now feeling like his old self again. He was in the process of going to find Jodar, who had summoned him to find this very woman that he was now holding tightly in his grasp. She looked up at him confused, and he laughed.

"Calm down, tall one. I don't need you to damage my knees again like the last time."

Sheye stopped struggling at this statement; she was very confused. Then she remembered the men whom she had attacked as he was trying to kill her beautiful Onyx and had then succeeded. In her fury, she had kicked her free legs out at his freshly mended knee. She knew she had damaged his knees to the point of needing surgery. This was that very man. How was he standing here now good as new? This was not possible, yet here he was!

Rage unlike anything she had known bubbled up with such ferocious intensity that she somehow managed to free her left arm. She raised her arm with an angelic speed and open palm smacked Tannor's nose so hard she could hear it crunch in a sickening yet very satisfying way. Green blood splattered everywhere. This was one of the men who had killed her Onyx, killed her Big Red; she wanted him dead. Tannor's eyes watered, and he heard his nose crunch and knew that it was shattered. Damn this woman and her ability to best him a second time. He started laughing though through the pain, but he dared not let her go and rearranged his hold on her so both her arms were pinned by her side again. She squirmed so much, and then she even screamed in his face.

Sheye suddenly stopped and just stared at him; something was not right here. There was blood gushing out of this man's face, but it was not normal. Sheye pulled her head away to get a better look. She had to focus on what was wrong here. The man holding her just grinned back at her with a smug smile on his blooded green face. *What is going on here? Is this a sick joke? Am I being super punked somehow by a movie studio for a new show?* Suddenly something dawned on her. "What the fu—"

The trooper that had chased her out of the Blue Cloaks' study had caught up to Sheye and was standing behind her watching the scene before him with humor. He knew that she had to be put out, or she would do even more damage than she already had. He could have stopped her from breaking Tannor's nose but waited to see what Tannor would do. When he saw what she could do with the great Tannor, he was stunned.

What a woman, he thought. What he had witnessed her do to his buddies back in the Blue Cloaks' study was honestly the most erotic thing he had ever seen a female perform. He was going to see if he could put his name in on this woman when the time came to claim a mate from their collections. Little did he know that she was being prepared for the supreme commander's son, Broud. If he had known that, he would have run in the other direction before Broud could say boo. He pulled out his rod and placed it on the side of the woman's neck just as she started to speak.

Tannor stopped smiling long enough to hand the woman over to the other soldier. He told him that she needed to go back to the holding room in sector 4, bay 1. Tannor sighed when he saw the demeanor of this soldier's body language change as the soldier held the beautiful woman in his arms and shook his head as he was dripping blood all over the floor.

"Just so you know, this is going to be Jodar's woman. Best keep your hands to yourself."

The other soldier's shoulders dropped in disappointment. If Jodar was going for this woman, he had no hope in hell at asking for her. He sighed and nodded at Tannor. There was honor among the troopers. Once a claim was made, then it was honored by all. The soldier did not even look at her with another thought of claiming. He took her back to the holding area she was to be kept in without hesitation. Tannor watched them leave, and his smile returned. Tannor flinched though as his nose began to throb and his eyes began to water even more.

Jodar is going to have his hands full with that one, Tannor thought. He turned back into the medbay to get his broken nose fixed. When Tannor removed himself from the spot he was standing, a clean bot raced out from the wall to clean Tannor's blood that was splattered all over the floor.

Chapter 7

Tannor entered Jodar's chambers soon after exiting the medbay for the second time with his nose completely fixed. Jodar swung around angrily.

"Where the hell have you been? I summoned you over two hours ago!"

Tannor laughed and retold the tale of what had happened to him only twenty minutes before entering Jodar's living quarters. He then collapsed onto the large sitting platform when he was just about finished explaining all the details.

"So she is safe and back at the medical level in section 4, bay 1. I just saved you having to go look for her, as now we know where she is at."

Jodar was very relieved that his woman was safe, but something nagged at the back of his mind.

"The supreme commander wants me to meet him at that exact area this very evening." As Jodar spoke of this, Tannor shifted forward from his comfortable position and leaned toward Jodar with a concerned look on his face.

"This does not bode well—I sense—my friend. There is only one reason why the supreme commander would be interested in your woman, Jodar. He already has a life mate, which means—"

Jodar tensed all over and then began pacing the room. He was beginning to turn red; he was so angry. "Tannor, if you say one more word right now, I am likely to take my rage out on you. I need to be alone to think. Leave me, my friend, before I do something you and I will both regret."

Tannor nodded and rose from his seat. Without a word, he exited the room; but before the door slid closed, he looked back at his friend and watched as Jodar slammed his fist into a wall in his chamber, leaving a small dent. This was no small feat as the wall was built with Sardanium steel.

Jodar was beside himself with such anger, but again, it was directed at himself. Tannor had warned him that his woman would indeed catch the eye of the Supreme family. He should have listened. He knew she was perfect, and so did the Blue Cloaks as soon as they had seen her. Now what was he to do? Broud would not touch her if he had anything to say about it. As he lived and breathed, Broud would never have her as his life mate. Jodar paced the floor a bit more till he calmed himself down with the thought of the knowing. He just knew this was how it would be with the woman he so wanted to have as his life mate. He had to remember that no matter what. He had to believe that together he and the woman would experience the knowing. Then it would not matter in the least if Broud wanted her or not. The law stood behind the knowing, and no one could break it.

Jodar was starting to settle down. He began thinking about how sacred the knowing was to his people. The supreme commander himself and his life mate experienced the knowing the first time they met. The entire planet was against the uniting of the supreme commander and his life mate though. She was from the very world that had caused so much terrible loss and pain to their own planet. Her world was why they were on this collection mission in the first place. When the knowing happened, no one could condemn their unity even if they had disagreed with it and wanted to speak up against it. This is how respected and ancient the knowing was to his people. It was becoming exceptionally rare as the generations passed and the people of his world were being mixed by other world races. It did still happen, even with off-worlders with his kind. It was very erratic, but it still happened. To keep himself in check, he just had to trust in what he believed. While Jodar prepared himself to meet the supreme commander, he kept himself calm knowing he was going to see his woman again within the next few hours.

*****

Sheye awoke in the white bubble room again. She sat up slowly this time and sighed. "Back to square one," she said out loud to herself. Before Sheye could think of anything else, several exceptionally tall; very slender men with long fingers; enormous, large solid blue eyes; and long white hair; dressed in full white cloaks flooded into the room. Behind the men entering came floating racks and trays with what looked to be small machine with lasers on it. Sheye bolted off her platform and scooted away from the strange men.

Oh great, Sheye thought. Now they were here to torture her for the trouble she had caused earlier. Men in costumes were going to torture her. They were sure into keeping up the appearance of whatever it was they were trying to film, do, or make her believe. Behind the strange men in the white cloaks came four of the large men in black armor. They each held one of the long metal rods. Sheye began to panic. Would she be able to handle being tortured? Would she make a complete fool of herself and beg? Sheye took in a large deep breath. *I will not scream,* she said to herself. *No matter how much it hurts, I will never give these people the satisfaction of thinking they have broken me.*

One of the tall, slim men dressed in the white cloak and weird facial mask stepped forward. He held his long hands in front of him with his palms faced up and open to show her that he had nothing to hide. When he noted that she had seen his empty hands, he clapped once, and a small bot came forward from behind the men and began to morph into a larger chair. Sheye was intrigued despite herself. She began to think that she must be in some secret government facility with technologies the world had not been introduced to yet. They sure had some supercool gadgets that she had never seen before. Sheye nervously looked at the costumed man as he began to beckon her to come and sit on the chair. When she did not listen, the armored men moved a little outward and forward with the rods out toward her. Sheye stiffened.

"Okay, her torture is about to begin." The head man standing closest to her spoke with a strange yet pleasant accent and thick voice. "Please come, sit. We are not here to hurt you. We are here to prepare you for the supreme commander's assessment of you."

Sheye stepped forward as her curiosity piqued a little. "So this is a military facility if I am to see a commander? What is it that you want from me and why?"

The tall, slim man blinked his large eyes at her. Sheye found it hard to look away from this man as his eyes were so uniquely beautiful. His makeup was strange yet so alluring. His eyes were so large and blue that she wondered how they accomplished these getups with masks and makeup. It was so real-looking and very unsettling. The tall, beautiful man listened to Sheye's sultry, smooth voice as she asked him her question. No wonder the commander wanted to see this one. She was indeed a flawless human female. He was sad that she may be given to the supreme commander's son, Broud. He had heard how all the women in the company of Broud had been beaten, bloodied, and broken. No female deserved to be treated that way, particularly this one. There was nothing he could do about it though. He was just here to perform his magic on her by making her even more stunning than she already was. The soldiers were only here due to her earlier antics as he needed the backup to keep him safe from this one. He did not want himself or his assistants to end up like the Blue Cloaks had earlier from this woman's ability to defend herself. News and gossip traveled fast in the ships among all the Cloaks.

The man motioned her toward the chair again. He only answered her questions with "the commander can answer your questions if he chooses, when he inspects you. All I can tell you is I am here to get you into a suitable outfit for your viewing. I am to style your hair and give you some facial enhancements." The man smiled slightly, shook his head a little, then added, "Not that you need any of this, I may add."

Is the tall man blushing? How is this possible through makeup? Sheye did not like the conclusion that her brain was suggesting, so she tore her gaze away and looked toward the strange-looking contraption on the floating tray. These still terrified her, so she backed up a bit.

The tall man regained his composure, raised his one long hand a little in a calm manner. "We are not here to harm you in any way. This device is our hair and facial enhancer. Would you please sit in this seat so I can get you prepared? We will be punished if we don't complete this task that has been given us."

Sheye sucked in her breath. *Will they really be punished, or is this a trick?* She did not trust anyone in this building and all its strangeness. She did not know who or what to believe either. She would never want anyone to be punished or hurt because of an action she chose though. Sheye looked at all the guards and shrugged, then she stated, "Oh, what the hell," as she stepped toward the chair. Sheye decided that if she did not move to the chair herself, they could easily use the rods on her and do whatever they liked to her when she was unconscious. This was something that did not bode well with her.

Sheye moved to the chair slowly and sat down on it. The armored men stood at ready in case she tried to pull anything or attack. Her heart was pounding hard in her chest. She prayed that this man was telling her the truth. She prayed that they were just going to pep her up a little bit and then leave her alone. Sheye almost bolted out of the chair when they brought the weird contraption around in front of her and began pulling it right up to her.

The man placed his long hand on her shoulder and, with a calm voice, again stated, "This won't hurt you. It is just here to assist me."

Sheye scrutinized the machine that was now in front of her and looked up at the tall man sceptically. The machine was octagon in shape with a flat bottom and a dome on the top. On each side of the concaved front were four pointing arrow like protrusions in a vertical line. Sheye eyed it warily for indeed it looked like a torture device.

The machine started to hover closer to her head; this is when Sheye did vault out of the chair and tried to knock it away from her. The armored men stepped forward laughing. Two guards caught hold of her and sat her back down in the chair. Then they clamped shackles on her legs and arms so she could not move out of the chair.

Oh god, Sheye thought, *this is it.* Her head was going to go into the center of this thing, and it would shove spikes right through her brain. The machine began to hover in front of her again, and she squeezed her eyes tightly shut and prayed for her dad to come and save her. When she knew that the contraption was at her face, she squeezed the chair handles to the point where she thought her fingers would break. There was no pain yet. She felt a very pleasant sensation stroke her face, like she was getting a facial. It felt like there were hands pleasantly playing with her hair. The device was quiet as it worked. With what seemed like only a minute passed by with no pain or spikes driven through her skull, she relaxed slightly. Then the device completed its task, floated away from her face, and settled back down on the tray. She opened her eyes and looked around bewildered.

All the men in cloaks stepped back and gasped. The armored men just looked at one another, nodded with appreciation at what they were seeing. The tall man walked around Sheye and fluffed her hair a little as he spoke. "Who knew that you could be even more spectacular than before, but here you are, even more astonishing. I can't believe my eyes that you are indeed real."

Sheye frowned at the tall, slim man for she had the exact same thoughts about him and his other men only a few minutes before. She wished she could flick him away as he fluttered around her with admiration like a beauty pageant mother. Sheye glared at the shackles that connected her hands to the arms of the chair. As if she willed them off, the shackled clicked open. The tall man held out his odd long, hand toward Sheye, and he beckoned her to stand up. As she did so, a solid screen wall silently slide out of the floor by the platform that she awoke on. The tall, slim man told her to stand behind it and to not move.

"It will feel a little strange at first, like a soft tingling over your body as the changer works on getting you dressed. Don't be frightened. The changer won't hurt you as I have said before as with the styler."

Sheye eyed the man up and down. She decided to go along with what he was asking of her for now. He did tell her the truth about the other contraption. She stepped behind the wall that was the same height as her neck, so none of the men in the room could see her behind it except for her head. The tall slim man then stated, "Now please take off your clothing."

"Oh, hell no!" was what flew out of Sheye's mouth as an answer to the tall slim man's request. "My clothes will stay exactly where they are, thank you very much, and that is on my body."

The tall man sighed and tried not to roll his eyes. "We can't see you if you are wondering. The changer can't do its work on you if you have unknown material from another planet. The fabric of your clothing is foreign to our machine. Thus, it won't work unless you are unclothed. We are not here to attack you or to peek at your nakedness. We would be punished severely if found to be ogling the possible choice for Broud by the supreme commander himself. We are just here to prepare you. Once again, you have nothing to worry about with us."

Sheye came out from behind the wall as the tall man was explaining. At first, she just stood staring at him open-mouthed, but then she suddenly burst out laughing, startling all the men in the room.

The armored men made ready once more thinking she was going to attack as she leaned over to the platform and rested her hand on it to keep from falling over due to laughing so vigorously. When Sheye calmed her laughter down and sucked in a lungful of air, she looked over at the guards and waved her hands in exasperation.

"Down, boys," Sheye stated to the armored men, and she held her hand up as she gasped for breath. "I have to admit, all this is pretty weird. Everything here is alien to me. What with the green blood, the rods, the pods with the women in them, your strange clothing, masks, and contraptions. You guys"—Sheye waved her hands toward the White Cloaks—"are the best so far though." Sheye turned to the tall, slim large blue-eyed man that was assisting her. "I mean, your makeup is astonishing if I must tell you the truth. I give props to your special effects artists. You almost had me until you just said what you said."

The tall man with the large blue eyes and extreme elongated hands looked confused. Sheye said, sighing heavily, "From another planet! Come on! Really? You honestly want me to believe you and all this"—Sheye waved her hands around the room—"are from another planet?" Suddenly Sheye was angry. "I am not going to play this game anymore. I am done! You can release me now. Your sick gig is up. Just take me to my friend, Mandy, and we will leave here." Sheye began walking around the room as the men watched her guardingly. They began to wonder if they had broken her. Had she lost her marbles as they watched, as she started speaking to the walls. "Okay, whoever you people are, I figured you out. You can stop the cameras now and let myself and Mandy out. I am not going to play this ridiculous charade anymore. You punked me, but I am done now. I may not even sue your asses if you just let me out of this debacle. Oh, and you better hope my horses are not hurt, lost, or hungry, or I will indeed sue you for everything you have. You can trust me on that."

The lead White Cloak came up to Sheye when she stopped ranting and just stood there waiting for someone or something to happen. "May I ask who it is you are yelling at?"

Sheye turned to look at him. "Your director or your producer. Whoever it is that oversees this fiasco. I have to say though, you are all amazing actors and stuntmen. I hope they are paying you very well for your performance."

The tall man was even more confused than before. "Please could you just get changed? And then we can talk about this producer-director person after! We are running out of time to have you ready for the commander. He will be here to see you very soon, and you are not ready."

Sheye could see that the tall man was sweating, with beads of perspiration showing on his brow. He seemed to be extraordinarily stressed now. He genuinely looked nervous and seemed worried. Sheye was impressed. "Wow, you really are good!"

They all held their characters and were still trying to convince her they had no idea what she was talking about. Now Sheye was developing a build in her ire as well. "Look, I am serious. I am done playing this game. Let…me…out!" Sheye took a step toward the tall man to reenforce what she was saying. Now she was fed up. All her amusement left her as fast as it had come. The armored men stepped forward, but she pointed her finger at them and yelled, "Stop!"

Surprisingly, they listened. Turned out it was not because of her; it was the tall man behind her that was waving his hand at them. With sudden calm authority, the tall man took a step toward Sheye, closing the gap between them, and with a steady gaze, he said, "I would really like you to change behind the wall. I don't want us to have to do this with you unconscious. Go behind the wall, undress, and we will complete our task with the changer."

Sheye was a little intimidated by his authoritative stand, but she was still disgusted with all this. Now she was 100 percent going to sue all these idiots. Sheye turned from him and tried to pass the armored men, but they all raised their rods toward her. "Fine, I will get behind your stupid wall." Sheye turned herself from the armored men and stomped like an angry child to the wall, went behind it, and stripped off all her clothing. "There, I am naked! Are you happy? Ready to molest me now?"

As Sheye was throwing her temper tantrum, she failed to notice the changer had positioned itself beside her and start to softly hum, nor did she feel the tingling sensation all over her body at first. What she did notice was the material that just seemed to be growing and appearing on her arms. Sheye stopped and gaped at the silklike material just magically placing itself somehow on her arms. The material felt alive as it slithered up and around her arms, torso, and down her back. Now she could feel the tingling, gentle sensation. Too in shock to do anything else, Sheye just held her breath and watched the progression of the fabric work its way around her body. This was so not normal! How the hell were they pulling this off? Had they drugged her, and now she was having a bizarre hallucination brought on by suggestion? The material was now flowing down and around her abdomen and her legs. She could see that this was to be a dress that was light and airy. It weighed next to nothing. The material seemed like a second skin.

The dress did not leave much to the imagination. On the top part of her body, the material was so tight it almost exposed everything without leaving much to have to guess at your assets, yet it was extremely comfortable. The cleavage was so low she felt naked. The bottom of the dress started to form, and to her surprise, it was uniquely beautiful. The material moved on its own, or so it seemed. It was, as if, a variety of translucent pieces of floating material hung in a way that none of her lady bits could be seen. The material overlapped enough as to not be seen through. As she moved, the material seemed to slip around her legs so she could expose the full length of her leg, yet it was not immodest. It was the most amazing sensation to have the clothing feel like it knew just how to show off what was needed to catch a man's eye and leave the rest to the imagination. But not so with the top. Other than her nipples not being exposed, Sheye felt very exposed indeed.

Sheye sensed she had just witnessed something that could not be faked. She did not feel drugged or altered in any way. *Where did they ever get this kind of technology?* Sheye's brain started to buzz in an unpleasant manner. What she had witnessed so far was just too peculiar to make sense of. Sheye mentally began to think about all the strange sights she had seen—there was the immense size of the men who had abducted her; the odd armor that the men wore; the silver rods that could render one unconscious; the pods full of women suspended in liquid oxygen for hibernation; the green blood; the small men in blue cloaks; the strange, tall, slim men with long white hair, immense blue eyes, and elongated hands and fingers; the weird devices and androids coming out of walls and floors; even the white room that seemed to have no connecting walls to the floor; and ceiling that made it seem like they were in a bubble; all the things that just floated above the floors and followed these people around like a pet. Now she had experienced the changer. As Sheye began to think about everything that she had witnessed in the last day, it was extremely unnerving. She had never experienced or heard of any of this before.

Sheye, without warning, suddenly bent over and vomited. Only bile came out as she could not remember the last time she had eaten. She heaved again, and the tall, slim man rushed around the wall and guided her to the platform for her to sit down and compose herself. He handed her a napkin to wipe her mouth, and she readily accepted it. Sheye let him lead her to the platform as she realized that this was not a prank or a reality movie. Everything she had seen came crashing through her head, and she just had the sudden realization that these men were not lying to her. This meant that they were indeed not of this world. Out of all she had seen this last day, it took the changer for her to believe. Sheye gagged again, and she became extremely dizzy and had to lie down for a moment.

Chapter 8

The supreme commander entered the holding cell with his life mate—Adrya, the mother of his son, Broud—only to find the woman of interest lying out on the platform with her arm thrown over her face, moaning softly as she rolled her head from side to side. The tall man was bent over her, whispering in her ear. The armored men immediately separated and bowed as the supreme commander entered the room. The White Cloaks all bowed their heads in a quick gesture toward their leader and his mate as well. The tall, slim man immediately stood up and nervously backed away from the woman so that the commander and his life mate could come closer to the platform for their inspection. The tall man was feeling uneasy. This was not how he intended the supreme commander and the mother of the next supreme commander to see this woman whom he had been directed to prepare, for assessment. The supreme commander and Adrya ignored the tall, slim man completely. They stepped forward, followed close behind by their personal protector.

Jodar had been excited to see his woman. When he entered the room behind the commander and his mate, his heart broke. He could see his woman was in a great deal of distress, lying the way she was on the platform. He wanted nothing more than to rush over to her, gather her up in his arms, and take her to his chamber where he could keep her safe. He knew if he did this though, he would be severely punished. It took every fiber of his being to hold back and stand quietly behind his charge.

"What is the matter with her? Is she ill?" The supreme commander directed his question toward the tall, slim man, even though he did not look in his direction.

The tall man cleared his throat before he explained. "I sense, the woman doubted that we are not of her world. She has just, this very moment, concluded that what we have been telling her was the truth. I believe she is overwhelmed now and is trying to process the news, my liege."

The supreme commander seemed satisfied with the explanation and nodded, but his mate, Adrya, gently scoffed at this. This woman was possibly meant for her son. She had better show more mental endurance than this. So far, Adrya was not impressed.

"What is your name, girl?" The supreme commander spoke with such fatherly authority that it made Sheye respond by putting her arm down and sit up. When she looked up at the man before her, they both gasped simultaneously, and Adrya took a step back and exhaled with her hand to her chest in disbelief.

Sheye inhaled her breath none too silently as she looked up at the man standing before her. He was the largest man she had ever seen in height and musculature. He was older, what seemed to be the age her father would have been if he had still been alive, yet he was in amazing shape. He had a strong, handsome chiseled face with shoulder-length, bronze-colored hair; she could not tell if it was brown or blond or red. It was a mixture of all those colors. He was clean shaven and had vast shoulders, accompanied with a chest the size of a small table. Sheye wondered if he had giants in his lineage. He must have stood at least seven feet tall. He was dressed in the same fashion of armor the other men in the room had on, only his armor was a gunmetal gray, and he had a dark-purple cape flowing down his back and attached at the shoulders with a large sword-shaped rod strapped to his side. The man standing before her held himself in a way as someone used to being in command, to having his every order followed. Yet he had kind gray eyes as he looked down at her.

The woman standing beside the giant of a man was something to behold as well. She was breathtaking. Sheye could not judge her age as she looked timeless. She had long black hair that flowed in beautiful waves down her back to her waist. It was pinned back regally to show all her perfect facial features with the most expensive-looking jewels Sheye ever had the privilege of being close to wrap around her hair and neck. The woman was about as tall as she was but with a little more curvaceousness. She was dressed in a similar dress to what they had placed Sheye in only hers was the same gunmetal gray tones as the large man she stood beside. She, too, had on a long purple cape as well. The woman had a heart-shaped face with full lips and a small pointed chin and a pert nose that any model would go under the knife for. Her eyes were large and so dark black you could not see her pupils. Her eyelashes went on for days. Sheye could not see a blemish on her perfect face. She was however taken aback by the look this woman was giving her. If looks could tear off your flesh and see inside your soul, this woman was doing just that to her at this very moment. Though this woman looked at her with malice, she had a smile on her face; it was still somehow evil. It was a smile that brought a shiver to one's spine.

The supreme commander was stunned at the woman before him. She had to be the most beautiful creature he had ever seen. She even surpassed the beauty of his Adrya, which spoke volumes, as his life mate's beauty was known throughout the twelve planets in their system. He was also staring at the live version of his son, Broud's, ideal woman he had created on his hologram. How could this be? He could not be happier at this very moment that she was Broud's idea of the woman he wanted. His son, Broud, was a huge disappointment to him with his cruelty to women and his petty jealousy of the man that stood behind his back at this very moment. The supreme commander caught himself many times wishing that his personal soldier, Jodar, had been his son and not Broud. Jodar was strong, clever, effective, honest, well-liked, and always the finest at whatever he set out to do. His son, Broud, was a perilous, an inconsequential man-child, always nipping at the heels of Jodar when ever he could. Broud would run to Adrya to be indulged by her to his every whim when things did not go his way.

Perhaps this woman would be able to change his son's outlook on life and finally be the man and leader he was born to be. The commander could not believe his eyes yet. Looking at this woman, he began to assume that someone was playing an extremely dangerous game with him. That someone had Broud's hologram image transposed to this holding cell. He shook this thought out of his head almost the second it sprang up. No one would dare deceive him like this. Everyone knew what the punishment would be to play with the emotions of the supreme commander.

The supreme commander came to his senses first. He looked over at his life mate, who seemed just as astonished as he felt. He noticed though the large smile that was on Adrya's face and knew she liked what she was seeing. He understood that she was also aware this was Broud's ideal woman. He looked back to the woman on the platform and again inquired, "May I have the pleasure of knowing one of such beauty's name?"

Sheye had the audacity to blush. This man may be her enemy and want to cause her harm. Here she was batting her eyes at him and blushing for God's sake. Sheye decided to go along with this god-and goddess couple for the time being and cleared her throat before she stood up. Sheye felt out of place before these two prime individuals. She felt like she should bow or curtsy for them. She was still a little dizzy from her grasping the true situation of this not being a hoax. With the speed at which she stood up, she stumbled and was about to fall right into the chest of the huge man standing before her. Out of nowhere, strong arms grabbed her and held her up and away from the supreme commander. Sheye thought that it was the commander who had caught her from falling into him, but when she looked up, she was met with the most magnificent amber eyes she had ever encountered in her entire life.

Jodar could not help himself. Without thought, he stepped out from behind his post, sidestepped in front of the supreme commander when he realized Sheye was about to either pass out or fall. Jodar could just tell that she was unsteady the second she stood up. His training was so instilled in him to not let anyone touch his charge without permission that without thinking he was already in action. Jodar was there the moment Sheye began to fall. When she looked up at him, he saw the astonishment in her eyes, and then there was suddenly something else. There was a strong sudden jolt that coursed between them both. It was so fast and so unexpected they both grabbed a hold of each other fiercely by the forearms. They could not unlock their eyes from each other. Suddenly, a small beam of light exited Jodar's eyes and entered Sheye's.

The lighting in the room began to flicker violently, like the flashes from a thousand cameras. Then without either being prepared for what was to come next, they were bombarded with each other's existences, flashing within each other's minds. Each of them experienced the other's feelings, thoughts, emotions, hopes, dreams, desires, needs and wants, losses and pains. These images and sentiments were so intense they leaned in and placed their foreheads together for support but kept eye contact. They were both panting as if they had run a marathon, and they broke into a heavy sweat. The sweat poured off both as if they were in an intense hot sauna. It was like they were suddenly in each other's body and experienced their entire lifetimes in a few moments. The strength of the emotions and images they were both experiencing became so powerful that they fell to their knees without letting go of each other. Their bodies were vibrating and sending off pulsing waves around each other, and it looked like they were being encased in a cocoon.

Jodar had been right. The instant he had laid his eyes on Sheye at the lake, he just knew. It was the knowing, and it was happening right now. As soon as they had looked into each other's eyes, the knowing had been triggered. Their souls were joining. They would feel emptiness if they could not be with each other for the rest of their lives, like identical twins ripped apart at birth.

The supreme commander and the rest of the room were in complete and utter astonishment. The only other person in the room that had experienced the knowing had been the supreme commander with his life mate, Adrya. It was so rare and unexpected for this to happen anymore. The commander could not believe the power of this knowing between Jodar and the beauty. He himself could only recall looking at his life mate as they experienced the knowing to be a strong buzzing in his brain, and then he blacked out and awoke with Adrya's life memories in his mind. His experience was not near as tangible as what he was seeing before him. The two were glowing and seemed to melt into each other, yet they were still two separate beings. You could feel the intense heat emanating from them.

You could see the vibrations surrounding them. The air was being mutated around the couple. The light became so bright for a second that everyone had to look away. As fast as the light emitted from the pair, it disappeared with a loud crack and absorbed back into each other and was gone. Sheye and Jodar fell utterly exhausted to the floor still holding each other's arms.

For a minute or two, the room was quiet. Everyone had backed away and were all in shock at what they had just witnessed. The only sound in the room was that of the two on the floor panting from their experience. Suddenly, the silence was broken.

Adrya screamed in anger as she dashed over to Jodar, "How dare you! What is the meaning of this outrageousness? This woman is to be given to my son, the man next in line to be supreme commander of our world, and you think you can just come in here and steal her from him? She will be my son's life mate. Broud will kill you for this." Adrya then slapped Jodar hard across the face before the supreme commander could pull her roughly back and away from the couple on the floor.

Chanlon was extremely angry as well, and his face showed it. Only he was not angry at Jodar or the woman; he was disgusted at the words and actions of his life mate. With a loud, booming voice, he turned to Adrya. "Woman! You dare go against the 'knowing'? We all just witnessed one of the most powerful 'knowings' that has ever been witnessed in over a century. I have only read of such 'knowings' in our ancient texts. Broud will have to settle on someone else we have collected as a life mate. This is my final word. This is the law. You have insulted our culture and our ways. I will have no more out of you on this matter. Go back to our chamber, and I will deal with you appropriately when I deem fit."

"Chanlon?" Adrya cringed at her life mate's words, but she did not obey him right away. She slithered seductively up to her life mate and stroked the armor on his chest with her delicate hand. "I don't know what overtook me, my love. I just want our son to have what is rightfully his."

Chanlon looked down in disgust at his life mate. "Obey me, Adrya. Do as I command, or I shall be forced to punish you in front of all these soldiers. Not one of them will stop me. They understand and accept the laws of our world unlike yourself. Begone from my sight."

Adrya looked defeated as she slowly backed away from her life mate. She had never seen him this angry toward her person. Nor had he ever talked to her thus. As she turned to leave, she ignored all the soldiers in the room. She held her head proudly and coolly exited the holding cell as if nothing untoward had just taken place.

Chapter 9

Chanlon sighed as he watched his proud, callous life mate exits the holding cell. The only reason he was with her was due to them experiencing the knowing together. He had found himself reading the ancient text many times about the knowing after he had been, in a way, forced to bond with Adrya. He felt cheated from his experience about how it was supposed to bond two people's souls together for life. He did not feel in anyway bonded to Adrya. He read how after the experience of the knowing, the couple would not be able to have a full, satisfying life without each other. He had never experienced this with his life mate either, even more so over the years as their son grew older. Chanlon and Adrya's knowing had been very mild because of Adrya being from another planet, or so Chanlon supposed. This idea though had just been blown out of the water as this woman on the floor with Jodar was not of their world either, and he had never, ever expected to see such a powerful bonding in his lifetime.

Adrya's planet happened to be continually at war with his planet. The only reason he had even met Adrya was due to a conference of the twelve planets assembling twenty-six years previous. The council had assembled to discuss a peace treaty between his planet Sarbus and Bionas. Adrya was the daughter of the supreme commander's commissioner from Bionas. Chanlon had learned before they were introduced. He had heard about her beauty, so all Chanlon had wanted from Adrya when he had first laid eyes upon her was to have her in his bed for the week of the conference. She had been the most beautiful woman he had ever encountered and lusted after her. He never in his life would have brought to his home an enemy of his world. But the first night he had lured her to his bed, the knowing happened.

When the knowing happens, it was the law to become life mates and to be bonded immediately. This is what Chanlon and Adrya did, and they were bonded under the insistence of Adrya and her father, the very next morning. There had also been a Blue Cloak in Chanlon's chamber at the time the knowing had happened. If there had not been a witness, Chanlon would have denied the entire event had even taken place. For one, he barely remembered anything other than a sudden strong buzzing in his head and then blackness only to wake up with Adrya's life's memories swimming in his head. Chanlon, being the supreme commander of Sarbus, had to uphold the laws of his world even though something did not sit well with him about what had occurred. Chanlon could have denied the entire event, but his guilt at not remembering parts of the night had him frustrated.

Chanlon did not want his people wondering if he was weak-minded. That he was a leader who consumed too much Jusberg wine while trying to bed an enemy of their planet, no matter how beautiful she was. No one would have interrogated the most powerful supreme commander in control of all the Sardanium ore, if he had completely denied what Adrya and the Blue Cloak had said happened. If it had just been Adrya claiming that the knowing had happened between them, he would have fully believed that he was being entrapped. The Blue Cloak, however, who had witnessed the event gave Chanlon pause. The Blue Cloaks were considered holy; no one believed that they had the ability to lie. Why would a Blue Cloak from Sarbus falsify evidence for an enemy that was trying to take over their planet?

The planet, Bionas, was the one world of the twelve in their system that continually attacked Chanlon's planet, Sarbus. They were endlessly at war. Bionas sought to seize the rights to own and control the Sardanium ore mines that were only found on the planet of Sarbus. The ore was also smelted only on Sarbus. Sarbians were the only ones with the knowledge on how to smelt the ore into the steel that was so coveted by the other eleven worlds. All twelve planets used Sardanium steel to construct and build everything from vehicles, buildings, short-distance and long-distance space vessels and cargo haulers. Sardanium steel was extremely lightweight, thin, and exceedingly strong. Using Sardanium steel cut massive amounts of fuel needed, as well as cutting the length of time needed to travel in space by over half the use and time. No other steel was comparable to being as durable and resilient as Sardanium. Sardanium was coveted as well as expensive.

The planet Bionas had tried different attacks on Sarbus many times over the centuries. The council of the twelve planets used to be the council of the fourteen planets many centuries ago, but two of the fourteen planets destroyed each other through using planet-annihilation weapons. The council of the fourteen became the council of the twelve. The rest of the council left, commissioned together eons ago, to never allow use of any type of massive destructive weapons that could destroy a planet. If any of the twelve planets went against the pact and used it against another one of the planets of the twelve, the council of the twelve planets would, without hesitation, destroy that said planet that used the weapon exactly as they had destroyed the one they used the weapon on. There was no law on wars against another planet of the twelve if weapons of mass destruction were not used to destroy the entire planet. So Bionas had tried to decimate Sarbus with everything but the use of outlawed planet-destroying weapons. They did uphold the council of the twelve pacts but tried in every other way to take over Sarbus.

First, Bionas tried to kill off all Sarbus's livestock. They did succeed with this, but the Blue Cloaks were able to invent a synthetic meat that sustained the population of the planet. The synthetic meat was so nutritious and tasted so close to the real thing Sarbus decided they had no real need to immediately repopulate any of the livestock. Then Bionas tried to wipe out all the vegetation on Sarbus. Again, the Blue Cloaks and their mighty brains were able to develop an atmospheric cure that annihilated all future attacks on their vegetation for any airborne, waterborne, or soilborne virus as well as any fungus, bacterium, insect, or infection. Bionas then flew in with fleet upon fleet of battle soldiers to attack on land and water. Unfortunate for Bionas, this was a complete failure. Sarbians were number 1 in war defense, war tactics, weapons use, and hand-to-hand combat. This third attack lost Bionas the right to any further trade or purchase of Sardanium steel by command of Chanlon. This threw the supreme commander of Bionas into even more rage. Then sadly, the next attack from Bionas was the most devastating catastrophe of all.

The last attack had almost succeeded in killing off the entire female population of Sarbus. The supreme commander of Bionas made the decision to have his scientists create a biological attack on the female population of Sarbus to hurt and decimate the population. Bionas thought that Sarbus would then give up entirely. All this genocide and annihilation for the single purpose to gain control of the Sardanium ore mines. A small number of Sarbusian females had survived. They survived only because of being off world when the airborne virus was released by Bionas terrorists. Within days of the viral attack, all Sarbian women and female children became severely ill and perished within days. The Blue Cloaks could not even begin to find a cure; it happened that fast. Now here they were taking women against their will from any planet that was overly populated and were compatible to their race for reproducing.

All the supreme commanders and the Senate of the twelve, minus the supreme commander from Bionas, gathered a week after the attack on Sarbus to inflict immediate justice. The heinous act of female genocide on the planet worried the Senates of the other eleven planets. Would Bionas's supreme commander and his terrorists begin coveting other planet's resources and commit the same terrorist attack against their planets as well. The council of the planets came down with swift action. They voted in less than an hour to sentence Bionas to be entirely encased by an impenetrable invisa-shield. No Bionaian would ever leave the planet again. They would have to become a completely self-sufficient planet. Bionas would immediately lose all trade rights, treaties, world's passports, travel rights, and all other amenities of any kind from the other eleven planets. They all mourned for the citizens of Bionas, but this was the only way they could be sure these attacks would not happen to any of the other of the ten unaffected remaining worlds in their system. The council hoped that the people of Bionas would be so outraged at their leader's actions against Sarbus that they would hunt him down and destroy him themselves. For some reason, Bionaians held their trust and belief in their supreme commander and his choices, and he still lived to this day.

Chanlon sighed again and shook himself from his thoughts. He stepped forward to the two on the floor and bent down. He gently raised the exhausted and perplexed woman off the floor. He was still in awe of what he had just witnessed as were all the soldiers in the room. They had all read and heard ancient stories of this somewhat powerful, undeniable knowing but had never dreamed of witnessing it happening. It was so rare now that Sarbians did not ever expect it to happen in their lifetime or anyone else's for that matter, especially since they had lost 99 percent of their world's female population. Sarbians were starting to choose one's life mates from off worlders by compatibility and attraction now.

Chanlon found himself envious of Jodar. If this were to happen to anyone, Jodar would be the one. Jodar never did anything half founded. Everything he lived for had been true, just, and with integrity. Chanlon knew of Jodar's insistence to never take a life mate unless he experienced the knowing with her. He had felt sorry for his favorite fighter, especially with his own experience with the knowing. Now he was envious and proud of Jodar's complete commitment to the old ways. Jodar picked himself off the floor and cracked his neck from side to side, shook out his arms, and turned to Sheye and Chanlon. When he looked at Sheye, he had the largest most enigmatic smile on his face, even with the reddening handprint left on his cheek by Adrya.

Sheye watched Jodar and was amazed at how smoothly he moved for the size of him. She was so befuddled now. She could not understand why she suddenly wanted to throw herself into the arms of this gorgeous stranger with the lion eyes and kiss him all over. As she watched him smiling at her, she was hit with the force of such love for him. This caused her to stumble back and land hard on her bottom when her legs hit the platform behind her. *Why do I know this man? How can I feel such powerful love for someone I have never met?* She could recite down to the very last detail everything about him and his life, yet this was the first time she had ever laid eyes on him.

Sheye smiled back at Jodar shyly. She truly looked at him now as he stood, continuing to smile at her like he had just received the best Christmas gift ever. What she saw, she very much liked. He was the most gorgeous man in face and in body. He was even better-looking than the large commanding leader beside them. He, too, was tall, large, and muscular. He could probably pick her up and carry her as if she weighed next to nothing at all. He was much taller than herself. This was an extreme bonus since she was so tall herself. This had made it hard to date a lot of men on her world. Suddenly reality hit Sheye again, and she realized what she had just thought. *Her world—oh god! Am I even still on Earth, or are we soaring through space at this very moment to God knows where?*

Jodar instantly felt Sheye's anxiety and moved quickly to her side and knelt beside her gently grabbing her hand. Sheye looked at the immense hand that engulfed hers. Her hand in his looked like it belongs to a child. His hand was so warm, so strong. In her mind, she thought how she never wanted him to move it away from hers. "What the devil?" Sheye jumped up and indeed did move away from Jodar. Every fiber of her wanted to jump into his lap and stare into those beautiful amber eyes of his forever. This was so not her; she was a strong, independent woman who had her own successful business and had never needed a man. Suddenly all she wanted was this man. Why was she so mushy, vulnerable, and lovey-dovey toward this stranger? Jodar let her go and understood her confusion. He now was able to sense her stress like it were his own. Even though her pain and emotional anguish bothered him, he was the happiest man in the whole universe right now. She was his. They would always be together. Broud would never get his hands on her. He would explain everything to her soon, and she would understand. They would be bonded as soon as possible. Jodar was over the moon. She was now and forever always his woman.

Sheye stopped pacing and looked at Jodar. His happiness was very contagious as it rolled through her like it was her own emotion. She walked over to Jodar and sat back down on the platform and placed her hand back in his. "You have a lot of explaining to do."

Just as Jodar was about to speak, Chanlon cleared his throat and stepped toward them both. His sheer size shot anxiety through Sheye again, and Jodar stroked her hand gently. "It will all be okay. I promise. I will explain everything to you soon as I am able. I have duties I must attend to first. I will have you taken to my personal chamber where I will meet you, and we will discuss everything. At that time, you can ask me any question you would like of me, and I won't deceive you in any way."

Without a doubt in her mind, she knew he was telling her the truth. She could feel his outpouring love for her. Sheye drank in it for a moment. It felt so pure, like the love she received from her father—no expectations or wanting something from her, just pure love. It felt so amazing that she could get drunk off it if she were not careful. Sheye snapped herself out of it, nodded, and forced herself to remove her hand from his. Was being touched by him what had her all twitterpated? Sheye tested this theory and moved herself away from him a little more. *Nope; I still want to give myself completely over to him, damn it.*

Chanlon looked at the two together. They would make an amazing couple when everything was taken care of. Chanlon shook his head slightly with the thought of again wishing Jodar had been his son and not Broud. How different life would have been. He had a hard decision to make involving his son, Broud, and the future of Sarbus to make very soon, but that would be dealt with after they returned to Sarbus safely. The precious cargo they carried to continue life on Sarbus needed to be placed and settled first.

Chapter 10

Adrya was so furious she was almost choking on it as she hurried off to her son's chambers. *How dare Chanlon treat me and talk to me the way he did in the holding cell and with all his soldiers as witness!* "Wait for him to punish me in my own chamber for protecting my son and our future? Not bloody likely." Adrya muttered to herself as she stormed down the corridor. Anyone she passed moved out of her way instantly without question. They knew that she had a temper and could easily take it out on one of them as she had done many times in the years past when Chanlon was not around. No one dared tell the supreme commander of his life mate's cruelty and behavior when he was not around. This was in case he took Adrya's side and punished them for attempting to tattle on his wife about her conduct.

Adrya was used to being treated like the queen she was always destined to be. Her father spoiled her terribly, giving her whatever she demanded of him as she grew up, especially after her mother passed away. No one dared even look crossly at her for fear of who her father was. All men adored and lusted after her for her beauty and her father's power. She could have had any man of her choosing to life bond with, but here she was stuck in a loveless bond with a man her father had forced her to seduce. She had agreed to do this for her father though. Only because she absolutely adored him, and he gave her whatever it was she ever asked of him.

This farce of a bonding would, in the end, be rewarding, not only for herself and her son, Broud, but for her home world as well. Before the conference of the peace treaty discussions between Bionas and Sarbus, her father had pulled her into his private chambers and told her of his dubious scheme. Adrya was willing to go along with her father as the reward in the end would be herself and Broud having total control of Sarbus if her father had all access to the Sardanium steel. Her father knew of her secret—the secret about her and the Blue Cloak. Her father used this knowledge to the utmost capacity he could. His plan had worked flawlessly so far.

Approximately a year before the peace treaty talks, Adrya had taken a hiatus with a few friends to the second moon of the planet Coslar. This moon was a go-to, for all the twelve planets as a vacation moon, with its beautiful beaches, lush vegetation, and perfect climate. On the first night of their voyage, Adrya and her friends had decided to all go out to a hot spot for unattached young travelers. That same night, a group of Blue Cloaks in training, were taking a well-deserved leave to the moon before they had to complete their preparation to their devotion as a true Blue Cloak. This was their last hurrah to get things out of their system before they devoted themselves to their studies. When Adrya and her friends saw the Blue Cloaks, they had dared Adrya to try to seduce one of them. Since Blue Cloaks were only from Sarbus, the rival planet of her father, she decided that this would be a fun challenge. Adrya was never one to dismiss a dare. Besides, she thought it would be a hoot to seduce a Blue Cloak and then leave him wanting, all for the entertainment of herself and her friends.

Adrya pulled out all her charms on the young group of Blue Cloaks, and one of them took the bait. The seduction worked. Adrya led the poor infatuated Blue Cloak to a secluded spot in the tavern. After they were comfortable, she swooned in on him and looked deep into his eyes; to Adrya's complete and total antipathy, they both unbelievably ended up experiencing the knowing. As their eyes met, an instant and strong connection melded them together for what seemed like eternity but only in reality lasted a few minutes. Immediately after the knowing ended, she was so disgusted with what had happened, she ran from the tavern and fled home instantly.

Adrya did not talk to her friends or even say goodbye. What had transpired between herself and the Blue Cloak was just too horrific for her to handle. Adrya was incapable of loving someone else but herself, so when she felt even an inkling of love for this strange young Blue Cloak from the planet Sarbus, she panicked. These feelings for the Blue Cloak were unwanted and foreign to her, and she did not like it one bit. She was far too embarrassed to admit what had happened between them to her friends as Blue Cloaks were looked upon, in their world, as unpleasant, awkward, unattractive scientists. The minute she returned home, she flew into her father's arms in tears and explained everything that had happened on her trip to the vacation moon. Adrya thought her father would be furious with the situation and hunt down and kill the Blue Cloak. She was counting on this of her father; Adrya wanted the Blue Cloak dead. This did not fit into her life in any way. Her father saw a much broader picture with Adrya's circumstance, and he intended to manipulate and use this new situation to its fullest capacity.

Adrya's father knew that Chanlon would desire his daughter, like every other man who had met her. The men usually changed their minds about Adrya after they had gotten to know how spoiled, selfish, and cruel she was. Adrya's father had a brilliant plan. He realized he could not have planned anything better if he had tried. He sat Adrya down and explained to her his plan. He stated to her that because of her cruel trick on the Blue Cloak, she had enabled him to thwart Chanlon more than he would have ever dreamed possible. With his plan in action, he brought Adrya with him to the conference to discuss the peace treaty with his world and Chanlon's. Adrya's father was Dorian, the supreme commander of Bionas. He only accepted the invitation to the conference to put his strategy into action. He would never sign a peace treaty with Sarbus. His hatred and envy for Chanlon ate at him daily. He also blamed Chanlon for the death of his life mate and mother to Adrya. Everyone looked at Chanlon to be one of the greatest supreme commanders within the twelve planets. Dorian would be that commander. Only he would earn their respect through fear and death. This was Dorian's time to be the head supreme commander of the twelve planets, and Chanlon's Sardanium mines and his planet would be his no matter what.

At the conference, Dorian had his top commissioner agree to introduce Adrya as his daughter when meeting the supreme commander of Sarbus took place. If Chanlon took the bait, it would then be up to Adrya to seduce Chanlon into taking her to his chamber, and then Dorian's plan could begin. The seduction had worked. Chanlon was in lust and wanted to bed Adrya. She had played it up that she was a willing harlot who wanted him as much as he had lusted for her, that she was a willing participant in entering his chamber when he invited her to meet with him. She made sure that she had averted herself from fully looking into his eyes as they talked and planned to meet. Then when she had him in his chamber, she had her Blue Cloak whom she had the knowing with enter the chamber "accidentally," just as she was staring into Chanlon's eyes. Of course, they had Chanlon drugged with the wine that Chanlon was drinking. While he was unconscious, her Blue Cloak who would do anything for her when asked had implants of fake memories placed into his brain much like their language program chips they implanted in their brains when traveling to other worlds. When Chanlon awoke, it was as if they had experienced the knowing and entrap him into bonding with her so they could begin their plan. Now they had a hold on the Sarbus by Adrya being bonded to Chanlon.

The plan had worked so flawlessly that it almost became a joke between herself and her father Dorian. Her knowing with the Blue Cloak from Chanlon's world had been such a fluke that worked in their favor it was almost as if it had been destiny. This was how Dorian viewed the way it had worked out for him. Dorian had the Blue Cloak found and brought to Bionas with the promise that if he did this for them, then he could be bonded with Adrya when the task was completed. He jumped at the chance to please his wanted life mate. The knowing was extraordinarily strong between him and Adrya. Adrya though was far too spoiled and selfish to really know love, so it did not stop her from using the poor Blue Cloak to their advantage. They had him strung along completely. Still to this very day, he hoped and prayed to the star's of Prantus that she would see the truth and finally join her life with his. Adrya would constantly give him little tidbits, morsels, and wonderful promises of the future with fake love, kisses, and letting him touch her here and there. He was so devoted to her he never believed that eventually she would do anything to him but bond with him. Twenty-six years and still, he was as devoted to her as if it had been the first day, they had experienced the knowing.

Adrya's father had wanted to kill off her Blue Cloak several times since then. He worried that one day he would come to his senses and realize that Adrya was never going to give him what he dreamed of and tell Chanlon everything. Dorian never understood the power of the knowing, especially since it did not seem to affect his daughter the same way it affected the people from Sarbus. Adrya had to convince him each time that they needed him. She did not really know why she defended her Blue Cloak each time her father decided to get rid of him. She just could not bare to see him killed. He was like a favorite pet to her. He had become so useful to them that Dorian seemed to ultimately like him around as well. The Blue Cloak wanted to please so much that it played on both of their egos to keep him around. In all these years Adrya or her father never even asked what the Blue Cloak's name was; they both just called him Blue.

*****

Adrya stormed into Broud's chamber without warning and walked up to Broud and his plaything for the moment and shouted, "Get out!" The woman happily scrambled away from Broud, who was becoming physically abusive with her and was about to hit her. She had experienced this with Broud once before and could not believe her luck at getting interrupted and told to get out. She did so with speed; without even donning any clothing, she ran out the door and never looked back. Broud spun around in a fit of fury until he realized that it was his mother and calmed down a bit. "Mother" was all he said as he gathered himself off the bed and strolled over to her and kissed her cheek. "What brings you to my chambers?" Broud stepped away from his mother and could tell that she was seething with anger. "What did Father do now?" Broud smiled down at his mother and then turned from her to grab something to cover himself and then he headed for a glass of wine.

Adrya paced a few moments and then smiled at her son. "My darling son, you are to ready yourself for a viewing immediately. We have found the perfect life mate for you. We must do this right away as your father is thinking of giving her to his pet, Jodar."

Broud straightened his back and stiffened when his mother spit out that name. He was instantly in a rage and threw his wine glass at the wall. "Jodar? Why would Father do this to me? He knows how I feel about his pathetic pet."

Adrya smiled and walked over to Broud and stroked his face with her hand that she had recently smacked Jodar with. "Don't concern yourself with your father's foolishness, for I have a plan. It will be set right, my darling. Just ready yourself and be at the viewing hall on level C in one hour. You won't regret my choice for you, my son. In fact, I think you will be over the moon with the woman your mother has chosen for you." With a true smile she only gave to her son, Adrya left his chambers and headed off to find Blue.

She would have to act fast before Chanlon found out her dubious plan and put a stop to it, or this would not work. Broud would have this woman no matter what knowing had occurred between Jodar and Broud's woman. She was destined for her son. She knew it the minute she laid eyes on her. Her son's happiness was all that mattered. This woman was the woman her son had always dreamed of. When Adrya first saw the woman in the holding cell, she was in shock. It was as if someone had brought Broud's hologram from his chambers directly into the holding cell. At first, she thought that it was a cruel joke. Then Adrya saw her move and talk. She was an exact replica of Broud's dream mate. For that first few moments she was the happiest mother alive until Jodar stepped in and looked into her eyes. Knowing—what a load of Kexar dung. It never affected her with Blue. Yes, she would never let her father destroy Blue, but that was because he was so useful, not because she loved him. This woman would be Broud's no matter what. She would fix this to be right for Broud.

*****

Chanlon, Jodar, and the other armored soldiers led Sheye back to Jodar's private chambers. They excused themselves after they had settled her in with a few instructions to not leave the chamber. Jodar promised he would be back as soon as possible, and then they would be able to talk. Sheye was still so stunned by what had occurred in the last few hours that she was very willing to remain in the chamber so she could think about all that had been told to her as well as all that had happened. Jodar's chamber was small but cozy. It had a small living space with a sofa of sorts, a large lounging chair, and a small table. There was an unusually large bed in the corner of the room. Before Jodar left, he squeezed Sheye's hands within his and looked her in the eyes with such love and happiness that it made her a little giddy. The butterflies flew around her stomach. He had the most amazing eyes that she could just melt into.

"Do you promise me that you will behave and not attack the troopers anymore? I will trust you if you trust me. Everything will be all right I promise. I will be back soon. Then we will talk." Sheye nodded at Jodar, still numb from emotions.

Sheye was far too exhausted from all that had happened earlier to even want to fight now. Plus, if what they were saying was true and they were on a spaceship, where could she even go? She had to trust this man. Before Jodar let go of Sheye's hands to take his leave, Sheye hesitated by squeezing his hands, and he stopped. "I don't even know your name."

Jodar blushed. He realized that he did not even know her name. He was just so over the moon that she was his that it had slipped his mind. Jodar bowed slightly toward Sheye and introduced himself, "I am Jodar of Sarbus, head combatant to the supreme commander Chanlon." Jodar raised Sheye's hand to his lips, and he kissed it gently. Even this small moment sent shivers down Sheye's entire body.

"Nice to meet you, Jodar. I am Sheye DuMontte of Earth, daughter of Joseph DuMontte." She giggled a little at how ridiculous she sounded, but Jodar bowed to her again.

"Sheye, that is a beautiful name. It matches you perfectly." Then Jodar smiled.

Sheye was amazed at how devastatingly handsome this man was. With one last look, he exited the chamber, and the sliding door slid back into place. Sheye went over to the large sofa and sat down. She was in a state of shock, and for once in her life, she had no idea what to do. She just sat on the sofa and stared at the wall. With so many thoughts going through her head, she had no idea which one to think about first.

Chapter 11

Sheye had only been sitting in Jodar's chamber for about five minutes when the door slid open. A small man in an orange cloak entered the room with a tray of food and drink. Behind him entered another cloaked man, but his cloak was blue. The man in the orange cloak never looked in her direction when she stood up from the couch. He just proceeded to set up the refreshment tray. Once that was complete, he turned and exited the room. The Blue Cloak stayed though. He stood by the door nervously looking in her direction and then back at the door. He never spoke as he pointed to the tray and beckoned Sheye to partake. Sheye was too nervous and stressed to eat anything, so she shook her head. "I am sorry. I will eat later, but thank you." The Blue Cloak became agitated and motioned to the tray again a little more aggressively than before. Sheye sighed. She just wanted to be left alone with her thoughts, so to make him happy and maybe get him to leave, she picked up the glass that had been poured for her and stared at the glowing contents. With a shrug and a tip of the glass toward the Blue Cloak, she closed her eyes and took a large swallow.

The fluid, whatever it was, was a perfect, cool temperature. It tasted sweet and tart at the same time. It was delectable. Before she realized it, she had drunk the whole glass. Sheye was much thirstier than she had thought. The Blue Cloak seemed satisfied and slumped his shoulders a little bit as she drank down the entire contents and then poured herself another. Within seconds after she poured herself a second helping of the delicious drink, she began to feel extremely strange. She felt a buzzing sensation start at her toes and then rapidly climbed to her legs and her extremities. She lost control of her motor skills, and before she could react or call out, she saw the man in the

Blue Cloak hurriedly stepping forward to catch her before she fell into unconsciousness onto the floor.

The drug had worked. Blue acted immediately and summoned Adrya. Adrya entered the room instantly, and between them both, they were able to get Sheye onto a movable platform that Blue had waiting just outside of Jodar's chamber. They covered her completely with a thin white sheet and transferred her to a medbay. The room was empty, and Blue took immediate action. He brought the floating platform with Sheye on it, toward the inserter, and punched in a bunch of codes. He then inserted a hose like contraption into Sheye's nostril and pushed a few more buttons. The computer panel lit up and a needlelike instrument inserted into the tube that was inserted in Sheye's nose. There was a whirring sound, and a slight crunching sound that followed. Sheye's body convulsed slightly but then stopped.

Adrya looked a little frightened and grabbed Blue. "Was that supposed to happen?"

Blue just nodded. "All is well, my love. The implant has been successful."

Adrya nodded, and Blue turned to her and pulled his hood down as he leaned toward Adrya. Adrya rolled her eyes, then she leaned in and gave Blue a soft kiss on the lips. "Thank you, my sweet. This gets us one step closer to being together forever."

Blue smiled at Adrya in admiration of her praise. He turned back to his patient and disconnected her from the computer and took out the tubing from her nose.

Sheye awoke slowly with a crushing headache. What the hell had happened? She remembered being in Jodar's chambers, but now as she looked around from the platform she was lying on, she was no longer in there. As she looked around, she was in a large hall with a lot of other women lying, sitting, and standing all around her. She groaned and held her head as she sat up. Man did she ever have a frontal lobe headache. It felt as if she was getting a bad sinus infection. After all she had endured, she sure as hell did not want to get sick on top of everything else. Sheye stood up and tried to walk a few feet forward toward one of the other women only to slam herself into something solid.

"What the hell?" Sheye stated out loud as she could not see anything in front of her. She reached out her hand, and it was stopped by an invisible barrier of some kind. She then took a few steps to her left carefully holding her hand in front of her and met up with another invisible barrier. The invisible barrier was all around her in a square surrounding the platform that she had awoken on. It was like a little jail cell without seeing the bars or the walls. All the other women were in the same kind of barriers and could only move a few feet to the right, left, forward, or backward. All the women were dressed up in the same kind of outfit that she was in and had been dolled up as well. Everyone in the room was beautiful and just as confused.

"You can't get out. I tried already," a beautiful brunette directly in front of Sheye stated to her.

"Where the hell are we?" Sheye asked the woman.

The brunette just shrugged and looked utterly baffled. "I have no idea! The last thing I remember, I was going for my morning jog. I remember that I was running away from these large men in black armor. Next thing I know, I am in this invisible box trying to find my way out. I am dressed in this extremely weird clothing that I don't remember putting on. My wrist hurts like it has been sprained. We are surrounded by all these other women who are just as puzzled as the both of us. Not one of us here knows what is going on or where we are."

Sheye looked around her and realized there must be at least fifty other women in the large room. "At least we aren't in the pods!"

The brunette frowned at Sheye as she had no idea what she was talking about. Sheye just shrugged and shook her aching head. "Never mind. You wouldn't believe me if I tried to explain."

Suddenly, the lights in the room began to get brighter. All the women in the room began to look around, talk, stand up, and some even screamed. At the far front of the room, a door opened; a few armored soldiers entered. Sheye thought she recognized the head soldier. He looked like the man whose nose she had broken earlier. Hatred flowed through her toward him, for he looked good as new again. She stepped forward and banged into the invisible barrier once again. "Damn it" was all Sheye muttered as she rubbed her nose and watched the front of the room. The soldiers were followed in by a Blue Cloak and the beautiful woman that she had seen with Chanlon and Jodar in her holding cell. Sheye felt a little more relaxed at seeing someone she had seen before but that instantly changed when a very tall, formidable-looking man with long dark hair entered behind the woman. The room's atmosphere changed in an instant. It felt like the devil himself had just entered the room. For some strange reason, Sheye instantly felt this man was not to see her. Something about him seeing her would end up being dreadful for her. Why she felt this way, she did not know. Flashes of images suddenly ran through her mind. They were images of the man who had just entered the room—life images, like she should know him, but it did not feel right. Sheye backed up and sat on her platform. What was happening to her? Her head began to hurt her even more.

    The large man was talking to the beautiful woman and the man in the blue cloak for a bit; he straightened and began walking further into the room. A few of the men in black armor, including the one that had killed her horses, walked behind the dark-haired giant as well as a few men in blue cloaks. The woman stayed behind though. She stepped onto a platform, and it began to rise. It stopped just high enough that she had a full view of the room. The intimidating man with the long dark hair walked slowly by the women. He paused at a few of the women and would look at them up and down. It almost looked as if he was viewing a car or a house he was wanting to purchase. It sickened Sheye as she watched. Some of the women, he did not even stop and view; he would just walk right by. Others he would look at for a moment or two and then move on. A few women he would examine a little closer but not for too long and then move on again. The closer he came to where she was, the more dread she could feel building up inside of her.

    This man must not see me... This thought kept running through her mind over and over. He was getting closer by the minute.

    The tall black-haired man stopped and walked around one of the woman's invisible cell. He walked around several times as if he were stalking his prey. The poor girl whimpered and tried to shrink away from him only to bump into the invisible wall of her small cell. Sheye noticed that he would admire the women with red hair the most. She grabbed a lock of her auburn hair and cursed under her breath. He had interest in the redheads that was for sure. This did not bode well. The brunette in the cell beside her started to weep.

"Do you think they are human sex traffickers who will sell us to some brothel somewhere?" The brunette was beginning to hyperventilate. Sheye felt for her but could not say anything that would calm her down. Her nerves were starting to fray as well. "Oh my god! That man is a giant. Do you think he will buy some of us? I can't be a whore for some greasy fat man in a hot country with no running water! I can't do this." The woman was really beginning to panic now. Sheye needed her to stop making a spectacle of herself as it was starting to draw attention.

"Stop it!" Sheye hissed. "The louder you get, the more you are making him come over here. Be quiet." Sheye tried to convince the brunette to calm down. She felt a little guilty about talking to her so harshly, but she needed the woman to be quiet. Of course, the brunette was not listening. She began to get even more hysterical, the closer he came.

Broud walked around the women. He was not impressed yet. There were several women he would like to bed, of course, but nothing that grabbed his attention for someone he would want as a life mate. He was excited though as his mother had promised him that the woman she had found, he would know her the minute he laid eyes on her. His mother had never steered him wrong yet. He trusted her. He was excited to see what his mother had in store for him, but they had to follow protocol; hence, the soldiers and Blue Cloaks were present as witnesses. He had to pick the right one. This viewing had to be documented to be valid in all ways to stay within the laws of the supreme family choosing a life mate. He was yet to be impressed though.

Suddenly, he started to hear one of the women farther in the room making a ruckus. She was beginning to make a lot of commotion. This in turn was affecting the other women. They, too, were getting tense and vocal as well. Broud was drawn toward the panic. He craved women that would cower before him. He loved to dominate a weak woman. It thrilled him to the core, yet he truly desired a woman who would stand up to him and challenge him. Even though he wanted a strong woman that could stand up to him as a life mate, the sound of a woman scared excited him as well. He stopped viewing the rest of the women near him and decided to see what this woman causing all the racket was all about. He did need new flesh to excite him in his bed for the night. If she were attractive, he would tell one of the Blue Cloaks to take her to his chamber so he could relieve some stress after the viewing.

Sheye noticed that the man was now beginning to make his way toward them and once again tried to calm the brunette down. "He is coming this way. Can you not see you are causing him to come this way? If you quiet down, maybe he will get interested in someone else before he even gets here to us. *Ssshhhh*, please." Sheye realized too late that this made the woman notice the man's direction change. This made the brunette become even more alarmed. Sheye sighed and looked down. She realized that she could not get this woman to calm down, and he would be here within a few moments. Sheye decided that all she could do was help herself. All she could think of was he could not see her. Why she felt so strongly about this, she had no idea. She immediately sat on her platform and brought her knees up to her chest and placed her head down in her lap with her arms curled around her knees. She spread her hair all around her so he could not get a glimpse at her face.

Broud approached the brunette who was pacing in her small cell around her platform crying and mumbling. She was beautiful, and she piqued his interest. She would sure thrill him if she were able to grace his bed for the night. Just as he was going up to walk around her cell to inspect her closer, something caught his eye. There in the other cell beside the brunette was a woman with her face and body crunched up on her platform. She had the most beautiful, long, wavy auburn hair cascading all around her body as she sat with her knees up against her chest with her arms wrapped around them. The color of her hair was the most beautiful auburn he had ever seen on a live woman. It was the exact shade of hair he favored. He even had this exact hair on his hologram woman. Very intrigued, he instantly ignored the brunette. He walked around her invisible cell; all the cells were noted with markings on the floor so no one would slam into the walls if they were walking around them and knew they were there. Broud approached the cell where the woman with the glorious auburn hair was curled up on her small platform. He studied her for a few moments, but she did not move. This frustrated him. He suddenly needed to see her face.

"You there, stand up," Broud commanded to the woman in the cell before him. Sheye knew the moment he noticed her. She could sense it as if she had been watching him with her eyes. There was no way she was going to stand up and let him view her like cattle. She sat silently without moving. Broud was slightly irritated at this woman not listening to his command. He was used to his every word being obeyed instantly. "I said to stand up, woman, show yourself to me."

Sheye could not help herself. "Go to hell!" Why she felt the need to say that she had no idea. She cursed herself for her pride. Maybe it was the tone of his voice that got to her, but she could not stop herself from responding. Broud turned red. No woman ever talked to him this way and not get a slap from him. His blood began to rush through his ears, and his heart rate elevated. Broud crunched his hands into fists but noticed in the three simple words she uttered, her voice was velvety smooth even though she was angry. This interested him even more. Broud tried a different tactic with the woman.

"I just want to have a few words with you if you will allow me the right. Then I will leave you be, my lady."

Sheye still did not move, but she responded to his statement. "Well, you just had a few words with me, so now you can move on."

Broud was caught off guard but in a very pleasant way, and laughter burst forth from him. He was impressed with this one. She was not only witty but quick-minded as well. Broud began to prowl around the cage. The soldiers and the Blue Cloaks stepped out of his way. Tannor was becoming nervous as he watched Broud. Broud's intensity at the need to see her face was growing. As he stalked around the cell, Sheye tightened her hold on her knees and shrank a little more so he could not get a good look at her. Broud was becoming aroused quickly. This woman excited him. It had been a long time that a woman truly made him feel a thrill. He needed to see her. Something told him that this was the woman his mother had found for him. He was not a patient man by any stretch of the word. He turned to the trooper behind him. "Tannor, open this cell immediately. I choose this one. This is the woman I will take as my life mate."

Tannor hesitated but then stood his ground. "I am sorry, Your Eminence, that would be against the viewing protocol."

Broud wanted to punch the soldier hard in the face but knew he was right. There were also too many soldiers at Tannor's back now for him to hit the trooper, so Broud turned back toward the cell. He had to follow protocol no matter how much he despised it.

Broud turned back to the cell. "Get up, now!" It was an order, and with that voice of his, she almost complied.

"No!" was all the response that Sheye would give him!

"I said, GET UP!" Broud growled only to be shouted back at by Sheye.

"No!"

Tannor smiled a little; he was impressed by this woman yet again. When he was told to get a few soldiers together for Broud to do a viewing, he knew exactly who they were going to view. He had warned Jodar that Broud would want this woman. Now here he was standing behind Broud watching the scene before him. He opened his com device and patched it to Jodar so he could hear what was going on and maybe get here with Chanlon in time. Tannor knew that this was not right. Chanlon should have been here as well for Broud's viewing for a life mate. Something was off. Adrya was up to no good; he could sense it. Jodar needed to know what was going on and would indeed get Chanlon here to stop whatever it was that Adrya had devised. Tannor besought silently for Jodar's woman to stay in her seated position long enough for Jodar and the supreme commander to make their way to the area.

Adrya watched the show from her platform. She was thrilled that Broud had found the woman who was intended for him. She had a sneaking suspicion that this woman would try something like this, so she had Blue install a special feature on the woman's platform in her cell. Adrya took a small cube device from within her dress and pressed a button on it. Sheye was suddenly shocked with a painful jolt coming from the platform. She released her knees and almost bolted from her seated position. She realized that she had almost exposed herself to Broud, so she held firmly to her knees again. Adrya hissed when Sheye did not jump up but then smirked a little. This one was going to be a well-suited mate for her son. She was strong. Adrya almost admired her will. She turned up the power a few notches and hit the button again. This time, the jolt was too painful for Sheye to resist it, and she flew up off the platform. She stopped just short of slamming into the cell wall and came face-to-face with the man whom she did not want to see her. As soon as Broud saw the woman's face, he was shocked and speechless. All he could do was stare at her as his breath caught in his throat at the sight of her. It was like the wind was knocked out of him. Was he dreaming? Was he back in his chambers looking at the hologram of his perfect woman he had created? Only this woman standing before him was even more remarkable than he could have ever created on a hologram image. She was flawless. Her hair flowed down her back and around her shoulders like a beautiful cape. She was tall and shapely in all the right places. Her breasts could make anyone's mouth water. Her voice was sultry like velvet. Her face was exactly as he had imagined it would be if his hologram would have come to life, and her eyes—he knew before she even looked at him that they would be the brightest emerald green, like the green from the coldest of waters fed by a glacier. He had never been so aroused in his entire life. He had to see her eyes.

Sheye tried to keep her eyes averted from him, but curiosity got the better of her. Maybe it was her dignity. She did not know, but she raised her head and looked directly into his eyes with as much malice as she could. Instead of malice, it quickly turned into something else. When their eyes met, there was a flash of light from above, all the lights in the room began to flicker, and some even erupted with loud popping sounds. A blast of wind came down from the ceiling and blew around Broud and the troopers. Broud and Sheye both stood fixed in place facing each other. Broud raised his hands up onto the invisible wall trying to touch the woman behind the cell wall, but the barrier stopped his contact. Blue went up to Broud by the cell as if he were going to pull him back. Blue reached out for Broud, but he had a hidden gadget in his long sleeve. He gently touched Broud's side with it. Just as Broud's hands touched the invisa-wall, he began to convulse. Sheye tried to back away, and when she touched the back of her legs to the platform of her cell, she started to convulse as well. A strong buzzing affected both their entire bodies. The lights in the room all went dim except for the one above Sheye's cell. That light continued to get brighter and brighter. The platform in Sheye's cell began to glow and shake.

Chanlon, Jodar, and several soldiers stormed into the large hall, and they all stopped in their tracks dismayed at what they had just come in to see. Jodar yelled out to Sheye and tried to head to her, but Chanlon and a few soldiers held him back. There was a large electrical charge that shot through the ceiling and then down upon Sheye's cell walls. Both Sheye and Broud were thrown back. Sheye landed on the platform, and Broud staggered back but did not fall. Everyone just stood around for a moment utterly confused at what just happened. Jodar was struggling to free himself from the other soldiers to get to his woman; he was very afraid for her. He could feel her pain as if it were his own. With him being in the same room as Sheye now, he could feel her stress as well as the pain of the shock she had just received. Suddenly, all the women in the cells began to scream and cower. Tannor, shocked at what had just transpired, turned toward Jodar and Chanlon with a look of utter distain on his face. They had not come in time.

Chanlon boomed out, "What is the meaning of this, Adrya! You have disobeyed me. Whatever has happened or has been witnessed in this room won't be documented as a true viewing for Broud. You went against me, woman. I won't allow it. Jodar and the woman have experienced the 'knowing,' already. They will be bonded immediately due to your dalliances. How dare you try to do this behind my back!"

There was a loud roar from Broud as he heard the words that came out of his father's mouth. He stormed toward Jodar and

Chanlon. "She is mine!" Broud had recovered from the shock of what had just happened. He grasped that the knowing was what he had just experienced with the woman. Did he hear correctly? His lifelong enemy, Jodar, had experienced the knowing with the woman as well? Possessiveness grabbed ahold of him immediately. That solved it. Broud raised himself to his full spectacular height and charged right into Jodar. Jodar was ready. He was as equally prepared to kill Broud as much as Broud was attempting to kill Jodar. They both were in love with the same woman. They both had experienced the knowing with her. They both hated each other to the extreme. They both wanted each other dead at that very moment.

The two men went at each other like a lion and a grizzly bear. It was a whirlwind of punches, grunting, splattering blood. Chanlon sighed and grabbed a rod from Tannor. When he saw an opening, he thrust it in to Broud, who dropped immediately. Another trooper did the same with Jodar. The two men lay in a heap on the floor. Tannor went over to Jodar and moved him slightly away from Broud. This was the only way to separate the two men who were trying to kill each other. Adrya smiled cruelly from up on her platform; her plan had worked. She made sure that there would be enough witnesses to testify that they had just observed that the knowing had happened between Broud and Sheye. Blue had made sure of that, with perfect timing and some well-timed special effects and trickery and voltage. Sheye now had fake life memories of Broud's implanted from the chip Blue had inserted into her head earlier with no one being the wiser.

Adrya had to thank the brunette who was in the cell beside Sheye as well, for her hysterics, which was an added and unexpected bonus. She felt like laughing as she had the platform lowered to meet Chanlon. She held in the laughter, but she did have a large wicked smile on her face. She could see that her life mate was angrier than she had ever seen him before. He was vibrating from it. She was quite satisfied with her deviant plan. Seeing Chanlon like this was quite the turn on. She had not felt this power over Chanlon for many years. Her father would be so proud of her. It was about time she was able to knock Chanlon down a notch or two again since her father and she first deceived him into bonding with her.

Adrya elegantly stepped off the platform. Before Chanlon had the ability to even speak any of his rage toward his life mate, Adrya held up her perfectly manicured hand. "Chanlon! Wait! I knew that this woman was special. I knew she was meant for our son even after we had witnessed the knowing between herself and Jodar. Now it has been confirmed as to why. As a mother, I knew this would happen. Therefore, I was so angry with Jodar. She has experienced the knowing with Broud as well. Ask anyone in here." Adrya swept her hand around at all the soldiers and the Blue Cloaks. "They have all witnessed it. They will testify that it is so."

Chanlon was slowly moving his way toward Adrya but stopped in his tracks and looked around at the soldiers who were in the room. They all had their heads bowed, or they were trying to avoid Chanlon's gaze from falling onto them. Chanlon spoke up, "Is this true? Tell me then, who witnessed this supposed event between Broud and the woman?" Chanlon scanned the silent group, quickly losing his temper with them. "Damn it, SPEAK!"

The soldiers looked extremely uncomfortable. Not one of them had been with Chanlon and Jodar when they first met Sheye for the viewing of her. They did not realize that the knowing had happened with this woman and their beloved, head trooper, Jodar. How was this possible? Jodar and the woman had the knowing, and now Broud and the woman experienced it as well. They were utterly astonished and appalled. They disliked Broud very much, but they had just witnessed something that they could not deny or explain.

Chanlon yelled at them all, "Tell me now!"

Tannor sighed. If he had only known that Jodar had experienced the knowing with the woman like he said he would, Tannor would have devised some way to have stopped this mess from even happening. Why had Jodar not told him? He could have tried to do something to help his best friend out so this would not have happened with Broud. He stood up from Jodar's unconscious body and stepped forward. He cleared his throat as he faced Chanlon and bowed slightly. He avoided looking back at his friend lying sprawled, unconscious on the floor as he spoke. He knew his best friend was going to experience great mental agony when he came out of stun. Tannor was a devoted soldier to the supreme commander. Friend or no friend, he had to tell the truth. "My liege, what your life mate states is the truth. We all witnessed the knowing between Broud and the woman. It is undeniable what we have just observed, Commander."

Chanlon's shoulders sagged at hearing this from the trooper Tannor. He knew how close he was to Jodar. He would not lie or jeopardize his friendship with Jodar to please his life mate. He looked around to the other soldiers, and they were all nodding, though it pained all of them. Chanlon looked over at Jodar's unconscious body, and then he looked at his son's. What had Adrya done? What a mess she had caused.

Only minutes before, Jodar had been the happiest man alive. When Jodar had completed his duties with Chanlon and had returned to his chamber to finally be with Sheye, to his utter dismay, he found that Sheye was missing. When Jodar communicated this with Chanlon, he knew in an instant his life mate had something to do with this. Within a few minutes of questioning the servants, they found the Orange Cloak who had served Sheye the refreshments in Jodar's chambers. They knew that Adrya was up to something. Then Jodar received an open page on his commlink from Tannor. They could hear everything that was going on, so they headed to the viewing hall immediately. Chanlon was so disappointed that they were not able to stop this outrage before Broud had seen Sheye. Now somehow, Broud and Sheye had experienced the knowing as well. How was this even plausible? There had not ever been a documented "double knowing" in all the history of his people. Chanlon was at a loss for words. For the first time in his ruling, he was doubtful of what to do. Right now, he would rather be in the middle of a bloody battle with Bionas than being in this room, trying to figure this whole mess out.

Chapter 12

Chanlon had to make a very hasty decision before Broud woke up. He had his troopers gather Broud's unconscious body and take him to the hibernation chambers. He had them prepare his son and placed him in his space hibernation tube for the trip home. This alleviated one problem. Broud would not cause anymore havoc with Jodar and the woman for the time being. Adrya was vastly displeased with the choice that Chanlon had made. She began to confront Chalon on his verdict. This was not what she had planned at all. Broud was supposed to immediately be bonded with the woman. Blue and herself had set up everyone to think the knowing had transpired between Broud and the woman so utterly perfect. She did not count on the bond that Chanlon had with Jodar. Nor did she count on Chanlon being suspicious of her motives.

Adrya never suspected that Chanlon would have their own son placed into space hibernation instead of Jodar. Broud should have been number 1 priority where Chanlon was concerned, not his bodyguard. Broud's knowing should have taken precedence over Jodar's. The bonding with a woman through the ancient ways of the knowing would have made her son's position stronger in the eyes of the people of Sarbus. After the bonding of Broud to a life mate, they could have forced Chanlon as the supreme commander to step down. Chanlon was aging. This would be around the time that a supreme commander would hand over the reigns to his eldest, who was now of age to take over the regime.

Adrya was so outraged with Chanlon. She could not help herself. Her spoiled, selfish nastiness bubbled to the surface. She started to germinate obscenities toward him and the soldiers, forgetting her position, her dignity, and her regal status. Adrya placed herself right in front of Chanlon and seethed her ire in his face. "How dare you choose a trivial fighter over your own flesh and blood! All these soldiers and Blue Cloaks witnessed the knowing between Broud and the woman. He even chose her, almost immediately from all these other women before the knowing even happened. She...will...be... Broud's, Chanlon! No daft combatant will stand in the way of *my... son*! You are too old to continue ruling over Sarbus. It is now time for younger blood to be the leader. You are old in your ways, Chanlon. You are becoming less of the fighter you once were each day that goes by. You are weak-minded, letting your feelings get in the way of what is right and what you think should happen. How dare you go against the ancient beliefs! You even said so yourself. The ancient ways of your planet will be upheld no matter what, but here you are taking the side of your pet, who is a worthless pile of Zardonus dung." Adrya was panting now; she was so incensed with Chanlon. Her plan should have worked; they should be bonding Broud at this very moment with the woman he chose. So the knowing was fabricated; no one knew this but herself and Blue. Not even Broud knew what had been planned.

Chanlon stood in silence as Adrya berated him in front of his troops. His fury grew with each word she spewed forth from her mouth. He was done with Adrya. He had let her spoiled, rotten attitude go on far too long. Something did not sit right with what had just transpired. All his years of being the supreme commander screamed in his head that something was amiss. Wherever his life mate and the Blue Cloak that Adrya called Blue were together, something happened that made things go Adrya's way. Why had he not seen it before? Blue was the Blue Cloak who had witnessed his knowing with Adrya in his chamber at the peace treaty conference. The night she had come to his chamber, Blue just happened to come in his chambers uninvited. He was also here by Adrya's side right now. He was hovering back, trying to be inconspicuous in the background behind Adrya with a nervous look on his face. Chanlon's brain began to click. Something was trying to connect, but he just could not put his finger on it. It tasted foul whatever it was, and he was about to get to the bottom of all that Adrya was trying to slip under his nose.

Without hesitation, Chanlon looked over at Tannor. "Take this menace to the hibernation pods and prepare her for the trip home. I no longer can stomach seeing her face nor listen to the rubbish she is tossing my way."

Adrya stopped her tirade and just gaped at Chanlon. "You can't be serious. I am the mother of your son and your life mate. You have no right." Adrya backed away from Tannor as he approached her with the other soldiers behind him. "Stop right there, you no good son of a brack's ass!"

Tannor hesitated. A brack was the worst offensive animal to ever grace a planet. Bracks were extremely ugly with shaggy, patchy long hair. Their legs were so skinny one wondered how they were able to stand, let alone run. They had scaly heads and tails with sharp teeth and claws. You could smell one coming before they even attack, which was the only warning you had before they wreaked havoc. Thank God they were extinct now, this being the only small benefit that the planet Bionas had rid for them when they attacked all their livestock in one of their viral attacks years before.

The brack was one of the nastiest beasts that had perished with one of Bionas's biological attacks many years ago. The offensive name-calling that Adrya had just thrown at Tannor was supposed to be extremely insulting, but Tannor just smiled at Adrya. He had waited many years for Chanlon to come to his senses after bonding with this female scum from their enemy planet, no matter how beautiful she was. She was evil and a threat to their people. Tannor always knew that something bad would come of their supreme commander bonding with the daughter of the high commissioner of their rival world. Now he was about to have the intense pleasure of watching her be placed in her space hibernation pod and be rid of her for a while. If only Jodar was awake to see all of this, what satisfaction it would have brought him. Jodar had been a bystander many times witnessing the callousness and cruelty that Adrya could dole out to their people.

Tannor approached Adrya again with his stun rod out. Adrya backed up toward Blue unconsciously. When Tannor reached out, Adrya yelled for Blue to help her. Blue instinctively sprang forward to help his love and was met with the rod to his neck. He dropped in an instance. Adrya screamed and fell to Blue's unconscious form. Seeing Blue comatose on the floor brought an unusual reaction out of Adrya. She panicked. She was not sure if he was dead or alive, and this disturbed her deeper than it should have. She was upset for Blue. She had feelings that she could not understand rushing through her. Before she knew what she was doing, she vaulted up and tried to attack Tannor. She did not make it off the floor though, Tannor blissfully stunned Adrya. She dropped lifeless in a heap beside her pet, Blue.

Chanlon frowned. Seeing Adrya's reaction to Blue being stunned was disturbing. She had always been quite emotionless to everything and everyone, except Broud, of course. Her rapport with the Blue Cloak had always piqued Chanlon's curiosity. He just assumed that because Blue had doted on her so much (like a lost puppy), he had become her favorite pet. Adrya's reaction just now was of a response from a lover, not a response for a favored pet. Chanlon needed to investigate; he had Blue's unconscious body moved to the holding cells. He told Tannor to pick only his most trusted soldiers to guard the cell. Blue was to have zero contact with anyone but himself, not even Jodar was to enter the cell unless he was with Chanlon.

Just as Tannor had gathered Blue and left the room, Jodar was coming out of the stun and sat up. He looked around and found that most of the women had been removed from the room, probably to be put back in the hibernation tubes. Broud, Adrya, and the Blue Cloaks were all gone as well. Tannor was nowhere to be seen. Chanlon was standing beside him, so he stood up quickly even though he was slightly unsteady. Chanlon held his hand out for his personal bodyguard and helped him up. Jodar immediately looked to Sheye's cell. Chanlon waved his hand toward the direction of her cell with a nonverbal approval for Jodar to go to Sheye. Without hesitation, Jodar ran over to Sheye's cell and picked her gently up from her platform. She was still unconscious from the episode earlier. Jodar was not sure if she had been electrocuted or if it was something else. He lowered his ear to her chest and could hear her breathing. It was shallow, and he needed to have her seen by a Blue Cloak immediately. He carried her the whole way back to his private chamber with Chanlon following close behind. When they entered Jodar's chamber, Chanlon ordered his personal Blue Cloaks to meet them there.

When the Blue Cloaks entered, Chanlon directed them to check over Sheye as she lay on Jodar's bed. When they began toiling over her to find out if she had been injured, Chanlon drew Jodar away to the seating area.

"We must talk, Jodar. I fear there is conspiracy within my family. I have noticed things this last few days that don't sit well with me. I must ask of you to investigate for me as quickly and quietly as you can. I fear Adrya wants me dead. Since the attack from her planet that shut them down and us coming to this world for our collections, something has changed in my life mate. She has become more withdrawn, agitated, secretive, and restless. I fear she aims for Broud to take over as supreme commander. She is building up to something. I am also concerned that Adrya, Blue, and her father have falsified the knowing I had with Adrya as well.

"This may be what has happened today with Sheye and Broud too! I think Adrya may be trying to find a way in which she can have Bionas released from the shield. I need you to find out how any of this was accomplished. We need to head home. I have had word that all the collections are completed, including the collections of plant life, wildlife, and livestock. I am placing everyone that is not needed to run the fleets back home into hibernation sleep. There will be no one snooping around that may hinder in your search. I need this done before we reach home, Jodar. I trust you with my life, and so I trust you with this."

Jodar readily agreed with Chanlon. He felt honored that Chanlon trusted him enough to carry out this investigation. Jodar mentioned to Chanlon that he would need a small team to facilitate with the investigation. He requested Tannor and his troops as well as Chanlon's personal Blue Cloaks. Chanlon concurred. After they had their discussion made, Jodar looked back at Sheye and watched her being worked over by the Blue Cloaks and sighed. Chanlon smacked Jodar on the shoulder.

"Don't worry about your woman, Jodar. What I witnessed with you and the woman was the true knowing. I have never seen such a powerful knowing before yours. She will be bonded to you when we get home. My son has no right to her. I give you, my word."

Chanlon had just made Jodar the happiest man alive once more. When he had seen Broud and Sheye going through what everyone, including himself, had believed was the knowing his heart shattered into a million pieces. How could the knowing happen twice with the same person? All he could think of at that moment was if he did not destroy Broud, he would lose Sheye forever even though they were connected in the most intimate way. He knew he would perish without her if he had to watch her be with another man. If they had not stunned him, he would have succeeded in killing Broud. Broud was larger and nastier, but Jodar had far more real battle experience. He had proven many times sparring with Broud over the years that he could beat him on every occasion. Broud would always try to cheat his way to the top instead of learning how to win. Broud was unpredictable and dangerous though. Jodar had to keep his wits about him every time they went at each other. He always managed to outmaneuver Broud in every fight so far, but now with Sheye in the mix, he figured that Broud may do something to kill him so Broud himself could have Sheye. He would focus his entire attention to the investigation for now. Then when they returned home, he would worry about what to do to keep Broud absent from Sheye's life with him.

One of Chanlon's personal Blue Cloaks walked over to Chanlon and Jodar and bowed. Chanlon motioned for him to tell them of their findings. The Blue Cloak looked confused but cleared his throat before he began speaking. "The woman is in perfect health. She was put through a massive surge that has rendered her unconscious. We are not sure as to what kind of surge went through her yet, but there will be no long-term side effects that we can find. She should be coming to shortly, as the surge effect wears off. We did find however an implant. We are confused as to why a language graft was implanted in the first place. The graft has also been placed in the wrong location. It is more in the location for memories."

Chanlon and Jodar gaped at the Blue Cloak as if they had misunderstood him. This made the Blue Cloak uncomfortable having not made himself understood, so he tried again. "Someone has planted a—" Chanlon cut the Blue Cloak off as he stood up suddenly and swore. The Blue Cloak staggered back, afraid he had said something wrong. "I apologize if I have made you angry in some way, my liege."

Chanlon began pacing the room in anger. Jodar thought for a moment, and suddenly, he had an epiphany. He let the Blue Cloak know that everything was okay, that he was not in any way in trouble, then approached Chanlon. "I have an idea, Commander. Would you allow your Blue Cloaks to scan you as well?"

Chanlon stopped pacing and stared at Jodar as if he had grown two heads. "With what we have just discussed, I feel it is in your best interest that I start my investigation immediately. I think you should be scanned as well, Chanlon. If my suspicion is correct, this may lead us to a huge break in what has transpired these last few days as well as the last twenty-six years. This may give reason for yourself with your distrust with Adrya."

Chanlon's curiosity was piqued. "You think I have a chip implant as well? You will, of course, find one, as we all have the language chip grafted so we can understand all this planet's languages."

Jodar nodded but continued, saying, "If my theory is correct, Commander, I think that you will have two implants."

Chapter 13

Chanlon stood for a few moments more as he processed the information that Jodar had just given him. A light went off in Chanlon's eyes as he realized what it was that Jodar was thinking. Chanlon went over to the large chair and sat down. He motioned to the Blue Cloak holding the scanner. "Scan me immediately! Look for two implants."

The Blue Cloaks looked at one another. This was extremely exciting to them as they loved a great conspiracy. It was in their entire nature to figure things out and fix it. This would make for an amazing tale to tell if they found a second implant in their supreme commander's head. Something sinister was afoot; they could feel it as well. None of the Blue Cloaks had any liking for Adrya. They only tolerated her because of their devotion to Chanlon. They lived for scientific and medical findings, but this was conspiracy at it is finest, and they were there to witness it at the very moment it was happening, how exciting. The Blue Cloak holding the scanner, in his eagerness to scan his supreme commander, tripped and fell into Chanlon's lap. Chanlon huffed at him, "Don't kill me before I am scanned, my eager young Blue Cloak!" He lifted the Blue Cloak off his lap like he would a child and placed him back on his feet. The Blue Cloak was embarrassed and profusely apologized. "Well, stop apologizing and scan me already."

The Blue Cloak stepped back to Chanlon carefully this time. He programmed the scanner, then held it up to Chanlon's forehead. The scanner plipped for a few moments; the Blue Cloak stood back with his eyes large and intense.

"My liege, you indeed have two chips planted within you. Our common language chip is there and in the correct placement. The second implant is in the same place as the woman's is."

Chanlon, Jodar, and the Blue Cloak stared at one another for a few moments digesting the information that they had discovered. Chanlon suddenly pushed up, off the chair in a rage, and knocked over the poor Blue Cloak in the process. The little Blue Cloak went flying over the couch platform but landed safely on the soft sofa seat.

"That conniving, manipulative wench! I want this implant taken out immediately. I want to know what it is and what is on it. I want to know now."

The Blue Cloak clambered off the couch and stood by his partner. "Right away, our liege. If you would follow us to medbay 4, we can extract the chip within the hour."

Jodar stood up as well and stated, "Let us bring Sheye, Chanlon. They can take out both chips at the same time. We can analyze them together. They may be the same, or they may be different, but we have to know what is on both of those implants."

Chanlon nodded toward Jodar. Jodar gently picked Sheye from the bed. The Blue Cloaks began to move the floating platform toward Jodar so he could place Sheye on it, but Jodar waved it away.

"I will carry her myself." He cradled Sheye in his arms gently, and they all proceeded directly to the medbay.

Sheye and Chanlon were laid out beside each other on exam tables. Sheye was still unconscious, but they gave her a sedative in case she woke up in the middle of the extraction of the implant, which would not bode well for her pain. Chanlon was sedated as well, and the two Blue Cloaks began the extraction after a bit of preparation and material gathering. It took them only a few minutes to remove both implants. They took them to a cleaning station and had the computer cleanse and disinfect them so they could place them on the chip reader. They had to wait for Chanlon to revive from the sedative. Jodar asked if they could keep Sheye under while they proceeded to view the chips.

Sheye would not understand what was transpiring, and Jodar did not want to cause her any more stress than she was already under. He also wanted to focus on what was on the implants and knew that if Sheye was awake, he would instinctively want to be by her side to make sure that she was okay and comfort her. Jodar wanted to explain everything in his private quarters alone with Sheye when she awoke to make it more relaxed for them both. He did not want to upset her with strangers around watching, listening, judging, or putting their two cents in. The Blue Cloaks did as Jodar wished. When Chanlon awoke, he sat up immediately, clear-headed, and demanded to see what was on the implant. The Blue Cloaks pressed a few keys on the virtual board and backed away, though not far enough away that they could not see what was taking place on the viewing screen. Their curiosity at learning what was going on was far too intriguing for them, even though it was none of their business.

The first implant chip they examined was Chanlon's. What flashed on the screen was code after code of symbols, numbers, and glyphs, which neither Chanlon nor Jodar could understand. Chanlon growled with impatience, turned to the Blue Cloaks, and demanded they decode the chip so they could understand what it was that the two of them were looking at. The Blue Cloaks scrambled over and played with the computer for a few minutes, and then suddenly, there was flash after flash of Adrya's life flooding the screen. Chanlon and Jodar stood back and then stared at each other. Chanlon was turning red, and he was flexing his fists. A Blue Cloak suddenly yet politely pushed his way through to the computer.

"Pardon my intrusion for a minute, my liege. I have noticed some things are not lining up on some of the codes when we were decoding them. There have been some interruptions and manipulations within the primary codes themselves, which is irregular. Someone has spliced in codes within the codes. If you give me a few moments, I can decipher what is behind the primary code if I may."

Chanlon backed off and nodded giving the Blue Cloak some space to work at the computers. This also gave him some time to cool off. He was distracted from his anger and was extremely interested with what else the Blue Cloak would find.

"My Eminence, I have detected that all the codes that seem to be altered with underlying codes are the ones that have Adrya's memories of her father involved. I am now going to peel away the false code and see what the real code is." As the Blue Cloak worked, the two men watched the screen. As the codes were fixed, the images changed—that of Adrya with the high commissioner, her father, to Adrya and someone else.

Chanlon leaned into the screen and stared hard at the images. "Freeze that memory." He almost yelled at the Blue Cloak, who jumped but did exactly that. Chanlon and Jodar stared at the screen in disbelief. There in the frozen memory the image stood Adrya with her true father. The man standing in the memory was none other than the supreme commander of Bionas, Dorian.

Chanlon smashed the console in front of him as he cursed Adrya's name over and over. He stopped and leaned on the platform beside Sheye as she was still lying in a sedated state. He had to get his rage under control before he stormed in to where Adrya was being hibernated for the journey home and do something he would regret, like committing murder. Chanlon watched Sheye slumber for a while, and then his shoulders sagged, and he sighed heavily. "I am disgusted with myself, Jodar. My lust to bed Adrya all those years ago had led me to possibly placing our world, once again, in peril. I was tricked into the knowing with Adrya and her true father. They haven't lessened their dirty plans to get our planet. They have only changed tactics. How could I be so blind, Jodar? I always knew in the back of my mind something was off between myself and Adrya. I always knew we had a weak knowing bond. Now I know it was not the knowing at all. This is treason at its finest. I have you as my witness, Jodar. Right here, right now, I am declaring that my life bond and the knowing with Adrya is invalid. Adrya can no longer claim she is my life mate. I renounce her as if she never existed."

Chanlon felt much better after denouncing Adrya. It was like a boulder had been lifted off his shoulders. He pushed himself away from the platforms and stood tall once more. Jodar could see that Chanlon was the supreme commander at top form once again as he used to be. The pity party he had was over. He was all business again. Chanlon spoke as he came up to Jodar and the Blue Cloaks. "Due to the nature of what we have found transpiring, we will need the council of the eleven planets to gather the minute we arrive home for Adrya's judgment." Chanlon turned to his trusted Blues. "I need you to arrange this with the council of the eleven. Don't explain what has happened, only say that it is of the utmost importance, and I have requested this trial personally. Tell them I will explain everything once we arrive."

The Blue Cloaks nodded and whisked themselves away to do as they were tasked in an excited manner. This had been the best thing that they have ever witnessed personally and been privileged to be involved in. They were extremely excited to be a part of taking Adrya and the supreme commander of Bionas down. They would also be the envy of all their Blue brothers.

Chanlon turned back to Jodar after he watched the Blue Cloaks hustle off to do his bidding. "We must discuss with the council the matter of Broud as well. He no longer has rights to claim the supreme commander's position from this day forth. I don't trust Broud even though he is my son, although, I am wondering if he is of my blood with all that has happened of late. It would not surprise me to find out that he is not of my seed." Chanlon sighed again but then reached out and placed his hand on Jodar's shoulder again. "Shall we see what is on your woman's chip, Jodar? Although I think we can both guess exactly what it is we will be viewing."

The two men viewed Sheye's implant, and it was exactly what they assumed. It was of memories of Broud as he grew up, and it had also been edited, especially the abuse he inflicted on all his bed mates, his cruelty, and his cheating, manipulative ways. He was made to look like Prince Charming. Jodar was now just as mad as Chanlon had been. Adrya would have stuck his Sheye with that monster. He would have beaten her and hurt her on a constant basis. It made him sick to his stomach to think of Broud even being able to touch her. He had been so close to losing her to Broud. Jodar thanked the fifth star of Prantus this would never come to pass.

Chanlon turned to Jodar. "We must interrogate Adrya's Blue Cloak. Something is not right with Adrya's relationship with him. I have come to the realization that one of our own is in league with our enemy. He is behind everything that Adrya has planned, and we need to find out how and why."

Jodar headed toward the computer to start to flip through more information and images on the chip, but Chanlon stopped him. "I must hear it in his own words, Jodar. I need to hear it coming from him. We may even, regrettably, have an execution this day, Jodar. Are you up to this?"

Jodar stopped what he was doing. "Of course, I understand that treason is needed to be dealt with swiftly, if it is found that Adrya's Blue Cloak is in leagues with herself and her father, then the punishment should be swift. I can't leave Sheye alone though. Would you mind if we had her platform follow us? I would appreciate her always being within my view, considering that we don't know who we can truly trust anymore or who else may be involved."

Chanlon nodded. "I envy you, Jodar. I envy what I have witnessed between you and your woman. I understand your wanting to protect what is yours. Yes, she can be brought along for you to safeguard. Have Tannor and his men with some Black Cloaks stand by at the ready by Blue's cell. We need to get to the bottom of this. I fear that we may not like the outcome."

Chapter 14

Chanlon's large formidable presence terrified Blue as he towered over him as he sat on the cell platform. Chanlon was looking down at him in a way that said he was already fully aware of everything it was that he had performed for and with Adrya. They had been finally apprehended. His beloved Adrya's plan had been discovered. Shame, quilt, embarrassment, and loathing for himself swirled around Blue as he thought of everything, he had done against his own world to make his Adrya happy. He knew right at this moment, his dream of one day finally bonding with Adrya was just that, a dream. He would be put to death for treason and rightfully so. He had accepted this reality when he realized he was in a holding cell when he became conscious from being stunned after the fake knowing for Broud, he had improvised at Adrya's command.

He had let his love and the knowing for Adrya blacken all that he believed in, trained for, and devoted his entire life to before he had met up with her, and for what? For something in his heart, he knew he would never obtain. He always understood, deep down, that Adrya was much too selfish and full of disgust for his world to ever bond with him. He had always longed and prayed to the fifth star of Prantus that she would eventually see their illuminated truth of their knowing and finally accept the inevitable. Now here he was with his supreme commander standing over him, ready to pass the death penalty, for the part he played in trying to bring Sarbus down. Blue welcomed it to finally be over. It was, in a way, an enormous relief. His tortured soul would finally be set to a close.

Chanlon looked down upon Adrya's Blue Cloak. He could see the shame written all over his face. Without speaking, Chanlon nodded toward his Blue Cloaks that entered the cell with him. They had just joined the group after they had sent the message to the council of the eleven. They punched a few commands on the floating computer council in front of them. Blue witnessed the flashes on the display hologram of all Adrya's memories from the implant that had been removed from Chanlon. Blue watched for only a minute and then looked away in humiliation. Chanlon nodded toward his Blue Cloaks, and they started to play another program. It was the recording of Sheye in her cell and the moment of Jodar and Sheye's knowing from her cell. Chanlon grabbed hold of Blue and forced him to watch the scenes that were being played out before him, without saying a word. Blue was undeniably astonished at what he was being forced to view.

Blue had not been with Adrya and Chanlon when they went to view Sheye for the inspection for Broud's possible life mate. He watched the recording and observed for himself the power of the knowing that Sheye and Jodar had experienced. It brought Blue to tears. It reminded him of his own formidable knowing with Adrya. How could he deny Jodar and this woman what they had experienced, especially since he knew all too much how it tortured his own soul when he was not allowed to life bond with Adrya after his knowing? He sold his soul to Adrya and her father in hopes that he would be allowed to bond with her eventually, some day, maybe.

These images finally broke through to Blue. Without further ado, he waved his hand toward the Blue Cloaks to shut off the recording. The other Blue Cloaks were so disgusted with Blue that they did not heed his motion to stop the recording; it took Chanlon's nod for them to stop the footage. Blue slumped his shoulders and sniffled, then sat up, and looked at Sheye lying unconscious on the floating platform by Jodar before he started to speak.

"For what it is worth, I am sorry for everything I have done. I am sorry for everything I have perpetrated against our world and to you, my liege. I don't expect you to understand, nor do I expect nothing less than be put to death for my hand in these treasonous actions. All I can do now is explain why I was implicated in these actions. I have kept a terrible secret for the last twenty-six years. I knew in my heart it would eventually be discovered. In case of any misunderstanding in why I was in league with Adrya and her father Dorian, I have kept on me my own personal records. If I may, would you be willing to watch what I have recorded over so many years?"

Chanlon was intrigued. He had yet to even say one word toward Blue. He could see the personal pain and guilt that was gnawing away at this small Blue Cloak. Chanlon was willing to entertain Blue's evidence.

Blue was ready to confess his implications without even having to be interrogated. Blue asked for one of the Blue Cloaks' instruments since all that he had on him was taken away. Chanlon nodded to one of his Blue Cloaks, who then tossed his med-tool, which they all kept on their person, toward him onto the floor. Chanlon's personal Blue Cloaks did not want to even approach the treasonous Blue. Throwing their special tool that they considered sacred on the floor was considered a terrible insult to a Blue Cloak. Blue nodded in understanding. He had lost all respect from his companions and brothers. He bent and picked up the tool from the floor, then pointed it at his arm. The laser sliced a small opening in Blue's forearm. They all stood by as they watched Blue extract an implanted chip from his arm.

After Blue retrieved his evidence from inside his own body, the other Blue Cloaks stepped forward reluctantly without eye contact. Blue place the chip onto a scanner on the floating computer panel. After a little maintenance, they inserted the chip into the program reader. They all sat and watched as the recording started. Stunned silence followed when the recorder switched off. Blue sighed, and he let a few more tears fall before stating, "I am ready for my sentencing now."

Chanlon's shoulders slumped; he, too, was upset by what they had viewed. He now had all the answers he needed to his questions. He knew what he had to do no matter how much he disagreed right now with Sarbus's laws. This is where being a supreme commander became unpleasant. Chanlon was a law onto himself, but he had to do what the laws of his world and of his people expected.

Chanlon stood up and moved over to Blue. "It saddens me to have to do what must be done, especially after seeing your reasons to why you did what you felt you had to do for Adrya and for your child. I am ashamed for you and what Adrya manipulated you into doing for her, and I am sorry for that. I, too, have been manipulated by that same family, and so has our world. If I would have known that you and Adrya—" Chanlon broke off his last few words and just shook his head. He felt so much anger toward Adrya and her father at this moment he was shaking. He not only lost his life mate by her treachery, but he now knew that Broud was also not his son. The night before he had met Adrya at the peace treaty was the only time that Adrya had let Blue be completely intimate with her. This had been the only way she had been able convince Blue to follow along with the plan for her father, Dorian. That was the night she had conceived Broud. Chanlon felt only sadness and regret for Blue at this moment. Blue was treasonous, but now he understood why. Chanlon placed his large hand on the smaller man's shoulder. "I will stop this madness that she and her father has caused. I will avenge your suffering."

Blue nodded but looked up with pleading in his eyes. "Please, for Adrya's sake, make it quick and painless after her trial. She knows no better. She is also a pawn of her father's abuse and exploitation. He spoiled her but only for his own gain. None of this is truly her own fault. So you know, Broud does not know I am his father. He is also a pawn in all this. Be easy on him. Please tell Adrya that I love her and that I said goodbye. Tell her that I don't blame her for what she has done nor for what I agreed to do for her."

Chanlon nodded. "I will. I will also promise not to place Broud on trial as he was not part of this conspiracy. Let your mind be at peace for your son's safety in not being tried with treason as well." Chanlon sighed again and patted Blue on the shoulder once more. "It is time." Chanlon nodded toward Jodar. Jodar called upon Tannor and the other soldiers to enter the cell. He could see they had all been moved by what they had heard as well. They were all in shock that one of their own, especially a Blue Cloak, being involved in such deception. They all understood what was about to occur. They all agreed with their supreme commander with what he had to do even though it made them miserable. Chanlon spoke with authority when everyone needed was in the cell. "I hereby pronounce for the record of Sarbus that Krenn Ly-Shann, also known as Blue, has been found guilty of treasonous acts toward his supreme commander, his planet, and his people. He knowingly admits to his crimes that he is being indicted for. For his said crimes of conspiracy to commit treason versus the planet of Sarbus, he is to be put to death immediately. You all, as my most trusted soldiers and Blue Cloaks, are here as my witness."

Jodar went slowly over to the cell door and opened it.

Through the cell door entered a large mechanical box, and two men in black cloaks followed closely behind. The black-cloaked men moved the box over to Blue and laid him down on the platform he had been sitting on. Blue complied without struggle. They placed a thin cable from out of the box and attached it to each side of his forehead. Blue closed his eyes.

"I am sorry for all the mess I have caused because of the knowing. I wish it had never happened to begin with. I do love Sarbus. I had just been so blinded by hope and dreams. Hail Sarbus forever and always!"

Chanlon nodded slightly toward the Black Cloaks. One reached over and pressed a button on the box hovering beside Blue. Blue convulsed, then his entire head and body turned to ash almost immediately. It only took a few seconds for Blue to become a complete pile of ash. After the box was finished with its duty, a hose came out of the side and sucked the entirety of what was left of Blue into it. Then with out a word, the Black Cloaks, the box, and the four soldiers left the cell.

Chanlon stared at the now empty platform where Blue had lain for a few moments. He had conducted many executions in his lifetime while being the supreme commander of Sarbus, but none had caused him such sadness, not one of the executions had been carried out on one of his own people. What he had witnessed from Blue's memoirs still spun through his brain. He had almost called off this execution. He nearly felt that there had to be some way around the capital punishment. He knew though because of the laws of Sarbus that this had to be done and placed on record. His personal Blue Cloaks would tell this tale for centuries to come. This would be a reminder to all that committed treason against one's own planet and people that execution would be the only way to deal with this kind of corruption. He had to be resilient, and he had to follow the laws. This execution had to be. He was still a man though, and he still had sentiments. This execution though had been the hardest decision he had ever had to make to uphold their laws as supreme commander. Chanlon internally cringed. Now he had to deal with Adrya. Adrya's trial though would have to be dealt with by the council of the eleven planets. This would thankfully be in their hands and not in his.

Chapter 15

Jodar found himself sitting back in his personal chamber with Tannor sitting by his side. Chanlon had excused himself right after the execution and had let Jodar go back to his chambers with Sheye to rest. There was no more trouble as of right now. Almost everyone had been sent to hibernation for the journey home. Chanlon needed some space to think about all that had transpired that day. Jodar and Tannor had not said two words to each other as they sat contemplating the last few days. Jodar was sitting beside Sheye as she lay on his bed. She was still unconscious. The Blue Cloaks had made sure that she would not wake up during the execution. Tannor was still thinking about all he had seen on the recordings before they had witnessed Blue's punishment. Suddenly Tannor spoke. "What did it feel like, Jodar?"

Jodar glanced over at his warrior friend a little confused. "What do you speak of, brother?"

Tannor stood up and went over to Jodar and looked from him to the beautiful woman on the bed. "The knowing—I mean, what did it feel like? You knew it was going to happen with her. You never had any doubt! How did you know? At first, I thought you were a little crazy since it does not happen so often anymore. I mean it did not even happen to the supreme commander as we have all recently found out. Your knowing has been the first in the last twenty-six years. Well, it hasn't happened since Adrya and Blue, yet you just knew."

Jodar shrugged but then became thoughtful. He thought for a moment about the first time he laid eyes on Sheye at the lake on Earth. "It was the minute I saw her. I felt like we were connected. I just had to have her. She was meant to be with me. I knew that it was not a mistake that I had come with you that day. There was a reason why I decided to join you for my day off from the commander. I woke up that morning, and something told me that I just had to join you. Even if you had said no, I would have found a way to go with you. When I saw her, it was like 'That's her. That is, it. This is the reason I am here today.'"

Tannor was enthralled and sat down beside Sheye on the floor facing Jodar. He seemed like a little kid waiting for the best story to be told to him. Jodar smiled at his lifelong friend when he asked, "What did the knowing feel like right when it happened? I know I saw it on the recording, but how did it actually feel?"

Jodar looked tenderly at Sheye's sleeping figure. "It was the greatest yet most terrifying emotions I have ever encountered, to be honest. At first, it was the connection of our eyes. When she looked directly at me, it was like our soul reached out for each other and intertwined in an intimate way. There was a strong jolt through my body that was better than any physical pleasure I have ever experienced, yet it was not physical at all. It was a mental connection. I remember the heat. It was so hot but not burning, nor was it uncomfortable. I never wanted to leave that heat. It was like I was being cloaked in the warmth of a mother's love. The love I felt pouring from her and for her was that of purity, wholesomeness, truth. I saw every intimate thing about her mind, her body, her soul, and her inner beauty. I saw everything there is to know and experience about her and her me. We could not hide anything from each other. Even now I can feel her peace as she dreamlessly sleeps, even though she is unconscious. She is not thinking about anything right now. She is just at peace. When she was being inspected by Broud, I could feel her hatred, her anger, her confusion, and her fear as soon as I entered the room. It is like we are not only connected physically, but we are also connected emotionally as well. I would die for her, Tannor. I never want to be without her now. It feels like a blessing and a curse at the same time, but I welcome it. I welcome it all."

Tannor was fascinated; he now wanted to have that experience with a mate. He saw how unbelievable it was with Jodar and sadly with Blue. He wanted to experience that kind of connection with someone. He understood Jodar more now with how he had always said he would not take on a life mate unless he experienced the knowing. Maybe all it took was to believe in something so passionately and so purely that it would make it come true. Maybe this was why his people were not experiencing much of the knowing anymore. The ancient ways were being lost with all the tragedies that had been happening to their people because of the attacks from Bionas for so long. Maybe his people had just lost hope.

Suddenly Sheye's hand moved, and it landed on Tannor's head. She smiled in her sleep as she gently stroked her fingers through Tannor's hair. Jodar was instantly possessive when he saw the pleasure of her touch in Tannor's face.

"Leave us for now, my friend. I want her to be alone with me when she comes to. Besides, she hates you, remember? Has she not attacked you more than once? She blames you for the loss of her beasts. You had better leave swiftly."

Tannor sighed; he always loved a woman running her hands through his hair. It was ever so relaxing, but he could see that it upset Jodar as she touched him. He laughed a little, nodded, and he stood up to leave. He turned back to Jodar when he was at the door. "I have the most amazing gift for the two of you when we get back to our home. I will give it to you both when you are bonded, my brother. She will come to like me, just you wait and see."

Jodar frowned. "Just remember, she is my woman, Tannor."

Tannor laughed heartedly at Jodar's possessiveness before he exited out the door.

Sheye moaned a little as her hand went to her head. The Blue Cloaks did warn Jodar that she may have a terrible headache when she came to because of the insertion and removal of the implants and all she had been through that day. Jodar had his medibot prepare his cure-all drink to be ready for her when she finally awoke. He gently touched her arm.

"Sheye, it is me Jodar. I have a drink for you. It will stop the pain you have in your head."

Sheye opened her eyes and blinked a bit to remove the fuzziness from them. When she could see clearly, her view was that of Jodar's handsome face leaning over her. A pure jolt of desire and love went through her, which made her sit up so fast she banged her head off Jodar's head. They both groaned and held their foreheads for a few moments, and then they both burst out laughing through their apology to each other.

Jodar smiled at her. "Wow, you have a solid skull."

Sheye gritted her teeth. "I can say the same thing about yours."

Jodar reached for the drink and handed it to her. Without hesitation, she drank the cooling beverage that tasted a little like honey and mint. She drank the glass without hesitation as she trusted Jodar to her fundamental core. Her head and body pain vanished almost immediately.

Sheye looked at the drained glass. She was impressed. Whatever was in that drink was a miracle cure for pain. It tasted surprisingly good too. Sheye sat up as she was beginning to feel self-conscious lying on a bed so near to the most attractive man she had every seen in her life.

"Uh, thank you, Jodar. That worked wonders." She collected herself off the bed and stood up. She was still in the strange dress that the tall, slim, blue-eyed man had made her wear before the inspection of her for their supreme commander. Sheye cleared her throat and looked over at Jodar. "I feel a little overdressed. Would there be something else I could change into that isn't so, well, so formal and immodest?"

Jodar frowned. "I think you look absolutely amazing. Is it not comfortable?"

Sheye sighed and looked down at herself. It was extremely comfortable in every way possible even with it being so tight in the bodice, but she did not like having so much skin exposed to the eyes of the man sitting in front of her looking like he would love to peel it off her at any given moment. Jodar blushed. He could sense her embarrassment as well as her growing arousal. His arousal was fast approaching his loins as well as he looked at her. This was not the time for that kind of intimacy. They had to talk. He was sure she had many questions. A little embarrassed at his hesitation, he quickly got up and went over to a computer console, punched a few commands into it. Near the bed, a closet popped out from beside the console with some clothing in it.

Sheye was again fascinated at the technology on this ship. There were no joints in the wall to indicate that anything was there, but suddenly, there was a closet where nothing was before. She walked over and investigated it. It was full of women's clothing. She was instantly jealous. She turned to Jodar jealously.

"If you expect me to wear your lover's clothing, buddy, you are sadly mistaken!"

Jodar understood immediately; he could feel her jealousy flowing through her to him. He stood up and calmly walked over to where Sheye stood. "These clothes have never been worn by anyone. They are all new. I just requested them for you. I have had the clothing styler make you something you would wear on your planet to make you feel more comfortable. It won't be of the material you are used to, but this is the best I can do for now. Oh, and I don't have a lover who has ever stayed long enough to leave clothing in my chambers."

Sheye could not stop herself. "So you do have a lover." Sheye blushed so red she was flaming hot with it. Never in her life had she experienced such jealousy before. It was so foreign to her. She was exceedingly embarrassed at her reaction. She wanted to bury herself under the covers on the bed. Jodar gently captured Sheye's hand and brought it to his chest and held it there.

"Don't be embarrassed or ashamed of your feelings for me. I have the same feeling for you. They are just as strong in me toward you as they are for you toward me. We had the knowing. The experience is an enormously powerful connection. No, I don't have a lover. It has been a long time that I have had a woman in my bed."

Sheye looked utterly confused and was still embarrassed by her jealous outburst. "I will give you a moment to choose something to change into. Then we will eat a meal, and we will talk for as long as you need."

Sheye turned back to the closet so he could not see her face flame up again. She also had to turn herself away from those damn amber eyes of his before she threw herself at him and told him to take her, no matter the consequences she would feel afterward. She busied herself looking at the clothing and decided on a pair of black tights and a simple white T-shirt. When she reached in to take them, she could not grab onto them. All the clothing in the closet were just a hologram. Jodar went back over to the console and punched a few commands in. A wall came out on the other side of her. As she stood behind the wall, she could feel the dress being removed from her body. She supressed a squeal as it startled her. Within moments though, the dress was gone, and she was completely dressed in the clothing that she had pick out. All she did was stand there, and the clothing magically appeared on her body like the dress did in her holding cell. This was going to take a while to get used to. All these strange unfamiliar technologies were so alien to her.

Suddenly, a thought crossed her mind, *Alien to her*. "Oh lord!" Sheye groaned out.

Jodar was instantly by her side behind the wall. "Are you okay? Are you experiencing pain again?" Jodar was looking all over her body to see if she had an injury.

"No, no, I am okay. I just had a realization about something, and it is a little disturbing for me."

Jodar looked at her with concern and led her over to the sofa. "Please tell me. I want to take away anything that disturbs you."

Sheye gave a sad laugh and looked at Jodar. He was so sincere. Here was this huge handsome giant of a man sitting beside her looking like he could crush anything with his bare hands softly stroking her hand to keep her calm. She just knew he would not lie to her, no matter what question she tossed his way.

Why do we have this connection with each other? She did not even know this man till that morning; if it was even the same day that she thought it was. *How is it I feel such a deep, powerful connection to this man? Okay,* Sheye thought, *I will ask him the most important question first.*

Jodar could feel her emotions; he knew she was stressed out when she removed her hand from his. He could also tell that it was too stimulating for her in a sexual way to have him touching her right now. He respected her withdrawal and sat there, waited, and no longer tried to touch her.

Sheye took a deep breath and started, asking, "Who are you?"

Jodar frowned but began to answer her. "I am Jodar, the personal—"

Sheye stopped him by waving her hand in the air, so he paused. "No, I mean what are you? Are you an alien?"

Jodar nodded with his understanding of what she wanted to know now. "Yes, to your world and your people, you would call me an alien."

Sheye nodded with a conclusion. "Here I always thought aliens were little gray men with large heads and big black eyes."

Jodar laughed. "That would be the Grays. They are from the Reticulum constellation. We trade with them from time to time."

Sheye just stared at him wide-eyed. He spoke so nonchalantly about it. Like they were talking about the weather. Jodar continued, saying, "We are from an old Globular cluster of stars that has reproduced our system of planets that we come from. Your astronomical community of Earth calls our area the Messier 4 cluster in the Scorpius constellation. We are approximately six thousand two hundred lights-years from your planet. We have shielded our planets to be seen from your Hubble telescope. Your scientists have discovered one of our planets though, on the outer edge of our system. It is no longer alive nor supports life due to it being destroyed in a war. It looks to your astronomers like an exoplanet that is orbiting around what they call a white dwarf star."

Sheye stared at Jodar like he had just said the most ridiculous joke, and she was trying to comprehend the punch line. "Um, okay then! Why do you have all the women on this ship? Why did you abduct myself, my friend, and all the other women I have seen here from Earth?"

Jodar new this would be one of her questions, so he was prepared for what it was that he was going to say. "My planet is called Sarbus. We are surrounded by eleven other planets. It used to be thirteen other planets, but two destroyed each other through a massive war between themselves many eons ago. There is another planet that loves war. This is the planet in our system called Bionas. They have made war upon my planet for many years. My planet has an ore that is very coveted by all the surrounding planets, but we trade peacefully with all of them except Bionas. They want the ore and the mines for themselves. The last attack from Bionas killed off 99 percent of our female population through a biological attack. Our planet will die. Our people will be wiped out if we don't have women to continue our bloodlines. Supreme Commander Chanlon, who you met already, asked the council of the other eleven planets if we could collect females from distant systems to continue our life on our world. The council agreed. They only agreed if it would not expose our system of planets in any way. We were also commanded that our collection of females would not lead to any death, destruction, or war. We only took women who did not have any real connections left on their planets nor were they mated or with children. We had to do it in secret, hence, what you call the abductions. It is the only way we can keep our world and our bloodlines alive in a way."

Sheye was able to digest the information, but then she became very scared. Jodar could feel her fear but sat still and let her ask more questions. "What is to stop this Bionas from killing all the new women that you bring to your planet?"

Jodar grinned at this question. "The planet Bionas has been completely shut down since the last attack. The council of the planets saw to it that Bionas would not hurt any other planet again by placing an invisa-shield around them. Bionaians may never leave the planet by any space travel again. They have been completely cut off from all the other planets in our system. They are on their own. No one can enter, and no one can leave. They are not allowed to trade with any of our planets within our system."

Sheye sighed with relief. That was a definite fear if they were not contained. "Wait, you said planets. There are alien women you have taken from other worlds on this ship as well?"

Jodar shook his head. "No, not on this vessel. We have other vessels that have collections from other planets on them, yes. Our planet has many diverse races on it. We have collected many types of females for all our people. Earth women have been collected for my warrior race. Other women from other planets have been collected for the other races that suit them the most biologically."

"What do you mean by other races? Do you mean like we have on Earth? Like me being Caucasian or like being Hispanic, German, Indian, or Asian? Is it in that sort of way?"

Jodar shook his head. "No, nothing like your world. Our races have always been diverse with species and not with skin color. I guess you could say. Myself for instance. You have seen us. We are the Warrior Cloaks, although we wear armor on missions when we are out of our system instead of cloaks. We are tall and strong. We are the protectors and are good at fighting, hand-to-hand combat. Then there are the Blue Cloaks, which you have also met. They look like us, but they are smaller. They are much keener when it comes to things like math, science, nature, medicine, technology, and our planet's ancient ways. You have met the White Cloaks too. They are the tall, slim, white-haired race with large hands and large blue eyes. They are exceptional in the arts of style, fashion, crafts, and architecture. They love everything beautiful. Our Black Cloak race would be a little more startling to you. You haven't met them yet. They are quite secretive. They have patches of scales on their backs, necks, arms, and the backs of their legs. They have large orange slit eyes, small tails, sharp teeth with a crest on the tops of their heads. The Black Cloaks are dark and private. They do all the nasty work on our planet like executions, interrogations, spying, covert operations, and they control our prison systems. The Orange Cloaks, even when extremely old, look as if they are young adults. They never age, or at least their appearance does not age. They are not immortal. They just don't age in a way that would be normal to you. When they die, they turn into an energy. Their energy is contained and is used to create more of their own kind. This is the only race on our planet that can still reproduce females. They don't need women from other systems as they can just use their old energy forces to recreate more. They love service to others, and they are amazing chefs. They are quite slim and are about your height. They don't speak for they have no vocal cords. They communicate by ways of telepathy.

"We have many more races. Each race from our world is good at a certain amount of thing and not so good at others. All our races on our planet are important to one another. We all balance each other out. One race would not survive without all our other races working together, but you get the idea. You will soon meet more."

Sheye was overloaded with information already. She had a particularly important question she just had to ask. "Is there any racism on your world, Jodar? Does one race feel more important, special, or think they are better than the other races?"

Jodar frowned at this question and sighed. "Our world has never understood other systems' ideologies that one race is more important than any of the others. All our races are of fundamental importance to one another. Without one race, the other races would fail. This is how it has always been. All our people have a reason, a purpose, and are all as equally valued as the next. It saddens us those other systems like yours don't understand this simple concept."

Sheye was astounded at the simplicity and yet powerful understanding that Jodar had on racism. If only Earth had these ideologies. How amazing her planet could have been? It saddened Sheye to think of how evil her world sounded compared to his.

"Don't worry yourself about that now, Sheye. Our world like any other has its issues. Racism isn't one of them though."

This was all so strange. She felt like she was living in a real science-fiction movie. She felt another headache coming on fast. She was fascinated, but her stomach decided to speak up and growled intensely. Jodar apologized to Sheye as he did tell her that they would eat before they talk. He could sit and talk with her forever. He stood up and went over to his console again and punched in some instructions. As he waited for the food to arrive, he poured Sheye another smaller glass of his headache cure and handed it to her. Sheye drank half down and thanked Jodar. Her connection to him still baffled her. She did not even have to tell him she was experiencing another headache; he just knew. There was a chime at Jodar's chamber door.

Jodar opened the door, and an Orange Cloak entered with a large floating tray in front of him. Whatever was on the tray smelled wonderful, and Sheye's mouth began to water. Even though Sheye felt like she had not eaten in weeks, she ignored the tray and was extremely interested in the fellow that was underneath the orange cloak. She wondered how young this one looked. According to Jodar, this was one of the races that never aged in body. She wondered how old he was and really wanted to ask him. Sheye was far too polite though, so she kept her mouth shut. The Orange Cloak suddenly looked over toward her and removed his hood. There stood a young man of about eighteen years of age.

Without a word from his lips, Sheye could hear a male voice in her head loud as day as if he spoke out loud. *I am one hundred and twenty-four years old.*

Then Sheye's eyes almost bulged out of her head. He smiled at her, replaced his hood, turned, and left as silently as he had entered, leaving the tray of food behind.

Chapter 16

Jodar had not lied about the Orange Cloaks being amazing chefs. All the food on the tray was completely unfamiliar to her, but she was so hungry she dived into everything and ate her entire plate. Everything was delicious. Jodar sat quietly and let her eat. He loved just watching her. He was still so elated that she was sitting here with him, and they would soon be life mates. Sheye looked over at him as she wiped her face with the back of her hand. The juice from the fruit she had just stuffed into her mouth squirted all over the outside of her mouth.

"Oh god, I am so sorry. This is all just so delectable, and I was so hungry. I must look a mess."

As Jodar handed her a napkin, he smiled. "You could never look a mess to me, Sheye. I enjoy a woman with a hearty appetite. Food is pleasure. We are lucky. The Orange Cloaks are able to control the food in a way that it sustains us but does not make us gain any type of excess fat."

Sheye choked on what was left in her mouth. "You mean I could eat and eat and not gain any weight?" Sheye snorted. "That is impossible."

Jodar just smiled and nodded at her. "The Orange Cloaks have added an ingredient that only they can create. It helps one feel full for much longer periods. It is impossible for one to want to overeat. The chemical in the ingredient that they add tells your brain to stop eating. Once the ingredient knows your body has what it requires, you will automatically not eat again until your body needs to be fueled once more."

As soon as Jodar had that explanation out of his mouth, Sheye suddenly did not want to put another morsel of food into her mouth.

She was completely sated. She still had a hard time believing what Jodar had just told her even though she believed every word that came out of his mouth. What a scientific revolution if this was true. How Earth would benefit with so many health issues abolished if they had this ingredient.

Suddenly, Sheye became quiet, and she placed her head in her hands. A few tears escaped, and she tried to wipe them away before Jodar could see them. He did not have to see them; he could feel her emotions. He slid off the sofa and knelt in front of her. He placed his large warm hands on her thighs.

"Please tell me why you are hurting, so I can take it away. The drink did not help this time?"

Sheye raised her head from her hands and looked directly into his eyes. Right now, they were looking back at her like pools of warm honey.

God, this man is too good-looking by far.

Jodar raised his hand and gently wiped a tear from Sheye's cheek. "Am I ever going to be able to go back to Earth, Jodar? Am I ever going to have my life back? I was happy, Jodar. My life. I am able to visit my father's grave whenever I miss him. I have my own business…what is going to happen to my business and my employees? My horses—" Sheye choked on the memory of Onyx and Big Red. Her tears burst out, and she could not help herself. Sheye was unexpectedly angry and dejected all at once. She leaped up in a rage, and Jodar almost fell back on his haunches with the speed of her movement. He managed to stagger back in time so they would not bang heads again.

"Why did that man have to kill my horses? They were just trying to defend themselves. I am going to find that man. I know he is on this ship. I even managed to break his nose before. When I find him, I am going to kill him." Sheye was seeing red; she tried to go out the door but did not know how to open it. She lost her mind suddenly at the memory of her horses.

Jodar placed himself between Sheye and the door. Her sadness rolled into him like it was his own, and he needed to explain. He held her away from the door and asked her to sit down.

Sheye, in her grief, screamed at Jodar, "Open this door, Jodar! I am going to find that murderer and give him a piece of his own medicine. My precious horses—they were my life. My dad gifted me those horses—."

Jodar tried to calm Sheye down and tried to start explaining, but Sheye would not listen. Suddenly she attacked Jodar but not with any real zeal. She just pounded on his huge chest as tears rushed down her cheeks. She was not hurting him, so Jodar just let her pound on him till she fell into his arms sobbing.

Jodar cradled her in his arms for a bit, then he swooped her up, and placed her back on the sofa. He stroked her soft hair till she stopped sobbing, then he placed both hands on each side of her face and made her look at him. When Sheye was calm enough, she looked at Jodar and sniffled.

"Your beasts are not deceased, Sheye."

Sheye pulled her face away and scooted to the end of the sofa. She had to back away as what he said made her surprised. "What do you mean? I saw them both go down from the weapon the men in black armor used. They were both killed. I saw it."

Jodar shook his head and shuffled closer to Sheye on the sofa. He shifted his weight so he could turn to her without falling off and making a fool of himself just as he was giving her the important news about her beasts. "No, Sheye, they were just stunned. They were rendered unconscious, just as you and your friend were when we took you."

Sheye crinkled her eyes and wiped the tears away as sheer joy pumped through her brain at hearing her precious horses were alive. Then what Jodar had just stated sunk in. She frowned at Jodar and then threw herself away from him even more to the very opposite end of the sofa. "When you took us! You were one of those men that took us?"

Before Jodar could stop himself, not utterly understanding, he stated, "I am the one who received your kick to my helmet. You even cracked it because your kick was so hard. I must say that was an impressive achievement." Jodar smiled at Sheye. He was trying to show her how awed he had been with her abilities. This had the exact opposite effect that he was hoping for though.

"You were one of the men who took me from my home, terrified me, stalked me, made me think you killed my best friend, and my horses and then abducted me? That was you?"

Jodar clued in immediately, realizing that he should have eased into this part of the conversation. He should have gotten her more used to being with him. Then he could have slowly explained to her why he had chosen her to be with him. He could feel the rage and disgust flowing from her. It was crushing his soul to feel her thoughts about him right now. Sheye had turned from the women he knew because of the knowing to a woman who absolutely hated him and was fighting the connection they had.

Jodar's fighter instincts kicked in, and he stood up and backed away from Sheye. He was preparing for her to attack him truly this time and needed to get into a position to enable himself to not get injured or for Sheye to injure herself if she did decide to throw herself at him. Sheye could see what Jodar was doing; he was getting ready for her to attack him. Smart man! She wanted nothing more right now than to make him hurt the way he had hurt her. She was so devastated and yet so confused. She was angry, yet she still wanted to throw herself into his arms and just have him love her. So instead of attacking him, she did the only other thing she could do. "Just leave." More tears began to flow down her cheeks as she choked this out. She hated herself for feeling so weak. Never had she cried so much as she had in the last few days. Why did women have to cry when they were so angry? It was either scream in rage at the one you were mad at, attack the one you were mad at, or when nothing else worked or was plausible, then the only thing left to do was cry. Right now, she did not want to think about the fact that she did not really want to attack Jodar. She hated him with her entire being right now. She knew that if he kept standing there looking at her like a wounded puppy, ready to be punished, she would turn to gooey mush and forgive him. She had to be alone; she did not want him around her. She was not ready to forgive him.

Jodar understood she needed time to process all the information she had discovered that day, especially about the last part. He looked at her sorrowfully, then turned to leave his chambers. Just before he exited, he paused and looked back at Sheye. "I am not sorry that you are here, Sheye. I loved you the minute I laid eyes on you. I knew we had to be together. I am sorry that I have caused you this pain though." Jodar then sighed and quietly left his chamber. The door slid shut, and Sheye just stared at the empty space for a few more minutes and let her tears fall. She started to pace around the room after her tears dried. She was mad again, but she was turning it toward herself. She began questioning herself. Why was she so upset with Jodar? Why did it bother her so much that it was him who took her away from Earth? She had a connection with him that she had never imagined could be possible with another person. She accepted him, and to be honest, even loved him before she found out that it was his group that had abducted them. He was still involved with all the collections. Why did it bother her that it had been him personally who had taken her?

Sheye knew why she was so upset. It was not Jodar. It was not that it was his group that had abducted her. It was the whole shebang combined. The pressure of realizing that her life had suddenly and completely been altered in every way imaginable was why she broke down, not because of Jodar. It was overwhelming, and she was taking it out on him. So her horses were not dead. Thank God for that, but they were all alone in the harsh wilderness. They still had their saddles and tack on. Would someone find them, hurt them, keep them, kill them? Would they become wild horses? Sheye felt completely depleted. She was drained from all that she had endured. Sheye looked toward Jodar's bed but just could not imagine snuggling into it right now. She knew she would be able to smell him on his sheets. That just would not do. So she turned back to the sofa. She flopped, none too ladylike on the sofa, curled up, and fell fast asleep out of pure exhaustion.

*****

After Jodar left his chambers, he went to seek out Tannor. He had to come up with an idea in which to have Sheye feel not so torn. He understood her emotions completely. She had every right to feel the way she did. She had been stripped of everything she knew. She did not have a choice in the matter. Everyone of the women they had abducted would be feeling the same way. He had to talk to Chanlon about this. Any way to ease this transition to make it easier to accept for all the women would help everyone. They needed to find a way so all the women would be able to cope better with their new situation.

When Jodar entered Tannor's chamber, all Tannor had to do was take one look at Jodar. He immediately poured him a drink. Without a word, he handed his friend the glass. Jodar drank it down in one large gulp.

"Thank you, my friend."

Tannor watched as Jodar paced his chambers but never spoke. He understood his friend enough that when he was ready, he would speak. Jodar stopped pacing and turned to Tannor. "I have been trying to come up with a solution to ease Sheye's emotions about what has happened to her. I made a mistake and just assumed that after the knowing, she would forget about everything, fall madly in love with me, and just accept us. I have been overly selfish. What do you think we could do to help Sheye manage, Tannor?"

Tannor thought for a moment and then smiled sadly. "I have an idea, Jodar, but you may not like what I am suggesting."

Jodar listened to Tannor. He thought long and hard about what it was he suggested, and then he turned to his best friend. "Yes, I think you may be right. We can deal with everything when we are home, in much more familiar surroundings. I agree. I don't like it, but I think this is the only option we have right now."

The two men downed one more beverage, then summoned a Blue Cloak to carry out the task. Jodar returned to his chamber when the Blue Cloak stated that he had completed what was asked of him. Jodar entered his chambers a few hours later; he found Sheye sound asleep on the sofa, curled up into a ball. He collected her tenderly. He held her on his lap in his strong arms for a few minutes. He caressed her cheek with the back of his hand enjoying her soft, warm skin. He then brushed a lock of her hair back behind her ear as he rubbed his fingers through its silkiness. He leaned down and placed a gentle kiss on her full lips before he tilted back and looked at her beautiful face for a few moments. Jodar relished in the moment and then sighed. He knew she could not hear him, but he still talked to her. "I am sorry that I had to do this, Sheye. We will talk when we get to my home. Everything will work out in time, my lady. I know this is difficult for you right now. This is understandable. I only hope you come to accept your new life with me. I can only pray to the fifth star of Prantus that you will recognize your love for me. I love you with all my being. It is time to place you into hibernation for the remainder of the trip home. Sleep in peace, my beauty."

Chapter 17

The voyage back to Sarbus was a prolonged and dreary one. Chanlon, Jodar, and Tannor spent most of their hours practicing their aptitudes with their weapons, exercising, and looking into how Adrya and Blue had been able to conceal their falsifications and schemes. Jodar was concerned that there was much more to Adrya and her father's plotting than anyone else guessed. There had to be additional persons than just Blue involved, but who? The three men spent many extensive hours going through security footage that had been recorded on the space transport ship over the period they had been out on the collections. It had been over a year since they had departed from their home world. They had visited and gathered specimens from many planets, not just from Earth.

So far, the three of them, combined with the Blue Cloaks' help, had not been able to find any tangible evidence that would lead them to detect foul play other than what Adrya and Blue had already accomplished. The footage captured of the two together throughout the trip was extremely pathetic and sad though. Blue was Adrya's lapdog, always looking for a scrap of her attention and affection. Anytime he would perform as Adrya requested, he would always linger for some sort of physical reward before carrying out her demands. Chanlon was disgusted by all of what he had seen on the footage. He refused to observe anymore than he had too. He asked Jodar, Tannor, and his royal Blue Cloaks to carry on without him. Chanlon locked himself up in his chambers formulating his speech and the evidence against Adrya, for the council of the planets when they returned home.

Jodar felt immense animosity toward Dorian, Adrya, and Blue. Chanlon had not only survived many battles between Bionas but had triumphed as well. Now he lost not only his life mate but his only son too, and yet he still held it together. Jodar was impressed at how well Chanlon conducted himself through it all with dignity. Chanlon was an astounding mentor to Jodar, who always showed respect, control, devotion, and honor to all his people and the council of the planets. Jodar would do anything for his commander. He would even die for him if it came to that. Jodar was bound and determined to find out all he could to solve the obstacles that Adrya had caused so Chanlon could focus on getting their world back up and running to it is full potential before all the battles and attacks had nearly destroyed them all.

Finally, the day had come where they were nearing their home world. Jodar was so mentally space-fatigued that he was vibrating with being able to stretch his legs on his home turf. Soon he would be able to have Sheye awake and by his side when they landed. He could not wait to remove her from her space hibernation and get their lives started together. Every evening after they had placed Sheye into hibernation, he would go down and watch her in her pod. She was so beautiful. He found it extremely peaceful to sit with her. He would catch himself fantasizing about their future together and even wondered what their children would look like and how many they would have. This excited Jodar since he had not allowed himself to think of family after his mother and sister had perished in the last attack from Bionas.

Jodar threw himself into his duties and refused to let himself dwell on the past or any kind of family thoughts for himself after the final attacks. Then he had found Sheye. Everything changed in that moment. Life had significance, possibilities, joy, and happiness for him once again. Jodar was about to go down to attend personally with the removal of Sheye's pod before joining up with Chanlon to organize the transport of Adrya and Broud's pods before the trial with the council of the planets when he was snapped out of his thoughts. Over his communicator, he was paged to urgently attend to a matter on the main deck. He growled to himself as he reluctantly turned away from heading to where Sheye's hibernation pod was and headed to the main deck. He just wanted to land already and get off this massive hunk of metal.

When Jodar entered the main deck, he was accosted by one of the lead pilots. "I was told by Chanlon to inform you of anything strange or unnatural occurring during our entrance into our atmosphere."

Jodar just nodded and waited for him to explain. "Just as we positioned the ship into the correct entrance position for burn, a transfer shuttle was released from bay 7."

Jodar frowned for a moment before responding. "Was it a malfunction?" Just as the pilot was going to respond to Jodar's question, Chanlon's personal Blue Cloaks rushed in breathless. Jodar frowned again, then began to feel anxiety start to well up in his stomach. He knew he was about to hear something that would not be pleasant. One of the Blue Cloaks had finally caught his breath enough to speak. "They are gone, Jodar!"

"Who are gone?"

The Blue Cloak explained, "We were going to prepare Adrya and Broud for transfer in their hibernation pods to the supreme commander's transport. Then we were to have all of us travel to the trial with the council of the planets as Chanlon had arranged. When we entered the chamber, the pods were gone. Someone has taken them."

A few very expressive words exited Jodar's mouth, then without hesitation, he ran out the main deck doors like a demon. He had never run so fast in his life. He prayed to the fifth star of Prantus that he would be wrong.

"Please let me be wrong!" Jodar flew like lightning down the corridor. As he ran, he paged Tannor. "Tannor! Meet me in bay 7 in five minutes. Bring your men."

Tannor paged back. "I don't like the sound of your voice, Jodar. We will meet you there in three, with a ship at ready."

Jodar was so grateful to Tannor at that moment. Tannor always understood exactly what Jodar needed without having to explain. Jodar entered the large chamber of hibernation pods and went directly to where Sheye's pod was located. He knew what he would find, and he was right. Sheye's pod was also gone.

Tannor was waiting with a shuttle ready with his men, Chanlon, and Chanlon's personal Blue Cloaks. Jodar nodded to all the men, thanked Tannor by slapping him on his shoulder, and bowed slightly to Chanlon. Then the shuttle doors closed, and they departed the main ship. Jodar went immediately over to the copilot. "We need to track the shuttle that departed our ship before our entry to Sarbus. Find out where they are headed."

The copilot nodded but soon turned to Jodar and Chanlon with a frown. "They must have dismantled their tracking device on the shuttle. I can't home in on it, sir. Our scanners are unable to pick them up either. I believe they have initiated their cloaking shields. I tried to page them. They are not responding."

Chanlon cursed under his breath, and Jodar clenched his fists in rage but held his tongue. Of course, they would do this to not be detected. That would be exactly what he would have done. Jodar thought for a moment and then turned back to the copilot. "Link to the main deck on the ship. I need to have them send us the footage of hangar 7. Finding out who took Adrya, Broud, and Sheye may give us an idea where they could be heading. Let me know when the footage is transferred."

The copilot nodded and instantly communicated back to the ship with Jodar's orders. All the men then proceeded to the seating quarters of the shuttle to come up with ideas of where they thought the rogue shuttle could be headed.

Chanlon spoke first. "I should have seen this coming. Adrya is far too cunning to have had only one person assisting her. I must apologize, Jodar. If I had thought about this sooner, I would have made sure you would have had Sheye safe. We know that they won't be heading to Bionas because of the shield. They will have to go into hiding as the council of the planets will put out an announcement to all the supreme commanders to be on the look out for them."

Chanlon snapped his fingers toward his personal Blues. "Bring up a map of our system. Let us focus on ruling out the planets that they won't be able to hide themselves easily."

Soon, their entire planetary system was hovering over the men by way of a hologram. Jodar stood and pointed to the planet Rueek and enlarged the planet for everyone else to focus on. "They won't be trying to conceal themselves here." Jodar enlarged the entire planet and spun it around. "We all know that the Rueekians only allow traders, council of the planet members, visitors, and royals to enter their planet and only at their visitor centers. They will attack and destroy any ship that enters without permission even if they link a distress signal."

Tannor stood up and pointed to the planet Dristk. "I don't think they would choose to hide on the planet Dristk either." Tannor placed Rueek back in its place and enlarged Dristk. "There is no place to hide on land here, considering it is all sand. The Dristk's live underground. I don't think Adrya would be able to handle the tunnels or the recycled air. I also heard that she is very claustrophobic."

Chanlon laughed and nodded toward Tannor. "You are correct. She stated that she would die before she ever set foot on that planet because of her fear of small tunnels and the cramped underground cities that are there." Tannor then continued, saying, "Also, Dristk just started their five-year drought a month ago. No one with any sense would go there when the drought is happening. It is far too hot. I can't see them going to planet Abenha either." Tannor minimized Dristk and enlarged Abenha. "It is 95 percent water. Our shuttles are not water submergible. One also needs permission from the queen and the supreme commander of Abenha to stay for any more time than a few days. One must get permission far in advance to stay over an extended period. They are never happy to have land dwellers stay too long."

Chanlon walked around the hologram of the planetary system. "So that narrows us down to seven planets." Chanlon turned to the Blues again. "Remove Dristk, Rueek, Bionas, Sarbus, and Abenha off the map. Let us look at the remaining planets that would be ideal to stay off any radar for a while."

Jodar slapped his forehead and turned to the Blue Cloaks. Why did he not think of this before? "We need to contact the other seven planets' security centers. See if they have had any unlawful, unscheduled, or emergency entries in the last few hours. Also, inquire if they have had any unusual blips or malfunctions on their systems of any kind that can't be explained in the last few hours as well."

Just as Jodar finished talking with the Blues, the copilot's voice came over the intercom. "The ship has sent over the requested footage, sir. Patching it through now."

Chanlon waved to the Blues, and they shut the hologram down and linked the footage to the center screen. The men all watched the footage. Around the time of the escape from bay 7, the feed just shut off. Chanlon roared at the Blues to fix the problem but was told that it was not an error in the footage or equipment. Someone had purposely shut off all the cameras to all the hibernation rooms, hallways, and shuttles in bay 7, at the time of entry to their planet.

There was absolutely no footage to be seen of who had taken Adrya, Broud, and Sheye. All the men cursed loudly in unison. Now they had to wait and see what the Blues would find from the seven other planets on any of the inquiries that Jodar had recommended. Waiting was not one of Jodar's strong points. Now Sheye was in even more dire trouble. It was torturing him to not know where she was, who took her, or if she was even safe. All Jodar could do was pace around the room as Chanlon, Tannor, and the rest of the men looked on.

Chapter 18

Sheye felt like she was drowning. Her lungs were burning like she had aspirated a gallon of water. She could not seem to breathe in deep nor open her eyes for the slime that was coating her entire face. She was freezing as well and felt sticky everywhere. She realized she was naked but had absolutely no idea why. What was happening? Why did she feel like she had just run a marathon in a field full of hardening cement? Her lungs hurt like hell. Had all her ribs been broken? Every breath she was now able to take felt like she was sucking in a handful of razor blades. In between all the pain she was in, Sheye thought that she could hear something, though she could not focus or understand what was going on. She was so disoriented; she could not concentrate. Again, she thought that she heard something. Her ears were full of the same slime that covered her entire body. A quick fluttering thought passed through her mind; she was wondering if she had an extreme case of pneumonia and a possible ear infection. Was she in a hospital? Had she been in an accident? Every time she tried to move, she would slip and slide as pain racked through her entire body. She was not on a bed. She could not seem to find a grip or a way to be able to stand up. She was on a cold hard floor.

"Stop moving and let us dry you off."

Sheye turned her head to the muffled voice that she thought she heard again. Was that someone talking to her? What the hell was wrong with her? Was she dreaming? Why did she feel like she was in a bubble? Sheye felt hands grabbing at her, and she tried to scream. She pulled away from the hands that were grabbing at her.

"Stop moving, stupid woman! We are trying to help you."

Sheye could hear two voices starting to argue. "Just get her cleaned up without insulting her. She is terrified. She just came out of hibernation without any support. She is disoriented." The other person scoffed but did as he was told. Sheye could feel hands trying to help her get up again. She realized that she had to accept the assistance. Whoever was trying to help her may be able to explain to her what was happening.

When all the slimy product was wiped away from her face and body, she was able to view the men who were helping her. There before her were two Blue Cloaks wiping her down and drying her off. She immediately felt extremely embarrassed at her naked state that she was in and snatched a towel away from one of the small men in front of her and wrapped it around herself tightly. Sheye was shivering with not only the cold but fear as well. Something was not right with this scenario. She was beginning to understand that she had been put into hibernation and was now being taken out. Now she knew how Mandy had felt when she tried to get them to escape the first time. She briefly felt terrible about that, but now she had to focus on herself.

Sheye looked around the room and realized that she was not in one of the bubble cells. Nor was she in Jodar's chambers where she remembered herself last being. It hurt to speak, but she asked anyways, "Where am I?" She was able to croak out those three words with not too much pain.

The Blue Cloak closest to her just smirked and looked her up and down. This made Sheye very wary. This was not the normal behavior from any of the Blue Cloaks that she had met before. A chill washed down her spine, and her spider senses were kicking in hard core.

"Where is Jodar?"

The two Blue Cloaks just laughed at her. One grabbed a pile of clothing and tossed them toward her. Then without a word, they both left the room.

Sheye glared at the door for a few moments before she gave up, then sighed. She would not get any answers yet, so she turned to the clothing on the floor and picked them up. It was a simple cloak and some undergarments, but it was better than nothing. She pulled on the underwear and then donned the cloak. She still felt filthy with all the sticky residues left on her from the hibernation fluid. Sheye was about to go try the door only to have it slide open, and the Blue Cloaks were standing on the other side. There was now five of them instead of two, and they all had a rod in their hands. Sheye backed up a little in fear. One of the Blue Cloaks waved her forward.

"We are taking you out of here. If you make any fuss, we won't hesitate to stun you. Don't make us hurt you. We just need to get you off the shuttle to where we have been told to place you."

Sheye frowned at them. "Chanlon and Jodar won't tolerate you hurting me. I will let him know how I have been treated by you when I see him. This is intolerable."

The Blue Cloaks all turned to one another and laughed. The Blue Cloak closest to Sheye turned back to her and stated, "We no longer have to worry about Chanlon and Jodar. We answer to a new leader now. He is allowing us to extract our revenge on the execution of our brother, Blue." Without another word, they ushered her out of the shuttle, keeping the rods charged and pointed close to her.

They proceeded to prod Sheye and led her out of the shuttle to the outdoors. They had landed on a world. It seemed almost like they had landed in the middle of the Amazon rain forest only it was not wet or raining. It was beautiful wherever they were. Sheye looked down at her feet and noticed the grass that she was standing on. It was unlike any grass she had ever felt or seen. It was as soft as angora fur and was light pink. She shifted her bare feet in the soft layer of grass and then turned back to look at the shuttle and gasped. It was undeniably a spacecraft. Somewhere deep inside, she had still hoped that all of what she had witnessed was on some secret military base on her own planet. With that thought in mind, something flew past her head, and she turned to watch the bird fly into a tree beside her. Not only was this a bird she had never seen before, but she also did not even know if she could call it a bird even though it had wings.

There were no feathers on this creature, but its smooth skin was shining like crystal. Its wings were smooth and featherless with clear membrane covering them. The top of the creature's head had a white tuff of fur on it, and its face looked like that of an owl only there was no beak. It had a mouth almost like a bat with small fangs. Its legs looked more like smooth, slender human arms and hands holding on to the branch that it had perched itself on. The Blue Cloaks pressed her forward with a poke of the rod. It only zapped her enough for her to keep going. Sheye continued walking but still took in her surroundings. The trees were all massive. The bark on them looked like snakeskin but was reflective like a dull mirror. Midway up the trees had gigantic red and blue flowers on the branches with the centers of the flowers dangling low and softly flowing back and forth in the calm breeze. Surrounding the flowers were immense leaves that one could almost use as a blanket. They were the strangest yet most colorful, beautiful trees she had ever seen. Looking up and past the trees, Sheye could see the sky. It was not blue though. The sky looked light purple with streaks of gold. The clouds were very puffy, and they were splashed with yellow and orange specks. Looking past the clouds, there was also a few moon-sized planets in the distant sky and a soft glowing sun farther away beside the planets that she could see. The smells and the sounds of this forest were peaceful and calming. She could close her eyes and believe that she was in an expensive spa only the superrich could afford.

They walked for only a few minutes when they turned down a trail that led to a large building. The building was inset against a cliff, and there was a large lake just below it. One could think it was an immense log cabin only the trees used to build the cabin had been the ones she had walked by. The bark had not been removed like cabins would have on Earth. The reflective bark was still on the material used to build this large cabin-like structure, and it glistened in the soft lighting of the planet. Again, Sheye was impressed by how beautiful everything was. The Blue Cloaks directed Sheye into the building. It was very gorgeous, open, and spacious. The far area facing the water was not even closed in with a wall. It was all open and a gentle warm breeze was flowing through the room. The room was luxurious with impressive large white furnishings. Sheye felt like she was on the deck of an expensive yacht. Whoever owned this beautiful home sure had good taste in decorating.

The Blue Cloaks directed Sheye up the stairs and onto another luxurious level. The entire front of the building had no wall. Every floor was open to the lake beyond. They led Sheye to a room and then turned away locking her in. Sheye was now all alone. Stupid Blue Cloaks! All she had to do was jump out the open where there was no wall to escape. This Sheye was about to attempt until she noticed what lay on the ground below. Nothing but jagged crystal-like rocks jutting sharply out of the ground. There was a small walkway making its way to the lake, but it was very narrow. She was also a lot higher up than she thought. The jump would certainly kill her. On the pier at the end was also a couple of large beasts sunning themselves. They certainly looked dangerous even though they were sleeping. They had short gray fur with red streaks like a tiger. They had the head somewhat of a bull but had long wicked-looking fangs, with three sharp horns on their heads and spikes around the top of their necks. These looked like they could gore anyone that messed with them. The beasts' front paws were enormous with vicious-looking talons, and they had hooves on their back legs. Okay, so jumping out the opening of this building was out of the question. If the jump did not kill her, those beasts surely would.

As Sheye was contemplating another way to escape, the door to her room slid open and a few tall, slender females entered. At least, she assumed they were females just by their beautiful faces, but their bodies were very unisex with no curves or feminine attributes at all, and their hair was like short spikes if you could even call it hair. They had large almond-shaped purple eyes. Sheye just stood still by the open wall.

What now? she thought. The beings almost floated toward her. She could not see them walk, but they were moving toward her. Sheye shook her head and closed her eyes for a moment. Everything was just so super bizarre and surprising. The being closest to her spoke first. "We have been sent here to get you cleaned up and prepared. Please step over here for us to begin. Sheye could not tell if they were female yet as even their voices were undiscernible. Suddenly, the thought of acting stubborn with these beings exhausted her. She was so very tired with all these surprises and weirdness for now that she just obeyed. These beings looked harmless enough.

They directed her to a large wardrobe-like area in the room and placed her in the middle. They told her to stand still. Suddenly, four glass walls emerged from the floor and enclosed Sheye in a small glass box the size of a shower stall. Sheye's heart rate became rapid when there was a gentle suction noise and a tickling sensation all over her body. The noise stopped, and the walls disappeared back into the floor. The whole thing only took a few seconds, yet Sheye felt completely clean just as she would have if she had taken a shower, but she was completely dry. The clothing she was wearing was also clean and fresh. Her heart rate went back down to normal as she realized this must be like a shower for them. How it worked was far beyond her comprehension, but she felt cleaner than she had ever been in her life. The tall slender beings motioned for Sheye to move to another section of the wardrobe area and sit. She was introduced again to the contraption that she had been so scared of with the tall slender man on the main ship. At least this time, she understood what it was for and just let it do it is work on her face and hair. It was very pleasant when you were not scared of it. Sheye felt refreshed. The beings gasped when the contraption moved away.

"You are so very beautiful, my lady. He will be very pleased."

Sheye frowned. She hoped they were talking about Jodar, but her spider senses were flaring up again, and she knew that this was not who they were talking about.

The beings then moved her deeper back into the large wardrobe area, and this time, a single solid wall came out of the floor in front of her. She was subjected to being dressed by the garment contraption like before. Sheye stood still as the strange material seemed to grow on her very skin. This was something she may never get used to. This time, the outfit was extremely inappropriate for anyone's eyes but a lover. The wall retreated into its place, and the beings gasped and nodded to each other but then quickly retreated out of the room. Sheye was once more left alone with no answers. There was a long mirror at the side of the wardrobe room, so she went over to it and gasped herself. There was no way on earth anyone would see her caught dead in this outfit if one could even call it an outfit. It was so sheer that it left nothing to the imagination at all. The color was very opaque, but it involved many different hues of pastel purples and blues. It was a two-piece with the top bodice reaching just below her breast and the neckline came up around her throat with no shoulder material that left them bare. The bottom piece had a thong undergarment with the same opaque see-through material swirling around her legs and large slits on both sides. This was the sexiest and most immodest lingerie she had ever worn.

"Nope, nope, and definitely nope." Sheye blushed while looking at her own reflection. No one was going to see her in this getup if she could help it. Sheye let her mind drift for a moment as she thought of Jodar. She smiled devilishly to herself. "Well, maybe Jodar one day." Sheye sighed again and removed that thought from her head and moved away from the mirror. She was going over to the bed to grab the spread to cover herself when the door slid open again. Sheye froze in her tracks. The hair on the back of her neck rose when she heard a man speak from the entrance of the door. Chills went down her spine, and she made herself turn slowly toward the door with her heart in her throat.

Chapter 19

Standing in the doorway with the look of pure lust on his handsome face was a man around the same age as Chanlon. For a moment, she thought it was the man that she had dealt with in the cell unit on the main ship who was inspecting all the women like cattle. He looked like Broud, only older and far more menacing even than the younger version. They both just stood their staring at each other for a few seconds. The man spoke first. "If you were not meant for my grandson, I would claim you. You are stunning."

Sheye sucked in her breath and took a step back even more aware of what she was wearing. The man was devouring every portion of her body with his hungry eyes. The man was about to take a step forward when they both heard a female voice come from behind him.

"Oh, Daddy, must you always be so vulgar? You know that she is Broud's soon-to-be life mate." The woman swept in past the man in the doorway with a gentle laugh.

Adrya was now front and center, standing in front of Sheye as she stopped and inspected her. "Very nice. The Charnals did a wonderful job with you, I must say. Broud will be so very delighted. I don't need to ask what my father thinks of my son's life mate as we already know you have piqued his libido as well. What is it about you that makes men fall at your feet? I have been the only one that has been able to do this in the past, and now it seems I have some competition." Adrya tsk'd.

Sheye could not tell if she was angry or just making a casual comment. Sheye took that moment to try to snag the blanket off the bed again, and Adrya jumped forward and snatched it out of her hand.

"Now, now, why so reserved? You have all the right qualities. Why not use them to their fullest capacity? Seems you have frozen my father in his worship of your body and his need for you. Oh, how my son will be so thrilled with his new plaything." Adrya laughed as she took herself and the blanket over to a large white chair and gracefully folded herself into it like a cat.

Sheye felt like a piece of meat standing there but stood her ground. She straightened her back and lifted her head high. She would not let this vile woman get the better of her.

"She has a backbone too! I am liking you more with every passing moment, my sweet." Adrya looked toward her father and scoffed. "Woman, show some respect since you are in the divine presence of my father, Dorian, the supreme commander of Bionas."

Sheye choked and gasped at this last statement. *How is this possible?*

Dorian's large figure moved into the room, and Sheye wanted to step back desperately but held her ground. Dorian came up remarkably close to Sheye. He then removed his lustful stare from Sheye to look over at his daughter.

"Do shut up, daughter. Your shrill voice is giving me a headache."

Adrya just sat silent and pouted at her father's rebuke in silence. Dorian looked back at Sheye and looked her up and down slowly. Sheye began breathing faster, which made her breast rise and fall. This excited Dorian even more. Sheye was disgusted and tried to keep calm as the bile rose in her throat. She kept thinking that this was the man who had instigated all the destruction, war, death, and annihilation of Jodar's world. This was the man who had put into motion the need for Chanlon to have to travel to other worlds and kidnap thousands of women to keep their world alive. This was the man who caused her life and all she new to be turned into a nightmare. Without thinking, Sheye attacked. She wanted to kill this man for all he did to her, Jodar, Chanlon, Mandy, and to all the other women. Dorian received a hard punch to his jaw, and it made him stagger back just a little. He looked down at Sheye with a smile that caused her to hesitate just enough that he was able to grab her in his large steel-like grip and held her tight against his body.

Adrya yelled as she jumped from her perch. "How dare you strike my father! Now you shall be punished."

Dorian just calmly told Adrya to shut up again and to sit back down. Dorian looked down at the magnificent woman he held in his arms. Right then and there, he knew that Broud would not claim this one. She would become his. He had never seen a more lovely, spirited, strong woman such as this before. She even surpassed his daughter in beauty. Dorian would make this fabulous specimen his life mate, and she would bare him many sons. Broud was a pathetic waste of skin anyhow. He had only just been introduced to his grandson earlier the day before and was not impressed with what he had seen. He would never accept a halfling into his life. Broud was half Blue Cloak. Dorian would never allow someone that carried Sarbus blood in their veins to be accepted as one of his own. He only convinced Adrya to seduce Chanlon for his own personal gain so he could take over Sarbus. Adrya did not really matter to him either. She was a female; she was his daughter, but he never wanted her truly. He craved a son. He let Adrya believe that he would one day let Broud become the supreme commander of planet Sarbus. It worked in his favor for him to have Adrya completely under his thumb and letting her continue to think this way.

Dorian had only spoiled Adrya so she would end up doing anything that he asked of her. When she grew up to be a beautiful woman, he had used her beauty to gain access to powerful men and to Sarbus. What Dorian wanted, he always got. The only thing that he never was able to obtain yet was Sarbus. This infuriated Dorian. He had schemed, murdered, corrupted, and manipulated his way to the top. He killed the last supreme commander of Bionas in a fair fight many years ago and had taken over that planet that he was not born to rule. After that, he murdered the remainder of the royal commanding family and ruled the planet with an iron fist. The people of Bionas were terrified of him, and that was exactly how he like it.

Dorian had set his eyes on Sarbus for the Sardanium steel mines, but he also wanted revenge on Chanlon. After he had been accepted by the council of the planets with his take over of Bionas, he set his sights on a life mate to produce sons for him. When his life mate had given birth to a girl and then lost several other pregnancies, he sent her away from him for a while as he was so terribly angry with her for not being able to produce a male heir. She fled to Sarbus, and Chanlon had taken her under his protection. Dorian's life mate had taken Chanlon's kindness too far and had fallen in love with him, but Chanlon did not reciprocate her feelings as she was a bonded woman. She ended up fleeing Sarbus in sorrow and returned to Bionas only to end her life right in front of him. She blamed him for everything and stated that he did not deserve her. She would leave him with the daughter that he did not care for and slit her throat right in front of him. Dorian did not blame himself for his life mate's taking of her own life; he blamed Chanlon.

Everyone adored Chanlon and worshipped him. The council of the twelve planets were even wrapped around his finger, but Dorian would change all that. Once he had Sarbus under his control, he would be the one that controlled the entire system of planets. Everyone would bow to him and the mines that he controlled. He would be the supreme commander of all. Dorian snapped out of his thoughts and looked back down at the beauty in his arms. He let the woman go even though she felt marvelous right where she was. He slowly made her body slide down his in a way that made her hips grind against his groin, and he moaned, then whispered, "Later," so only Sheye could hear him.

Sheye stumbled back away from Dorian to get some distance from him. He smiled evilly and then turned to Adrya. "Come, daughter, let us prepare for tonight's festivities."

Adrya unwound herself from her perch and walked out of the room but not before she grabbed Sheye's arm and squeezed it painfully with her nails digging in as she glared at her. Sheye did not give her the satisfaction of trying to pull away and glared back at her. Adrya tsk'd again, and then she walked out of the room with her father close behind her, and they shut the door. Sheye stood and stared at the space Dorian and Adrya had just vacated. The man terrified her more than anyone had in this entire fiasco. *How is it even possible that he is here?* Jodar had told her that the planet Bionas had been shut down completely with the shield. No one could enter nor leave. Sheye went over to the bed and sat down heavily. *Did the Blue Cloaks in his control have something to do with his escape from the shielded planet? Did they find a way to get him out?* Sheye knew that she was on the right track, but other than that, she could not figure it out. *Oh god, Jodar, I need you. Please find me.* Sheye had no idea how her connection with Jodar worked, but she sure prayed that it was telepathic in some sort of way.

*****

As Sheye was sitting on the bed contemplating how Dorian was able to escape the Bionas's shield, Chanlon, Jodar, and Tannor were hard at work trying to figure out where the rogue shuttle had disappeared. They were all looking at every schematic they could find about the planets and the possible places that the shuttle could have hidden when the copilot's voice came over the intercom. "We finally have all the security reports that you requested of the seven remaining planets, my liege. I am patching them to you now."

All the men stood up and returned to the large screen to view the reports. They skewered through all the information that had been sent to them. There was not one thing to show any illegal, unusual entry, or disturbance into, around, or on any of the planets. There was not one piece of evidence that would help them at all. At last, Tannor threw himself onto one of the sofas exhausted. Jodar would not give up though as he began to go over the reports again to see if they had missed anything at all, even one small detail.

Out of the blue, Tannor sighed loudly and stated, "To all the stars of Prantus, I am in desperate need of a vacation."

Jodar immediately stopped what he was doing, jumped up, and headed to where Tannor was splayed out on the sofa. "What did you just say?"

Tannor sat up quickly and apologized. "I am sorry, Jodar, for my exhaustion. I know we must find the shuttle and bring Adrya back for her trial and get Sheye back by your side, but damn, I will need a vacation after this is all over."

Jodar whooped and slapped Tannor on his shoulder; he ran over to the Blue Cloaks at the computer panels and told them to bring something up on the hologram.

Tannor and Chanlon joined Jodar at the hologram station and watched as the vacation moon Sreigar of the planet Coslar came into formation.

"Why didn't I think of this before?" Jodar enlarged the planet and spun it around before he turned to face his companions. "This is the place they are hiding. I just know it in my bones. There is lacking security tracking on the vacation moon. You can get any kind of drug. You can gamble, drink, lose yourself in sexual fantasies. The black market is huge on this moon. They allow anyone to come and go without a second glance. Everyone turns a blind eye to the illegal activity there. What happens on Sreigar stays on Sreigar."

Chanlon clamped his hand on Jodar's shoulder. "I think you may be on to something, Jodar. This is the perfect place to hide and not be found for a while."

Jodar turned to Tannor. "Thank you, Tannor. I would not have thought of this if it weren't for you."

Tannor smiled and nodded at Jodar. "Does this mean we are going on vacation?" Jodar had a renewed hope and smiled back at his best friend.

"Yes, we are, my friend. Yes, we are."

Chanlon spoke into the intercom and told the pilots to change course to the vacation moon immediately. Then he told the men to prepare for a possible battle when they arrived.

*****

As the festivities started, Dorian was standing at the head of a lavishly laden table full of exotic foods and drink. He was toasting the Blue Cloaks who were seated around the table with Adrya and Broud. The Blue Cloaks all had beautiful women on their laps, and they were all laughing, eating, fondling the women, and having a grand time. The Blue Cloaks were all celebrating with their new leader they had recently pledged themselves to. Dorian had promised them the positions of head inventors when they were able to get back on the planet Bionas. They were guaranteed whatever they would need and dream of to create their inventions and whatever they wanted to develop. They would be showered with riches and all the beautiful women they could handle.

These Blue Cloaks had been the five friends who had been with Blue vacationing on this very moon years before letting off some steam before their true training commenced. They had all thanked the fifth star of Prantus that it had not been them who had been seduced by Adrya that night. Because of their silence, they were now reaping the rewards for not telling Chanlon what they had witnessed when Blue went off with Adrya. They had protected their friend's secret for over twenty-five years. When they found out about Blue's execution, they knew that they, too, would be discovered soon when they found out about Jodar's investigation. They gathered themselves and used their intelligence together and came up with an idea. They were able to develop a device that was able to not only communicate with Dorian but also open a small wormhole in the Bionas shield. They were able to remove Dorian in a small personal transport shuttle from one side of the shield to the other. They were only able to keep the wormhole open for a few minutes without being detected by the council of the planet's high security, and they had succeeded. Now here they were being rewarded for their efforts, living their dreams without the worry of being discovered and executed for the secret they did not divulge by Chanlon.

Dorian raised his glass and toasted the small men at the table. "If it were not for your brilliance and fast thinking, I would not be standing here with my daughter and grandson now. Because of your loyalty to me, I will keep my end of the agreement and shower you with power, riches, and women. Drink up, men. Drink as if you would not see the new dawn of tomorrow."

All the Blue Cloaks cheered and pounded their drinks back. Dorian himself went over to them all and filled their cups again. Adrya watched the scene before her in silence. Broud was beside her fondling a woman quite inappropriately and was not paying attention to anything else in the room other than the woman on his lap and his own drink. Adrya was watching the little men in cloaks and was feeling slightly guilty. She missed her Blue terribly. She had realized that she did indeed love Blue as much as she could love anyone besides herself, her father, and her son. Adrya missed his worship and devotion to her. She missed his constant shadow always within earshot to complete any task that she requested of him.

When Adrya had been told of Blue's execution for treason when she came out of hibernation, she flew into a rage. She destroyed everything in her path. She ripped, tore, screamed, and smashed anything she could get her hands on, then collapsed in tears. Her father could not even console her. The only thing that finally aroused Adrya out of her morning was her father's promise to capture, torture, and kill Chanlon. She had made him promise her that she could be the one who gave Chanlon the final killing blow. As she watched her father carry out his task for the evening, she looked forward to its end. Then she would take her son upstairs and show him her surprise. She had not told Broud yet that the woman he so desperately wanted was just in the room above them. It would be so satisfying to see that woman put in her place, and Broud was just the man to do this. Adrya sat back again and swirled her wine in her glass as she drowned out the party sounds of the Blue Cloaks. She smiled to herself as she let her mind drift as she thought about what weapon she would use to crack open Chanlon's skull.

Suddenly, one of the Blue Cloaks started to gag and choke. Blood flew up from his lungs and splattered onto the thighs of the woman who was sitting on his lap. She screamed and jumped off. The other Blue Cloaks also started to choke simultaneously and gob up streams of blood. All the ladies sitting on the Blue Cloaks' laps jumped up and left the room in fear. The Blue Cloaks' skin began to shrivel and age with startling speed. They all looked around in fear realizing that they had been poisoned, and they had been deceived.

One of the Blue Cloaks removed a remote out of his cloak with a shriveling hand and pushed the buttons on it. He croaked out, "Your wormhole will no longer function. You will never be able to return to Bionas." As he said this, blood spewed forth from his frothing mouth.

Dorian casually walked over to the shrivelling, dying Blue Cloak and grabbed his withering skull in his hands. "I care not of Bionas, you traitorous scum. It is Sarbus that I want, and it is Sarbus that I will get." Then Dorian crushed the Blue Cloak's skull in with his bare hands.

Chapter 20

When Chanlon's shuttle landed, they immediately entered the visitor center. The men were disgusted with the lack of security and headed over to the main security bay. No one questioned them or tried to stop them, except to stare or run in the other direction. All kinds of humanoids from all around the system were at the center for their vacations. The ones ducking, running, or hiding themselves away were all illegals, but this did not concern the group or deter them from their mission. These other people were not any of their concern for why they were here. The group of soldiers entered the security bay, and Chanlon's booming voice awoke the four guards from their slumber on their chairs. "I need all the data on every shuttle entry to this planet from the last few days immediately."

All the lazy guards jumped up from their chairs in anger. "Who the hell are you? This is a secured area. You are trespassing. Get out, or you will all be arrested."

Jodar stalked up to the belligerent guard who had spoken and grabbed him by his throat and lifted him with ease off the floor. All the other guards began to step forward to defend their buddy, but Tannor and the rest of his soldiers stepped forward as well, which made the three guards think twice and stand down. As the guard grabbed at his neck while he dangled helplessly in Jodar's grip, Jodar spoke. "Never speak to the supreme commander of Sarbus that way ever again."

The guard's eyes bulged out partially because of Jodar strangling him as well as the news he had just heard. The guard choked out an apology, and Jodar roughly threw the guard away from him. The guard regained his footing as he rubbed his neck and stumbled over to his buddies. Chanlon had his Blue Cloaks sit down at the control panels at the security main frame, and soon, they had the data of all shuttles entering the planet from the last few days.

The men were looking at the screen when Jodar pointed. "There, enlarge that area in the southernmost quadrant of the moon."

The Blue Cloaks obeyed.

"That's got to be them. This section is the best vacation spot on the moon. This part of the moon is visited only by VIPs, the rich, important, and royal supreme families. These are the only ones that can purchase property for vacation retreats in that area of the moon. Two vessels have landed in the last two days. One of these must be the shuttle we are looking for."

Jodar turned back to the four guards who were cowering in the corner. "We are leaving you with the supreme commander's Blue Cloaks to keep watch over you all. Don't try to warn anyone in this sector. They have permission by the supreme commander himself to kill you without question if you even move. Do you understand?"

All the guards just nodded. They were all far too underpaid for it to be worth trying to go against these formable soldiers. It was an easy job, and they were not willing to jeopardize their posts for some rich family they did not even know. They all nodded, and then the soldiers with Chanlon, Jodar, and Tannor left the security room. The Blue Cloaks smiled at the guards, and they all sat down uneasily not wanting to piss off the little guys in blue.

*****

Sheye was just about to sleep on the bed when she heard a racket coming from outside of her door. It was a male and a female voice, but before she could sit up, the door slide open, and this time, it was Broud who filled the doorway.

Adrya slipped in again and turned to her son. "Surprise." She turned back to Sheye with a smirk that said, "This is what you get for standing up to me."

Sheye almost jumped off the bed when the door slid open until she remembered her near-naked state, so she clasped the blanket around her like a shield.

Adrya turned back to her son as she left the room. "Enjoy my gift, darling."

Sheye found herself alone in a bedroom with a man she knew would have no qualms about raping her. Just one look at his face told her all she needed to know about what was about to occur. She would not go quietly. He would have to kill her before he would touch her in that way. Sheye screamed in her head again, *Jodar, help me!*

Broud entered the room and shut the door. He pressed a few pads on the sliding door, and she instinctively knew that he had locked it. Broud stalked slowly up to the bed. He was larger than Jodar and lacked any of the kindness and love that she felt exuded from the man she had been connected with the knowing. The look on Broud's face was that of ownership and control.

Sheye slowly moved to the other side of the bed never taking her eyes off him. Broud was breathing heavily, and his black hair was falling over one eye. He stopped on the other side of the bed and swept the hair off his face in one swift movement of his hand. He was handsome but a very cruel, evil handsome, like Dracula.

Without a word, he began to unbutton his shirt. Sheye stepped off the bed and backed away.

"Remove the blanket." Broud's voice was strong but quiet.

Sheye stood tall and grabbed the blanket closer to her body. "No." Oh god, why could she not just keep her mouth shut? Why did she feel like she had to say anything to him at all? It just seemed to ignite the flame in his eyes even more.

Broud smiled at her as he slowly moved to the end of the bed like a panther stalking its prey. "The minute I saw you, I knew that you had to be mine. You were made for me, Sheye. We are destined to be together."

Sheye could not help it and snorted. "I highly doubt that." Again! What was wrong with her? Had she lost all her senses? Why did she feel the need to have to provoke this man? If she made him mad enough, maybe he would charge at her; maybe he would even tumble off the edge of the open wall, or she would be able to get a few good kicks in before he was able to overpower her.

"You are mine now. I have wanted and desired you long before we even met. I won't hold back tonight. You won't find pleasure in my need for you. It is too great. I won't be gentle with you on our first joining. It will be fast and powerful. I will be gentler with you on our second joining, maybe."

Sheye could feel her panic rising. He was the size of a bull. How would she be able to survive his onslaught on her body? "You are welcome to try, Broud." Damnit, he just made her so mad. She was unable to keep her stupid mouth shut where he was concerned.

Broud took this as a welcome, enticing challenge. He was getting closer, and she was almost backed up to the opening where there was no wall. *Will death be better than this man taking my virginity?* The thought crossed her mind, but she just could not do it. She would fight him. She would keep her dignity and give it all she had. She realized that she had to get him to attack her so she could shock him with a return attack. He had yet to see her abilities, and she may even get in a good enough hit to knock him out.

She tried to bait his rage. "When Jodar finds you, he will kill you."

Broud just laughed as he looked around and came closer. "I don't see Jodar here. Where is your protector now?"

Crap, that did not work. What else would anger him enough? She was losing space as he closed in on her. "Did your mother tell you that Chanlon is not your father?"

Broud hesitated and frowned.

Okay, she was on the right track; she had to keep this going. "I know who your real father is! Remember, Blue, your mother's lap dog?"

Broud stopped and growled. "You lie."

Sheye had him right where she wanted him. "Really, then why don't you go and ask Mommy dearest? Blue is your father. You have polluted Blue Cloak blood running through your veins." Sheye was disgusted with herself. She had nothing against Blue Cloaks, nor thought they were dirty or polluted in any way, but she knew that this would piss off Broud. She had to get him off his guard. He had to attack. It worked. Broud leaped toward her. Sheye was ready. She threw the blanket that she had been readying in her hands on to his head and darted to the side. Instead of him charging over the wall like she had hoped, Broud slid and crashed into the side wall just missing the opening.

He growled as he threw off the blanket. "Smart girl. You don't have another blanket, so now what are you going to do?" Broud was smiling from ear to ear. Not only did she have the exact look of the woman in his dreams, but she also had intuition and a pair of balls. She was everything he could have hoped for and more. A woman who could finally stand up to him and not cower was a fine woman indeed. He would have so much fun with her. He hoped she did not break too soon. This was the most turned on he had ever been in his life. He was rock hard with wanting to feel her fighting under him as he penetrates hard inside her over and over. He was almost ready to orgasm just thinking about it.

Without warning, he charged at her again; she was ready. Sheye jumped up in the air and slammed his jaw hard with a left kick. His neck twisted cruelly with the force of the kick, and he grunted in pain. He stumbled back a few steps and then touched his lip with his fingers; he pulled them away and found blood on them. Now he really was excited. No woman had ever drawn his blood. Sheye assumed he would have to recover for a moment, so she started to look for something that she could smash over his head, but she was wrong, he was already charging at her. This time, Sheye was not prepared with an assault, and he tackled her. She landed on the floor so hard she had the breath knocked out of her for a moment.

Broud took advantage of Sheye not being able to catch her breath and had her underneath him in one swift move with his strong arms. He pinned her there on the floor, and he tried to unlatch his pants. "Now this is where you belong. You belong beneath me with my cock buried deep inside you."

Sheye gagged and tried to open palm his nose, but he grabbed her hand before she connected.

"My god, you are beautiful." Broud was looking at her breasts as she struggled beneath him. She bucked her hips up to try to unmount him, but he had his strong muscled thighs securely in place, pinning her hips down so she could not get a full rise out. He forced both her hands over her head and held them there with one hand as he unbuckled his pants. His manhood sprang out of his pants hard and hot, already dripping at the tip. Once his throbbing flesh was released, he reached under him and fumbled with Sheye's thong. She heard it rip as he tore it free from her body and flung it across the floor. "I must taste you." Broud dipped down and had Sheye's mouth smashed to his. His tongue forced past her lips, bruising them in the process. She bit down instinctively, and he grunted. He pulled away and slapped her hard. Sheye's ear began to ring, and her eyes watered. Damn, that had been a hard slap.

Broud reached in between her legs and shoved his fingers inside of her. Sheye screamed but not in pain. She was raging with anger. Broud withdrew his fingers and brought them up to his mouth and sucked on them and moaned. "You even taste divine."

She was becoming exhausted and sick to her stomach. He was so strong. Her arms were still above her head in his one hand. She tried everything to get him off her, but nothing was working. He was just too damn big. Broud lifted one of his legs and planted it between hers. He was forcing her legs open. Oh god, he was about to drive his manhood into her with no idea that she was a virgin. This was excruciating, and it would only become nastier if he manages to penetrate her. Sheye was panicking. Broud was breathing hard now; his hair was hanging in her face. He grabbed his cock and was trying to guide it into her as she continued to try to buck him off. Sheye could feel the tip of his manhood near her entrance trying to find its way in. Sheye found brand-new strength in her dread and raised her free leg.

Using the back of her foot, she drove her heel as hard as she could toward the area of his back on his kidney. Broud jerked and lost the hold he had on his manhood. He slapped her again. This time, the slap was so intense she instantly saw stars. Unexpectedly, there was a loud grunt, and Broud's weight was removed off her. Sheye was trying to get the stars to stop spinning in her head. Was he going to pick her up now and throw her on the bed? She had to get it together to fight him some more, but nothing more happened. She noticed she could hear scuffling combined with grunts and groans.

Then nothing. She could hear some heavy breathing; she did not know if it was hers or Broud's.

Soothing large warm hands lifted her up and off the floor. Wow, Broud had hit her hard. Her eye was already swelling shut, and her vision was extremely blurry. Who was helping her? She did not care at this very moment, so she just buried her face into the large strong chest and cried. The man was soothing her by stroking her hair as she hid her face in his wide chest. She was safe now; whoever it was that saved her was warm and gentle as he held her. She was sat on the edge of the bed with whoever it was still holding her in his arms. She sniffled and pulled away with a grateful thank you on her lips. As she looked up at her rescuer, she saw Dorians's face looking down at her. "Don't worry now, my beauty. He won't harm you again. You have my word."

Sheye was very confused and too startled to pull away. Had Dorian killed his own grandson to save her from his ravishment? Sheye looked around the room and saw Broud crunched up on the floor, but he was moving on the floor in pain.

Without warning, the door slid open once more, and Adrya rushed in. She screamed when she saw Broud lying on the floor. She went to him immediately and placed herself on the floor as she looked at her son's wounds. "You wretched woman, what did you do to my boy?" Adrya looked up with a look of death toward Sheye. Then her glare went from murder to absolute shock as she saw her father holding the perplexed and beaten Sheye in his arms.

"I warned you, Adrya. I told you not to tell Broud she was here, and you went against my instructions when I was cleaning up the mess of our previous engagement downstairs."

Adrya grimaced at the intensity and disgust in her father's voice but argued anyway. "This woman is Broud's property, Daddy. He can do to her whatever he chooses."

Dorian stiffened and gently placed Sheye away from him. He stood away from the bed, stalked over to his daughter still on the floor with her son, and scowled down at them both. "She is no longer Broud's concern. She will be under my protection from now on. If he ever tries to touch her again, I will kill him."

Adrya sucked in her breath sharply, and Broud growled out, "No, she's mine! You can't take her away from me." Broud tried to stand up, but Dorian placed his foot onto his grandson's chest and forced him back down.

"This is my final word on this, boy. Don't experiment with my patience. I never threaten. I always do."

Broud looked over at Adrya. "Mother, do something."

Chapter 21

Jodar stopped in his tracks as they were searching for the shuttle that they knew was within their proximity. Suddenly, he felt fear, revulsion, and frenzied rage, but it was not his. It was Sheye's emotions. Then suddenly, he could hear her voice in his head like she was right beside him. *Jodar, help me!* Jodar spun around looking everywhere frantically.

Tannor stepped over to his friend. "What is it, Jodar?"

Jodar gasped out. "We are close. I can sense her. She is in severe danger. She just called out for me. We need to search every building in the area now. She is so close. Damn it, where is she?"

The men spread out with new concentrated swiftness. They began to search each vacation home that was within their vicinity with no remorse or explanation to the vacationers. The bad thing was, they happened to be on the opposite side of the lake that Sheye happened to be on.

After they searched the area, they were in completely; they finally decided to go to the other side of the lake. They had yet to find any sign of Sheye or the shuttle they were searching for. Time was running out. As they proceeded to the other side of the lake, Tannor and the other soldiers were in the lead with Chanlon in the center for protection. Jodar was flanking the group, hanging back a little to make sure there was no ambush from behind. They noticed a large house lining the lake half embedded into the side of the crystal cliff. That could be the place, so they decided to go check it out first. It was sizeable for a vacation home, extravagant, and yet elegant. This place would be somewhere that Adrya would approve of since she always had to have the best of the best for herself and her son. Then they noticed the shuttle from their transport ship sitting a way off, back in the trees. They were finally at the right place. Jodar wanted nothing more than to charge into the building but knew Adrya was cunning, and Broud loved to ambush his adversaries with traps instead of fighting face-to-face. Broud had always been a coward in that way. Jodar hung back knowing that they would have Sheye safely where she belonged soon. This gave him the patience that he needed to stay calm and focused on the task at hand. He needed to keep Chanlon safe as they save Sheye and capture Adrya and Broud.

*****

Adrya dragged Broud out of the room instead of helping him convince her father that he was in the wrong. Dorian stood tall and menacing as he watched the two of them scurry out of the chamber.

Broud yelled at his grandfather as they left, "This is not over, Grandfather! I will be seeing you soon, and this time I will be prepared."

Dorian scoffed as he watched them leave. "Pathetic." He then turned to the intercom. "I need a medibot sent up to me immediately."

Within seconds, a medibot entered the room. It proceeded over to the still stunned Sheye, who was sitting quietly on the bed. It gave her a medicated drink, which she took, and then it quickly scanned her face and body for injuries. Sheye felt a small uncomfortable tingling as it fixed her up as good as new. Within moments, her pain vanished, and her face felt entirely healed. The medibot with its job completed turned and exited the room. Sheye felt her face and blinked. Would she ever get over the complexity of their amazing technologies? She looked up at Dorian and tilted her head at him with an unreadable expression.

Dorian admired her for a moment before he spoke. "You look confused, my beauty?"

Sheye took a deep breath, but she did answer him. "I know you did not save me from Broud for my benefit. I am just a pawn in your larger scheme. So when are you going to ransom me to Chanlon?"

Dorian's eyes glinted with pleasure. This woman would truly make him an ideal life mate. She was smart as well as beautiful. He looked forward to getting to know her more. She was far from boring. She was much more beautiful and exciting than Adrya's mother had ever been.

"I won't have to ransom you in any way, my sweetling. Chanlon is already here with his guards looking for you right now."

Sheye gasped, and Dorian stepped closer to her. He placed his hand under her chin so she could not look away. He was not rough, but he was firm enough that Sheye did not attempt to pull away from his touch, or he would possibly slap her as Broud had. She had more than enough of being slapped for the rest of the day if she could help it.

Dorian smiled slightly. "You see, I have the upper hand. Chanlon does not know I am here. They are walking into my trap. They believe I am still stuck behind that ridiculous shield on my planet. Chanlon, the arrogant man that he is, is here with only a few guards to collect Adrya, Broud, and yourself. So today is a superb day for me." Dorian leaned down so his face was only a centimeter from Sheye's. "I am going to kill Chanlon and his guards, then my new life mate will warm my bed this evening and celebrate my dominion." Without warning, he kissed Sheye gently on the lips but pulled away with a malevolent smile. "I will see you in my chambers later tonight. Be ready. You won't deny me, my new life mate." Without another word, Dorian caressed her face softly and then left the room locking the door behind him.

So she was to be raped tonight either way, only this time by an even more despicable man. God, what was it with men wanting to take her against her will lately? She was pretty much done with this whole disgusting family. *Jodar, please where are you? I need you.* This was not going to happen to her again. Just thinking of this man laying his hands on her in an intimate way sent nasty goose bumps running down her entire body. Unexpectedly, Sheye felt a panic that was not her own. She heard Jodar's voice spring into her thoughts. *I am here. I am so close. Hold on, my lady.* The panic left her body immediately. Jodar was here. He had found her.

She was so relieved she could cry. She choked her tears back though. She could now sense Jodar's presence. She could feel the anger he experienced rolling off him toward her captors. Sheye became acutely aware of intense imminent danger. She recounted what Dorian had just mentioned to her a few moments ago:

> You see, I have the upper hand. Chanlon does not know I am here. They are walking into my trap.

She had to warn them. She had to find a way to get the hell out of here and escape herself. Then she would find Chanlon and Jodar so she could warn them that Dorian was here. Sheye knew her only way to escape would be out the front opening in the nonexciting wall, but how the hell was she going to get off the front wall? Sheye thought for a few moments, and her eyes lay upon the blanket that she had tossed at Broud still thrown in the corner. *Why not tie blankets together like a good ole-fashioned rope?* She was proficient with knots due to working with horses her entire life. Now was a great time to put her knowledge to use and save herself from falling onto the jagged crystal rocks below. Sheye hastened her idea by shredding a few of the blankets into threes and got to work tying them together. Within a few moments, she had the blanket rope anchored to the bed. she began looking for a way that would be the best possible place for her to get down. She spotted an area on the side of the opening; closest to the cliff, there was a flat spot lower on the cliff.

She would have to swing herself over quite literally in order to reach the small shelf, but she had to give it a try. It was either do or die or be raped. Without a second thought, Sheye traversed down the rope a little and was happy with its strength. Her knots held brilliantly. She placed her feet squarely on the small floor separator and leaned in. With a swift thrust of her body outward, she swung out hard, and then she directed her body to the right and landed again on the floor separator. Then she repeated the process again only this time she swung to the left to get more momentum. She went back and forth a few times. Each time she was getting closer and closer to the edge until she finally took the last swing and threw her body off and away from the rope and onto the shelf of the cliff.

Sheye hit her chest hard on the rock shelf knocking the wind out of her again for the second time in one day. She made her body move though to get herself up on the shelf so she would not lose her grip and fall to her death. Once she was on the shelf, she rolled onto it painfully and just lay on her back for a few moments to regain her wind. When her lungs were full again, she stood up gingerly so she would not topple over the edge of the small rock shelf. She quickly inspected herself, noticing only a few cuts and bruises on her arms, chest, and face. Nothing awful enough to impede her from further escape. Now she had to figure out if she was going to go up or go down. The jagged crystals were still below and then the lake beyond that looked quite deep. She had no idea what kind of creatures lay beneath the waters in this alien lake. Nope, she would not be able to dive past the crystals and make it to the water without killing herself, so she looked up.

The top of the cliff looked easy enough to climb up to, so she decided to go up. The jutting crystals in the cliff's wall were solid, so she made it to the top without much difficulty. She only slipped a few times but was able to secure her footing and continue to the top. When Sheye reached the top and caught her breath, she soon found out that the only way down was to walk across the roof of the house she had just escaped from as the cliff's edge was sheer, and the large trees lined the edge, and she did not know if the bark on the beautiful trees was slippery, dangerous, or even poisonous to the touch. So she cautiously stepped out onto the roof of the vacation home.

Just as Sheye was sneaking across the roof, she noticed several figures of men coming toward the house just in sight at the line of the enormous trees. They were cautiously making their way closer and walking like you see in military movies. They were alert, methodical, and quiet as if they were waiting for an attack or ambush. Her heart rate rose as she recognized Tannor in the front. She hated this man, but he looked like the most beautiful person she had ever seen right at this moment. He was here to help rescue her, and that meant Jodar was close as well. Her heart skipped a beat and then fluttered as she thought of Jodar. She squashed down her intense feeling about Jodar and made herself concentrate on the task at hand. She could not get all mushy and nonsensical now. She quickly made her way to the edge of the roof. She looked around to see if there was any of Dorian's guards or beasts around, and when she did not see anyone or anything, she stood tall at the edge of the roof and began waving her hands frantically trying to gain the men's attention.

Tannor noticed her immediately. He used his magnifier on his helmet and was able to see that it was Sheye who was on the roof, and she was waving her hands like a crazy woman. He felt guilty as he watched her as a blush rose on his cheeks. She was in the sheerest of clothing that he could see every detail of her as she stood in the moonlight. Jodar was indeed a lucky man. He took only another moment to appreciate the view but then looked toward his men and gave them quiet signals to approach with caution and pointed to Sheye on the roof. The men in front with Tannor quickly neared the door just below where Sheye stood on the roof, with Chanlon close behind. Sheye kneeled on the roof when they were near enough to loudly whisper, "Tannor, it's a trap. Dorian is here. He escaped the shield..."

Tannor stopped. "What did you say? Dorian—he's inside?" Tannor took another step forward as he looked up at Sheye to hear her clearer.

When Chanlon heard what Sheye had said, he too stepped closer to the group with a shocked look on his face and stated, "Tell us what we need to know."

Before she could explain anymore, she heard a loud click. Tannor looked down on the ground where he stood and noticed a small device stuck in the ground under his foot, then stated, "Shit, Chanlon it's a—"

Before anyone could do anything, there was a long purple arch of electricity that looked like lightning streak from the ground and connect through each of the men. Within a second, Tannor, his men, and Chanlon were all violently crumpled and convulsing on the ground. Sheye placed her hand over her mouth, so she would not scream. The front door to the vacation home was thrown open, and some men came out. Sheye backed quickly away from the ledge with her heart in her throat and lay as flat as she could to conceal herself on the roof, praying that they would not see her.

The men dragged the now unconscious men into the house as one of them said, "Dorian was right. So much for the so-called super warrior race of Sarbus. Tell them to raise the shield to the house now that we have them." They all laughed and joked as the door closed behind them.

Oh god, what am I going to do now? As Sheye was trying to think coherently, she could hear a soft hum and looked back onto the center of the roof to notice a glowing light coming from a small satellite-looking device. The glow spread up and then arched to cover the house in a dome-like structure. This must be the shield they had said to raise to protect the house. "Shit, shit, shit." With the shield up, she could not get out and away now. Sheye may have escaped to the outside, but she was still a captive. It would only be a matter of time till they found that she was missing and come looking for her. She had to figure something out. Sheye smacked her forehead over and over as she sat on the roof. "Think, think. Come on, Sheye, you can do this." Sheye had to get that shield down somehow so she could go and get some help.

Sheye quietly crawled over to the device that controlled the shield to examine it. She noticed a small control panel just beneath the curved plate where the beam was coming from and laughed sarcastically. On the panel, there were a few small indiscernible mechanisms and lights, but in the center of the panel were two larger buttons—one was red, and one was green. "It can't be that easy, can it?" she asked herself, and then without a second thought, she pushed the red button. Sure enough, the humming stopped, and the shield beam was cut off. Sheye was so ecstatic that she almost let out a celebratory whoop but remembered that she needed to stay quiet just in time. She did a couple of fist pumps in the air though and then crawled lightly and hurried over to the side of the house opposite the lake. She was able to use ledges and her fantastic agility to make her way down to the ground. She remembered that there still may be traps laid out all over the ground, so she plastered her back flat against the wall of the house and began to sneak her way around to the front.

Chapter 22

Just as Sheye was coming up onto a large window, she crouched down to try to sneak by, but as she did, she could not help but peek in to make sure no one would see her. To her horror, she could see Tannor and Chanlon manacled to the side wall. They had been stripped of their armor, and their chests were bare and bleeding with large deep cuts all over their upper torsos and shoulders. The other guards who had been with them were lying in a pile in the corner. They were obviously dead as they were covered in green blood and were motionless. Dorian and Adrya were also in the room taking turns torturing Tannor and Chanlon with a device in their hands enjoying the agony they were inflicting on their captives. She covered her mouth as she gagged and sagged against the wall. Was her sweet Jodar in the pile of dead bodies? Sheye realized that she was crying. She never sensed any harm or pain coming from Jodar. Did he die quickly, and therefore, she did not feel him pass on? She was not familiar with what was entailed with the knowing or one's full capacity with their connections to the other.

Sheye took a deep breath; she had to know if he was in the pile of bodies in the corner. Maybe she could see him. "You need to know if Jodar is in there, Sheye. You can do this." She peeked back in to see if she could glimpse Jodar within the bodies. What she was witnessing was of the cruelest nature. As she was trying to see if Jodar was in with the other men, she could hear Adrya demanding to know where Jodar was. Sheye almost collapsed in gratefulness as she understood that Jodar had not been captured. She listened in carefully.

Tannor lifted his head proudly even though he was in tremendous pain, looking Adrya right in the eyes. "I have already told you that he stayed on Sarbus to arrange everything for our return."

Adrya sneered at Tannor and hit him with her weapon again. Tannor hissed at the pain. "You liar! Chanlon is never without Jodar by his side. Remember, I have been in Chanlon's life for twenty-five years. He never went anywhere without his puppy, so I ask again. Where is Jodar?"

This time, Chanlon spoke to Adrya to defend Tannor's statement. "Woman, know that it was I who made Jodar stay behind to prepare the return of the collections. He is the only one I trust to fill in and get things done right while I am absent looking to deal with you and your treachery. I told him he could not come because of his attachment to the woman you stole from him. They are truly bonded through the knowing. We could not afford for him to lose control when he got here and find her."

Adrya shifted from one foot to the other as she knew Chanlon. What he said made sense, but she went over and slapped him anyways just for the fun of it. Chanlon just glared at her. He did not give her the satisfaction of looking away from her or even flinching. Adrya stepped back and hit Chanlon with her weapon. Another large wound opened on his left shoulder; he flinched this time, which seemed to satisfy Adrya for the moment. She backed off, and her father laughed at the men hanging on the wall. Sheye could not watch this any longer. Jodar was somewhere safe. That was all that mattered now, but if she left to try to find help now, Chanlon and Tannor would be dead by the time she returned. Dead like the other soldiers from the group who now lay discarded and forgotten on the floor in a pool of blood.

Sheye was full of rage again. This twisted, psychotic family could not get away with this. Sheye wiped away her tears and had a new sense of purpose. Get back in the house, find a weapon, kill this perverted family, and rescue Tannor and Chanlon, then find Jodar. Sheye took a couple of deep breaths. "Okay, you've got this. You can do it." Sheye moved quickly and quietly as she snuck past the window. She flattened her back against the wall again as she continued around the corner to the front door. She avoided the front door. It was a sliding door that may have an alarm, so she went past it to the front of the house that faced the lake. Sheye peeked around the corner of the house through the opening where the wall was absent. No one was in the large open living area. It was empty. She climbed over a smaller jagged crystal and made it back inside easily. She ducked behind a large lounger to catch her breath. *Now where would they keep weapons?* Sheye thought. She needed to find one of the rods that they all seemed to bear. She could at least stun anyone she came upon as she worked her way through the house to the room where Tannor and Chanlon were being tortured.

Sheye looked around to see where she needed to proceed. To her utter delight, there in between the bar and the sliding front door stacked against the wall were five of the rods she was looking for. Sheye immediately scrambled on all fours toward the rods.

Just as she reached for one, she heard a voice behind her that she wished to never hear again. "Maybe I will use that very weapon on you when I have you beneath me while I am fucking you."

Sheye froze with her hand wrapped around the thin metal rod. She took in a deep breath and then turned around to face her foe. Broud was leaning against a large beam at the front of the room with a sneer on his face. He had obviously used a medibot as he looked good as new again. She slowly straightened her back and stood to her full height to show him she was not intimidated by her attempted rapist. He had bested her once before, but she would not give him a second chance.

Sheye replied calmly, "I would love to see you try."

Broud's grin turned into a wide smile as he pushed his muscular frame away from the beam he was casually leaning on.

Sheye relaxed her stance into one of her preparation stances to brace or prepare for an attack. She placed her mind into a calm Zen, as she learned to do this in her martial arts training. She could not let him get her mad or throw her off her concentration. She was ready this time. Broud did not stalk her this time; he prowled. She watched him as he circled around the room as he spoke, slowly closing the space between her and himself, watching, preparing.

"On the stars of Prantus, you excite me so you understand. You are mine. When my grandfather kills Chanlon and his men, I will then take the opportunity to kill my grandfather. My father, his pathetic pet Jodar, and my sociopathic grandfather will all be eliminated. There will be no one to stand in my way any longer. I will take you and my mother back to Sarbus to take over my rightful place as supreme commander. You will be by my side as my life mate."

Sheye grasped that Broud had no idea that Jodar had not been captured. She kept that tidbit to herself and snorted back. "I feel sorry for you, Broud. You still think Chanlon is your father. I take it you forgot to ask your mommy about that certain subject I had mentioned earlier. Oh, right, maybe because that conversation was right before your aging grandfather wiped your pathetic ass all over the floor." Sheye remained calm as she spoke, but this hit a deep nerve in Broud, although he was desperately trying to hide it. He sneered as he circled closer.

"I won't let your taunts distract me, my wildcat. I will punish you for that wicked tongue of yours when you are naked and underneath me."

Sheye hit a nerve. She pretended to nonchalantly move the rod back and forth as if playing with it, then stopped it in a position so she could raise it up and use it on Broud if he decides to charge at her. Sheye baited Broud again. "It seems that you only have the balls to force women to fight you instead of fighting a man. You can't even call yourself a man. You are just a boy in a man's body. Only thinking of raping women to gain some partial control and power over a female because you can't defeat a true man in battle. You, boy, are pathetic. I would rather have your grandfather's cock in me than yours any day. Now Dorian, there is a true man. He bested you in a heartbeat, did he not?"

Broud snapped. He charged her like a rhino. "You will wish you had never spoken those words."

Sheye raised the rod, and with a wide, clean stroke, she smashed it against his knee and skipped away unharmed. Broud's knee buckled, but he recovered quickly and spun to face her again. She could see his arousal. He was hard and throbbing within his slacks. He was a real man in that capacity, an exceptionally large man indeed.

Sheye maneuvered herself to the center of the room where she could have more open space to battle. "You can only get a woman that you have to force into your bed. Tell me, has any woman come to your bed willingly, boy?"

Broud was about to charge again when another voice interrupted. "Did I come at a bad time?"

Sheye had never thought she would hear this incredibly smooth, sexy, deep voice so soon. They both spun around to see Jodar casually leaning against the side of the open wall at the very place she had snuck into only minutes before. Jodar had been hanging back from the group to make sure they would not be attacked from behind. He had noticed that the men had quickly moved out to the front door to talk to someone on the roof. He was just about to get closer to the group after realizing that it was Sheye they were talking to on the roof when suddenly the men were ambushed with the lightning trap. Luckily, he was not near enough for the bolt to travel to himself.

Jodar was able to cloak himself just before the guards came out of the house to drag the soldiers and Chanlon inside. He was amazed to see that Sheye had managed to escape and then watched her as she dismantled the shield, to his great relief. He thought that he would have had to go all the way back to their shuttle to communicate with the Blue Cloaks who were waiting back at the security center to see if they could dismantle the shield, which would have squandered precious time he did not have. Thank Prantus, his woman was as intelligent as she was beautiful. After she dismantled the shield, he watched as she jumped off the roof to the far side of the house. She was either gone or captured as he waited for over five minutes for her to come around to the front. He was just about to go and search for her when she peeked around the back of the house and then began to sneak around the front to his immense relief.

He watched Sheye slip around the front of the house and then sneak back inside. "What the hell is she doing? Why is she going back into the house instead of running away?" He cursed as he realized, she was going back in to try to rescue the men. He could feel her intentions; she was scared but incredibly determined. He had to follow her. He could not live with himself if anything happened to her. He ignored all her panic and intense fear that she was feeling, so he could concentrate on getting into the house himself. Then he overheard how brave Sheye was in confronting Broud. She was amazing. He fell in love with her even more at seeing how she taunted him so he would lose control and charge at her, but enough was enough. Now it was his turn to take on Broud. He had waited many years for this day. Broud would now die by his hands. He would die because he had scared, hurt, humiliated, and touched his woman. For any one of those reasons, he would delight in killing his lifelong nemesis.

Was that fear Sheye saw flash for a moment across Broud's face as he turned toward Jodar? She was sure of it. Sheye had never been so happy to see anyone in her life as she did at seeing Jodar so casually leaning against the outer wall. She did not say anything though. Jodar may have looked calm, but she could feel his wrath and revulsion rolling off him in the direction of Broud. He was in extermination mode. Sheye would not be the one to distract him, so she backed away from Broud slowly. Jodar pushed himself away from the wall. He then began to slowly take his armor off. He wanted the fight to be fair, man to man. Flesh to flesh. Fist to fist. Broud smirked. Sheye had a bad feeling about Broud's smirk. Did he have something up his sleeve? The two men slowly entered the center of the room and faced off with each other, staring each other down. They were both massive as well as rippling with bulging muscles. Sheye feared for Jodar. She had thought him dead already. She did not want to lose him a second time.

Without warning, the two men charged at each other at the exact same moment. They struggled as each one's hands went around each other's necks and heads. Then they were pushing and shoving. Broud was able to get his hands free first and got the first good punch in. Jodar did not even recoil. He connected with two good punches to Broud's head and a few good punches into his kidneys. Broud stumbled back to reassess the situation. He had never beaten Jodar in a fair fight in their entirety of training. Jodar did not give Broud the time to access his situation. He was on him like a lion. Furniture, fixtures, and everything else that was not bolted or fixed to the floor was destroyed, broken, shattered, or strewn everywhere. Blood was spraying all over the floor, and both men were glistening in sweat. As Sheye watched on in tense silence, she saw Broud get in an uppercut to Jodar's jaw, which had Jodar staggering back. Sheye sucked in her breath. As Jodar staggered back, Sheye watched Broud slip something out of his sleeve. It was small, but it looked wickedly sharp.

Without thinking, Sheye raised the rod she was holding. Jumping toward Broud screaming, "Charlatan," she slammed the rod into Broud's back as she did so. Sadly, the rod had not been turned up to full stun, and it only caused enough of a jolt to put Broud down onto his knees. This was enough of an advantage for Jodar though. He grabbed Broud by the neck and maneuvered in behind him with the speed of a cat. Without a second of hesitation, Jodar's large hands twisted Broud's neck. With a loud crack, Broud went limp, and Jodar let his body slump to the floor. Jodar stumbled back breathing hard, bleeding from his brow, jaw, and nose. He looked at the ground where Broud had collapsed and spit on him. Then he saw it. His eyes focused on the small implement that was lying close to Broud's hand. He bent down and picked up the small weapon that had dropped to the floor when Broud collapsed. Jodar's eyes widened, and he looked astonished as he looked back at Sheye. "You just saved my life, Sheye. I am forever in your debt."

Sheye furrowed her brows together. "It was nothing. No one brings a knife to a fistfight and gets away with cheating, no matter what."

Jodar bent down and carefully picked up and held the small weapon so Sheye could see it. It was a very pointed crystal quill of some kind.

"This is not a knife, Sheye. It is a quill from a creature called the vantar. It is a small creature like your hedgehog on Earth, but it is extremely dangerous. The vantar is the most poisonous beast to ever live in all the universe that we know of. On your planet, you have a tiny creature called the blue-ringed octopus and its venom can kill up to twenty men. That is pittance compared to one tiny scratch from this vantar quill. The vantar has hundreds of these quills on its body. This one quill can kill you in less than a blink of an eye and can be used over a thousand times with one tiny scratch. It could kill one thousand of your planet's elephant beasts in seconds before its potency begins to fade. If you had not seen what Broud was about to do and stepped in to stop him. It would be me dead on the floor now, not Broud." Jodar smiled brightly as he looked at Sheye. "I do apologize for what I am about to do."

Without warning, Jodar stepped over to her and swooped her into his arms, planting the most amazing kiss she had ever experienced onto her lips. Sheye clung to Jodar. They kissed hard and fast. When Jodar pulled away, she looked into his beautiful lion eyes.

"Why do you feel you have to apologize for that?"

Jodar laughed. "Because now you are covered in my blood and sweat. That is not acceptable, but I just had to kiss you. I was devastated when you were stolen from me. I felt my world had come to an end when I found you gone. You are now my life, Sheye. My heart and my soul belong to you. Without you in my life, I would no longer want to exist."

As Jodar still held her in his strong arms looking down at her with so much love in his eyes and hearing those words, Sheye realized that there was no place she would rather be. She, too, would no longer want to exist if he was not in her life. Sheye grabbed Jodar's face in her hands, and she kissed him passionately again. "Blood and sweat don't bother me, my strong warrior."

The look that Jodar gave Sheye at that very moment melted her heart. She realized right then and there her heart and her soul belonged to him as well.

Jodar sighed and placed Sheye gently away from him. "As much as I want nothing more than to scoop you away from all of this, keep you in my chambers for the next month with nothing else on but our birthday suits, sadly we must now rescue my supreme commander, my best friend, and his men. By the way, I have been dying to tell you. I love your outfit."

Sheye looked down at herself and blushed. She had completely forgotten her lack of attire and the sheerness of what she was wearing. She laughed and gave him a slap on his large bicep. As the two of them teased each other, they heard a groan come from the direction of Broud.

The two of them both turned to see Broud trying to move. Sheye was astounded. Hadn't Jodar broken his neck? Broud should have been completely paralyzed! Jodar sneered. He went over to Broud and grabbed him by the shoulders. "Looks like we need to finish this once and for all." Jodar pulled Broud out of the open wall and onto the narrow path leading to the dock.

"Wait! Jodar, there are two vicious beasts tied at the end of the pier."

Jodar just smiled at Sheye. "This I already know. I observed them when I was listening to you banter with Broud."

Sheye tilted her head in confusion; she then shrugged her shoulders and followed Jodar, who did not seem to be worried about the beasts. He dragged Broud close to the end of the dock and then proceeded to lift him up over his head. This was no small feat as Broud was a massive man and must have weighed over 250 pounds. "Here, kitty, kitty." Jodar then tossed the groaning Broud to the beasts that were already pulling at their tethers, snarling and snapping their jaws at them. When Broud landed on the dock, the two beasts tore into him, shredding him to pieces within moments as they gulped and swallowed Broud down almost whole. Sheye had to look away but did not feel any remorse for the despicable man. He had gotten what he deserved and nothing less. She was glad that he would never be able to touch her again.

With that thought in mind, Sheye wondered how they would deal with Dorian. Sheye suddenly realized that Jodar was still unaware that Dorian was even here. Sheye grabbed onto Jodar's arm.

"Wait, Jodar, Dorian is in the house. He escaped by way of Blue's friends. They made a contraption that was able to open the invisa-shield for a few minutes, and it enabled Dorian to get out. The Blue Cloaks did this for revenge for Blue's execution."

Jodar spun around to look at Sheye. "What?" Jodar was so stunned that Sheye felt that she had to apologize.

"It's my fault that they were all captured. I distracted Tannor when he saw me, and he came over to me to get me off the roof. I tried to tell him that Dorian was in the house. They all stepped closer while talking to me. Therefore, he stepped on the trap. If I had not distracted him, they probably would not be getting tortured as we speak. Oh my god, Jodar, I saw them. The soldiers are all dead except for Tannor and Chanlon. They have them chained to a wall, and Dorian and Adrya are torturing them right now. We must save them. They may even have killed them as we stand here idly talking."

Sheye began to hyperventilate, and Jodar quickly grabbed her into a big bear hug. "My Prantus star, you are not to blame for this. This was a very well-thought-out plan. You were just put into the middle of it all. Dorian has wanted to kill Chanlon for many decades." Within Jodar's strong, comforting hug, it hit her. She pushed herself away from his warm embrace and quickly stated, "I think I have an idea. Can I use the vantar quill? I need to somehow get it secured to the rod weapon." Jodar frowned for a moment and then walked back up to the house and went over to his armor. He came back to Sheye with a tiny vial of black sticky liquid that looked like tar inside of it. "We use this if we have been severely injured in battle and can't make it to a medibot or medbay. It can glue the most grievous of injuries back together till we can get to one. What are you thinking of, my precious one?" This man just kept on making her heart melt; she had to look away from him and catch her breath so she could concentrate on her plan.

Jodar did not like this plan of Sheye's, not one bit, but he had to admit it was an incredibly good plan if everything went as intended. All he could think of was she would not be able to use the quill on Dorian if he even came close to touching Sheye, for he would snap and kill Dorian himself, but this may give Adrya a chance to kill both Chanlon and Tannor if he screwed things up due to his jealousy. Sheye led Jodar back up to the chamber where she had been kept captive in. She made him show her how to work the shower, the hair and makeup designer, and the clothing contraption. He growled at her when she asked for the sexiest outfit that he could muster up, but he did as she asked. He did not like anyone seeing her dressed like she was as if she was ready to join in sex. This should be for his eyes only. Resentment raged through him, and Sheye had to calm him down. "Remember we are saving Tannor and Chanlon's life. This is the only way it can be done." Jodar growled low in his throat but accepted it. Sheye promised to tell him everything Dorian had done and said to her when they were all safe and back on Sarbus.

When Sheye was completely made up in hair, makeup, and clothing, she came out from behind the dressing wall. Jodar sucked in his breath; he began pacing the room. "No way! I know I said that I was okay with this. No, no, and no. We will find someway else to draw Dorian out of that room. Dorian won't see you like this. I can't accept any other man seeing you this way. It makes my heart hurt." Even though it was a roundabout compliment, and she could feel Jodar's jealousy and pain rack through her body, she walked up to him again, reached up, and grabbed his face in between her hands.

"This is the only way, Jodar. How much do you love Tannor and Chanlon?"

Jodar looked down at Sheye with sorrow in his eyes and then sighed in defeat. "I would die for them." Sheye smiled sweetly at Jodar and then gently pulled his face to hers. "Then let's us get this over with, shall we?" and then gently kissed his lips.

They crept down the stairs with Jodar in the lead. They came across two guards in the back hall guarding the door where Dorian and Adrya were torturing the men. Jodar quickly despatched the guards without much noise by using the rod with the quill firmly glued to the tip. After Jodar removed the bodies, he then placed himself in a cervix in the wall by the door and handed Sheye the rod back. Sheye walked in front of the door with her heart pounding hard in her chest. She looked over to Jodar and winked, showing him everything would be okay. Without further hesitation, she knocked on the door. It opened almost immediately by Dorian, who was yelling, "I thought I told you both to only disturb me if it was an emergency," but as he slid open the door, he stopped in his tracks, and then his eyes lit up with instant desire.

Sheye could see his immediate lust traverse throughout his entire body as he looked her up and down. As he admired her, Sheye took the opportunity to look demure as she glanced behind him and into the room. She could see that Tannor and Chanlon were both hanging unconscious, and Adrya was sitting on the soldiers' bodies having a glass of wine. Sheye hid her loathing and disgust at what she saw. She quickly looked back at Dorian and fluttered her eyelashes at him shyly. She cleared her throat before she spoke. "I apologize for the interruption, your grace. I wanted you to know, I have thought about what you said, about me being your new life mate. You are such a strong and formidable man. You frighten me to my very core, but you also have set a fire within me that I can't explain. I haven't been able to stop thinking about you since you left my chamber. I have concluded that I want you. I want you more than I have ever wanted another man before. I just wanted you to know this. I must ask where your chambers are so I can wait for you to join and lay with me." Just saying this had bile rising in her throat, but she swallowed it down and used it as a shyness that she was extremely embarrassed to confess her feelings to him.

Dorian stood at the door listening. He could not stop staring at this beauty standing before him. He still had suspicion in his eyes, but his lust for her took over his doubt at her words. Dorian called out to his daughter, "Adrya, have another class of wine. I am leaving you for a while. Don't kill Chanlon while I am gone, or there will be hell to pay."

Adrya stood up and looked past her father. She stormed up behind him and glared at Sheye with murder in her eyes. "You disgust me with your lustful ways because of this slut. If you must have this woman against my wishes, as she was supposed to be Broud's, then do as you must. I can't stop you. Maybe we can come to an agreement where yourself and Broud could share her in both your beds."

Dorian just snorted at Adrya. "You and that boy of yours will soon come to realize, I don't share what is mine." Then he quickly dismissed her from his mind.

Adrya scowled at her father's back, then proceeded to go back to the jug of wine, and poured herself another large glass as she mumbled under her breath. For her own shits and giggles, she picked up her weapon and slashed it at Chanlon's face, slashing open a large gash across his cheek. Adrya then looked back at Sheye with ugly loathing. Chanlon jerked and moaned a bit, then fell silent as blood dripped from his face onto the floor.

Sheye held her breath. She wanted nothing more than to spit in that woman's face for her demon ways. Jodar, too, jerked at what he was hearing but held his ground in the cervix in the wall.

Dorian smiled at Sheye. "You won't regret your decision, my beauty. You will be satisfied in my bed as well as by my side as my life mate."

Jodar jerked again and almost lost his mind, but again, he just scowled and stayed put. He had to trust Sheye. He did trust Sheye. When Dorian stepped forward, he reached out and gently stroked Sheye's breast. "Oh, you are going to give me so much pleasure, my sweet."

Jodar growled under his breath and clenched his jaw hard. He wanted nothing more than to kill this repugnant man so desperately. He could taste the blood from his tongue as he was biting it hard for him to stay in his hiding place. He could see it was taking everything in Sheye's power as well to let Dorian stroke her as he was. Jodar knew she was only tolerating his touch so he would step out of the room a little bit more. Then she could take him by surprise. Sheye pulled back just a little, so he had to reach for her; this made him step a little closer so he could stroke her nipple. Perfect. In a flash, she pulled the hidden rod from behind her back. She stepped back and smiled all the while as she aimed the rod at Dorian's face. Just a little scratch. Dorian did not even have time to flinch; he just stopped, looked at her confused, then dropped dead in a heap on the floor.

It was that easy. Adrya heard her father's body crumple to the ground. When she looked up and saw her father was down, she immediately threw her wine in Sheye's direction and charged, screaming like a banshee with her weapon still in her hand, intent on using it on Sheye. All Adrya was able to get out before Sheye raised her fist was "You slut." Before Jodar could even push past Sheye, she stepped forward and drilled Adrya with the hardest punch she could right square in her nose. Adrya dropped like a sack of potatoes. Jodar stepped behind Sheye and viewed the room. He was immensely impressed with Sheye at this moment. *And she's all mine,* he thought as he grabbed her from behind and swung her around. "My stars, you are amazing." He placed her back on her feet and then instantly went over to Chanlon and Tannor. Without hesitating, he cut them down as gently as he could and was on his commlink to the pilots of his shuttle to get their asses to their coordinates asap with the medbay ready for two.

Chapter 23

They were finally on their way back to Sarbus. They had gotten Chanlon, Tannor, and Adrya on the shuttle with the help of the pilots. Chanlon and Tannor were immediately placed in the medipods to heal all their wounds, but they did not give that luxury to Adrya. Sheye had broken her nose but good. Right now, she was not looking like her beautiful self, what with all the swelling, black eyes, and blood smeared all over her face. They did not even give her the luxury of cleaning off any of her blood that had splattered all over herself. She sat there and glared at them all as she demanded to be given at least one of the healing drinks. Jodar was exhausted. Adrya's ranting and demands were too much to take. He had enough of her. He went over to her with the stun rod and turned it on to high. He smiled at her and poked the rod onto the side of her neck as she screamed at him. Adrya slumped where she sat, still in shackles.

They picked up the Blue Cloaks from the visitor center, then they were off at warp speed back to their own planet. Jodar and Sheye were so weary, and with Adrya now out of commission, it was nice and quiet. Jodar and Sheye looked at each other; without even having to speak, Sheye knew exactly what they both needed. She got up and went over to where Jodar was sitting. He lay down on the soft sofa in the seating area, and then Sheye laid down with him and snuggled into his long, warm body alongside of him. Jodar placed his arm around Sheye so she would not fall off the edge of the sofa, and they quickly fell asleep that way.

*****

Chanlon entered the seating room and sat down. He observed the young couple sleeping peacefully. As he watched them, he began to contemplate about his life—Adrya, Broud, Jodar, Dorian, disputes, wars, his people, his reign, the knowing, almost losing his planet several times to the man whom Jodar had managed to eliminate. He was a strong man who had fought and won many battles. These last few years had done him in though. He felt much older than he was. He was tired. The last year, especially the last few days, had put him over the edge. He felt like such a fool for being duped for all those years by Adrya. He glanced over to his ex-life mate's slumped form. How had he been so blind? Chanlon would have understood why he did not see Adrya's deception if he had been in love with her. He had not genuinely loved her. He tolerated her because of him thinking that he shared the knowing with her. Sure, he had spent twenty-five years of his life with her, so how did he not sense even a small inkling of her deception until the last moment?

Chanlon reflected on the loss of his son, Broud, who it turned out, his true son he was not. Chanlon realized he was not displeased in finding out that Broud was not of his blood. He was also not disappointed that he was dead. He found that he was relieved that Broud was gone. He had been such a menace. Broud had always been an embarrassment to him. He was not as broken up about losing Broud as he was about losing his good men whom he had lost yesterday for being so unprepared. He almost lost his life as well. He thanked the fifth star of Prantus, Jodar, Sheye, and Tannor were safe. He had caught himself wishing many times over the years that Jodar had been of his seed. What a delight it would be if someone said that they had discovered Jodar was of his blood. Chanlon would be so delighted to hear that kind of news. It would make his life all the simpler to have such a man as his son.

Now that Dorian was eliminated, Broud was no longer alive to relentlessly pester him to step down and hand over his leadership, and Adrya was now awaiting trial. Chanlon wanted nothing more than to rid himself of all responsibility and begin to enjoy his life. Dorian had been a constant thorn in the side of his planet and his people. Chanlon had been on his guard for over thirty years dealing with that psychopath. Now it was time to breathe. He wanted to experience happiness with a woman whom he could love, who would love him back for who he was and not what he was. His thoughts drifted back to Adrya. He scoffed to himself. He had decided that execution was much too good for Adrya. He had a much better punishment waiting for her when they returned home. He also had a colossal announcement to make to the council of the planets as well. Now that Dorian was deceased, Sarbus and his people were safe. Chanlon could move on.

Jodar awoke sensing someone watching them. He lifted his head slightly to see who it was without disturbing Sheye, who was still fast asleep. Jodar spotted Chanlon sitting quietly across from them in the dimly lit room. Jodar slid himself off the sofa slowly. Sheye only protested a little in her sleep, then rolled over with her face toward the back of the couch, and snuggled in again when Jodar placed a blanket over her sleeping form. Jodar stepped over to where Chanlon was sitting and sat down beside him concerned. "Are you all right, my liege? You look troubled."

"No, Jodar, I have never been clearer than I am at this moment. It has been so many years since I have felt this kind of calmness and relief as I do now. It feels wonderful."

Chanlon turned to Jodar, so he faced him completely. "Once again, I find myself in your debt for saving my life, Jodar. I thank you with my entire being. I wish to repay you in a way that only I can."

Jodar stopped Chanlon from saying more. "Your Eminence, I can't take the credit for saving your life this time. Sheye was the one who saved yourself and Tannor. I did dispatch Broud but only after she distracted him. Then she saved my life as well. I was only backup for her." Jodar explained everything that had happened to Chanlon while he was being tortured. He explained how Sheye had escaped on her own, how she took out the protection shield and her fight with Broud, and how Broud was almost able to use the vantar quill against him, and that she had caught him trying to cheat. He then explained Sheye's plan and how she was able to accomplish carrying it out perfectly. When Jodar was finished explaining everything, Chanlon chuckled and turned back to look at the woman lying on the sofa.

Chanlon was stunned at what he had heard. Sheye was the perfect match for Jodar. When they returned home, they would have the grandest of bonding ceremonies anyone had ever seen. That was the least he could do to show Sheye his appreciation for her saving his life. He turned back to Jodar. "I still owe you my life, Jodar. You have outdone yourself in the protection of my person many times that I can't keep count anymore. I have thought about this for many weeks now about what it is I am going to tell you. Jodar—" Suddenly there was a horrible scream coming from the direction of where Adrya was confined.

Chanlon and Jodar just rolled their eyes at each other, and when Jodar went to get up to deal with her, Chanlon motioned for him to sit back down. "It is high time I deal with her myself, Jodar."

Jodar nodded, and Chanlon walked over to Adrya and scowled down at her.

She screamed again as she glowered up at Chanlon, "You son of a rotten Strackez carcass, release me this moment! How dare you treat the mother of your son this way."

Chanlon smiled and raised his eyebrows at his ex-life mate. "Oh, yes that. I completely forgot to inform you that I have been made aware that Broud is not of my blood."

Adrya sucked in her breath and looked away. Chanlon leaned in so his face was only an inch away from Adrya's. "Your pathetic excuse of a father and son are no longer among the living, my dear Adrya."

Adrya swung her head back around, and she looked into Chanlon's eyes. Adrya could see the truth within Chanlon's eyes; she did not doubt what he said for a second. She spit in his face.

Chanlon stayed where he was and grabbed part of Adrya's dress and wiped off his face with it. "However, Adrya, I am still trying to come up with a civil means to keep you from causing more mess than you already have. You have committed vile crimes. You understand you must be punished severely for them."

Adrya cringed inwardly. She had lost Blue, her father, and her beloved son. No one worshipped her anymore. The only people who loved her were all gone. She no longer wanted to live. She welcomed her execution that awaited her part in the treasonous rebellion against

Chanlon. She looked at Chanlon again with her head held high. "I welcome my execution. I will no longer have to pretend to love you or pretend that your touch excites me. You know, Chanlon? Blue satisfied me in ways you could not. He gave me the son that you could not. You are not a man, Chanlon. You are a fool. How I was able to get away with so much due to your inability to think for yourself without your Blue Cloaks or your pet guards around is a wonder. You are nothing, and now you have no one."

Chanlon chuckled low at Adrya. "Still trying to get in the last word? I see. Oh, Adrya, if only I was going to have you executed. No, I feel that execution is much too good for you. You see, the Black Cloaks have wanted to get their hands on you for years after all your mistreatment of everyone when I was not around. I have finally given in to their wishes. You are going to go with them when we get home. I have told them they can do with you as they see fit as long as they don't kill you or let you kill yourself."

Adrya started to choke on her own spit as she tried to beg Chanlon to kill her. "No, Chanlon, please! Anything but the Black Cloaks. Please execute me, just get it over with."

Death would be welcome if she did not have to go to the Black Cloaks. As she choked on her fear, Chanlon turned back to Adrya with his stun rod in hand and zapped her unconscious. Her reaction satisfied him. He knew he had made the right choice in her punishment. "Damn!" zapping Adrya was so extremely satisfying.

Jodar was proud of his supreme commander; even though Adrya spewed insults his way, he kept his composure. He never lost his temper or yelled at her. Someday, Jodar hoped he could become as calm, collected, and as strong as Chanlon. He watched Chanlon immobilize Adrya again and saw the pure pleasure cross Chanlon's face and laughed inwardly. He, too, felt the same way when he was able to stun her. Chanlon walked back over to Jodar and joined him once more. They both looked over at Sheye, who still slept like a rock, even through all the ruckus that Adrya had just made. They were both impressed.

"She must be very tired." Chanlon sounded concerned. "She has gone through much because of us, Jodar. I am surprised she has not had a complete mental breakdown for all that we have put her through. Let her sleep if she needs, Jodar. I still would like to tell you of my gift and what it is I would like to give to you."

Just as the two men were about to start their conversation again, Tannor barged into the room from the medbay. "I feel like a new man, Jodar. I have been fixed up better than new. Where is that woman of yours? I have been told we owe our lives to her and that she killed the beast of Bionas. I want to give her a great big thank-you hug. Then I want to convince her to leave you and choose me as a life mate."

Jodar jumped up, ready to pummel Tannor. One for his loud voice, and two, even though Tannor was like a brother to him, jealousy kicked in. Tannor would not touch Sheye if he meant what he said. Jodar would see to that, brother or not.

Tannor laughed heartedly. "Calm down, my brother. I would never step on your territory. I like my head where it is, thank you very much." Jodar grinned but still punched Tannor in the arm, none too softly. Tannor stumbled back onto another sofa and laughed again. "You will always have to protect that one, Jodar. Every man but myself and Chanlon will try to steal her from you, just saying, since we have already experienced it with Broud and Dorian. She will be able to bring down kingdoms if she realizes her power over men, Jodar."

Jodar growled at Tannor, but then he smiled. He would fight for her every second of every day for the rest of his life if that is what it takes to keep her safe and to keep her his.

Sheye began to awaken with all the new commotion, and she sat up groggily. Jodar went over to her and sat beside her. She curled up under the arm he cradled around her and snuggled into his side. Chanlon sighed to himself but then smiled inwardly. He realized that it was not the right time to spring his gift onto Jodar right now. All the interruptions were a sign. He decided that he would hold off his announcement until after Jodar and Sheye's bonding ceremony, then he would give Jodar his gift during his announcement. He stood up and excused himself from the three of them and went to tell his Blue Cloaks to open a link to the council of the planets. He needed to invite them to Sarbus for the bonding ceremony and to be prepared for his announcement before they returned home.

Chapter 24

They were, finally, ultimately home and landing on Sarbus. Stepping out of the shuttle into the docking bay of their planet seemed almost surreal to Jodar, to Tannor, and to Chanlon. So much had changed. It had been over a year since they departed to other star systems collecting what the planet needed to keep it alive, thriving, and no longer on the brink of dying. Chanlon was extremely excited to be able to revive the planet he once loved back to the glory it had previously been. With all they had collected from the other star systems, their planet would now be a planet worth saving. They would have a unique array of species and diversities that no other planet would have because of all they had collected. Their planet would now have a unique ecosystem with new combined plant life and animals like no other planet in existence. Their planet would be a combination of many planets merged. It would blend the remainder of what Sarbus could contribute as well as what they had collected from other planets. Sarbus would create and meld everything in unique ways that had never been done before. Sarbus would now be a planet that could survive no matter what.

*****

Sheye was a bit more tentative than the others as they departed the shuttle to the visitor center on Sarbus. Treading onto an alien planet other than Earth was an altering experience for her even though she had been on the vacation moon, but she had been so stressed that she did not really focus on it being an alien planet. She had accepted that she wanted to be with Jodar no matter where they were, but she was still trying to acknowledge the reality that she was on an extraterrestrial world, and this was plenty to overcome and accept in her reality as being genuine. So far, everything looked quite dispassionate to Sheye, and she was somewhat disappointed. The visitor center appeared like a large, open, high-quality office lobby. Sure, it exhibited some unusual plant life and unique furniture, but if one were not paying attention, it would not appear so abnormal. She did observe that there was a great number of soldiers, Blue Cloaks, and many additional men arriving to welcome their group home, and she was beginning to feel slightly besieged.

Jodar felt Sheye's rising panic and decided to take her away from the throng of men who were beginning to surround the group. There were lots of back slaps and congratulations being thrown around. He was accosted as well and, for a few moments, smiled and nodded, laughed and acknowledged the group's enthusiasm and compliments. As soon as the interest started to turn toward Sheye, Jodar decided it was time to politely exit. He made sure that Chanlon was safe, and Tannor accepted to take over watch on Chanlon so Jodar could take Sheye away after he explained Sheye's apprehension to him. Tannor watched with a bit of envy as Jodar swept Sheye away as casually as he could with the least notice possible.

Jodar and Sheye exited the main visitor lobby and went into another bay that had much smaller transport vehicles. Jodar signed out his two-seater that had been stored there for over a year and placed Sheye in the passenger seat. It felt so wonderful being back in familiar surroundings. Sheye was unusually quiet, but Jodar knew that she was okay. She just had a lot on her mind, taking in all her new surroundings and sights. He decided to show her some of his planet as he took her back to his home for the rest of the day until the festivities began on the next rising. They both needed to be alone with each other for at least one night to become a little more familiar.

As Jodar exited the bay, he maneuvered the hover craft in the direction of their main city where Chanlon resided and reigned over the planet. Jodar's home was on the outskirts of the city as he detested urban living. He had to work within the walls of the city daily, so he preferred to live in a more peaceful environment when he was alone. Sheye sat forward in the vehicle as they began their travels. She was quite shocked how much the landscape looked like the province of Saskatchewan on Earth. There was a lack of vegetation or any kind of large trees anywhere. It was open and vast where one could see for miles. Jodar piped up as he felt her curiosity rise. "This area used to be like an oasis, believe it or not. Sarbus was much like the vacation moon we just left for its beauty. After all the attacks on our land, wildlife, and people from Bionas, this is what we have been reduced to. Therefore, we had to do the collections from other thriving worlds, or our planet would eventually die or become a barren dessert planet. With the technologies created by our Blue Cloaks, they have estimated that we can have our planet back to the new normal within several years."

Sheye was saddened as she listened to Jodar. She could feel his deep sadness at the loss of his old world, but she could sense a new excitement within Jodar as he looked forward to the new future for his kind as well. Sheye was losing all her anger toward her abduction by the minute. Yes, she was upset that she may never see Earth again, but she really did not lose much as she only had her business that kept her from losing her mind and being alone. Mandy was here somewhere as well, and they would be reunited soon. Mandy also did not have any family left on Earth, so she hoped that she also would eventually be happy and adjust to her new life as well. The only thing that really had Sheye regret her abduction was the loss of Onyx and Big Red. She missed them so much. They had been her only true friends for over a decade. Not knowing what had happened to them or if they were okay preyed on her mind daily.

Sheye buried her melancholic thoughts about her horses when she noticed a large ridge of mountains off in the distance and commented. "Wow, that is a massive mountain range. All of them must be taller than our Mount Everest on Earth. They are beautiful."

Jodar smiled. "That is one of our main ranges that holds huge quantities of our Sardanium ore. The entire range you see there is one continuous mining operation within and underneath. One day, I will take you there to see the process and the impressive layout of it all." Jodar became silent for a moment. "I just wish you could have seen how beautiful Sarbus once was. It was breathtaking to live here. We had the vastest array of wildlife and plant life. It was the most fruitful planet within our system. We also have and, still do, the most diverse humanoid species here as well that coexist together in harmony. We were immensely proud of that, and therefore, we could not let our planet die. Sarbus is worth saving. Now that Dorian is dead, we can start to rebuild without having to worry that he may destroy everything again. The threat of him is gone."

In the distance to Sheye's right, she noticed something gleaming and realized that they were coming up on a massive city. To her amazement, the city was completely white and cream colors, and all the shapes of the buildings were oval. There was a high white wall surrounding the city that reminded her of the Emerald City in the movie the *Wizard of Oz*, minus the emeralds. It was beautiful. Everything looked so smooth and elegant. There was not a square, rectangle, horizontal or sharp edge in this city anywhere. Even the bridges were rounded off in a way that seemed curved and smooth. "That is Sryzon. It is the largest city of the four we have on Sarbus. Sarbus is about the size of your moon on Earth. All the planets in this system are approximately the size of your moon or slightly smaller. Sryzon is the central hub of all Sardanium steel inventions, creations, manufacturing, trades, sales, banking, you name it. This is also where Chanlon resides. His palace is the central building there that stands the tallest above them all. Chanlon's residence is at the top so he can view his city from every angle unobstructed."

Sheye frowned at what she was seeing as they passed by. "Jodar, there is vast amounts of vegetation and trees within the city. How is this possible?"

Jodar nodded at her comment. "Luckily, all the cities have shields that the attacks weren't able to penetrate." Sheye turned to Jodar. "Then why did you not just use the plants from the cities to regrow your destroyed plant life?"

Jodar nodded again. "I see what you mean, but the cities only have certain plants that never lose any leaves or make any messes. There are only a few varieties of our plant life in the cities. These plants don't produce any fruit, so they are just for aesthetics per se." Sheye raised her eyebrows and nodded as it made sense. They zoomed past the city and entered a bushy area that had a bunch of low-laying bushes. Within the bushes were a few oval buildings, but they were small in comparison to the cities. In a few minutes, Jodar pulled up alongside a small oval building with a few connecting ovals and stopped the vehicle. When they exited the craft, Jodar turned to Sheye. "Welcome to your new home."

They were both nervous when they entered the home. Jodar was nervous for he wanted Sheye to like it and feel comfortable and know that this would be their place together. Sheye was nervous as well since this was were Jodar resided before they had ever met, and she was apprehensive at what she would find in a bachelor pad. She was extremely pleased though as she entered, and she was also surprised. When you came to the home, it looked solid white, and one could not see into the home. There were no windows, so Sheye was concerned that it would be dark and dingy, but it was the exact opposite. Now she understood why there were no windows. She could see through the walls. When you entered, it was like you were outside and not within a building. It was open and had high oval ceilings. Each room did have a wall that one could not see through for privacy, but all the outer walls were like they were not there. The furniture was massive and looked wonderfully comfortable. It was clean, arid, but very cozy, not what she expected at all.

Jodar showed her around his small comfortable home, and she noticed there was no kitchen area. It was just the central seating area like a living room, a section where one could do their toiletries, and a sleeping quarter.

"Jodar, how do you cook anything as there is no place for it?"

Jodar had a sheepish grin on his face when he answered her. "I am one of the lucky ones. Being the head guard of commander, I have my meals delivered whenever I choose. One of the perks I guess, so I have had no need to have a cooking area in my home. I only moved out here when I received my posting with Chanlon. I used to live in Chanlon's palace for a while, but I was not happy there. I needed my own space, my own peace. So when this was built for me, I opted out of a cooking section. If you would like one, I can always have it built."

Sheye laughed and turned to Jodar. "I would not even begin to know how to cook with your foods and ingredients. Having meals prepared for now is fine by me."

Jodar then took her to the sleeping chamber. The bed was the focus point of the entire room as it was massive. Sheye turned to Jodar and pointed at the bed with a look of humor on her face. Jodar scratched his eyebrow sheepishly.

"I like a lot of space to sleep."

Sheye tilted her head. "That is a bed for recreation, not for sleeping, Jodar."

Jodar's face flamed red, and he came up to Sheye and held her hands in his and faced her. "I know you don't mind that I had physical relationships with other women before we met, but I need you to know that it has been an awfully long time, and it was never in this bed. I have always been different from my friends and colleagues about sexual relationships. I believe that intimacy is something to not be just given to any woman. Yes, I have had relationships, but nothing that ever lasted. I craved to experience the knowing with someone so desperately. I always have. I always believed it would happen to me, so because of this, it held me away from a lot of intimacy with women. Now that I have you, and the knowing has been shared between us, my dream has come true. You are all that I need, Sheye, forever and for always. I am yours."

Jodar melted her heart. She knew what he said was the utmost truth as she could feel his sincerity of what he said as if it were her own. She stood up on her tiptoes and gently kissed his lips. "I need you to know I have never completely laid with a man, Jodar. I... I... am a virgin. I guess deep down I, too, wanted that special something before I became intimate. This feeling for a man has not once transpired for me until now."

Hearing that Sheye had never coupled with another man before made Jodar full of delight. She truly would be his and only his in every way. Their planet did not frown upon sexual encounters. Sexual meetings were not something that was forbidden or frowned upon in their system. It was considered natural until you were committed to someone and bonded your life to them. Then the act of laying with others than one's life mate was extremely taboo.

Jodar returned Sheye's gentle kiss. Her lips were soft and supple. She tasted so right. Jodar deepened the kiss and just enjoyed the feeling of her body pressed against him. His hands began to wonder as did hers. She was the most perfect fit for him, and she was tall enough that he did not have to bend down much to reach her derriere as his hands traveled downward. Sheye moaned as he cupped her bottom in his hands. "So perfect," Jodar commented in her ear as his lips grazed hotly against her neck. He was the most amazing kisser she had ever experienced, and she was becoming aroused at a speed that was intense. They were both becoming one. Their need for each other and to touch one another other was becoming a desperate passion for their minds and their bodies.

Before long, Sheye was removing Jodar's shirt, and then hers followed and landed on the floor, forgotten. They explored each other with their hands as they continued to kiss. Sheye loved the feeling of his large muscles under her fingertips. He was so warm and solid as her hands ventured around his torso. He made her feel like she was the only woman on this planet who would ever matter to him. Jodar was thinking the same thing as his hands glided over her breasts, back, and abdomen. She was perfectly proportioned as her breasts fit his hand perfectly. He stroked her hardened nipples with his thumb, and she moaned in ecstasy. He ended the kiss and stepped back a little so he could just soak up the vision of her before him. She began to remove her pants, but he stopped her.

"Please let me." Jodar kneeled on the floor and slowly slipped her pants past her hips. By Prantus's stars, she was so perfect, so beautiful. He exposed her hips and planted a kiss on each hip bone and then one just below her belly button. Sheye sucked in her breath. The feelings that he was causing her body to experience were delicious. She never wanted this to end. He continued to remove her pants and undergarments together, then flung them on the floor. He sat back on his heels for a moment and drank in the sight of her standing naked before him. Jodar groaned and leaned back in. He grazed hip lips over her pelvis, and then he flicked out his tongue and began to massage her in the most intimate of places. Sheye's legs almost buckled beneath her. She held herself up by placing both hands within his beautiful long hair. His tongue was like magic. Sheye shifted her stance so he could have more access to her swollen womanhood. He glazed his tongue across her pleasure area a few more times, then bit with his teeth in a gentle but maddening way. "Oh lord," then he began to suckle on her private area with his mouth.

"Oh god!" She was in heaven.

The pressure of his lips with the pulling, sucking, and massaging on her womanhood was almost too glorious to take. Sheye moaned so loudly that it startled her. Jodar stood up, and the heat in his eyes took her breath away. He scooped her up and gently placed her on the edge of the bed.

"Lay back, my beauty."

Sheye did not hesitate to do as he instructed, and as she lay back on the bed with her legs still bent over the side, he spread them wider. Again, she was taken to heaven as his tongue worked on her flesh. The most wonderful warm, tingling sensation began to build deep in her loins. It was hot and powerful. Sheye could not stop moving; she bucked and pulled in a deep breath when his tongue went deep inside her.

She called out his name as the heat continued to build. Jodar changed tactics and trailed kisses up her pelvis and over her stomach, enjoying the taste and feel of her skin. He placed himself half on top of her and claimed one of her nipples in his mouth. Sheye gasped and clung to his shoulders. His suckling her nipple was sending intense pleasure right down to her groin. Jodar worked on her nipple and then proceeded to claim the next one with his exquisite mouth. Suddenly he backed away. Sheye opened her eyes to watch him removing his pants, and her eyes flew open when his manhood was exposed. It was the most beautiful appendage that she had ever seen. She was a little afraid at the size of it though.

Jodar felt her fear. "I will be gentle, my sweet one."

Sheye was calmed immediately and drank in the sight of his magnificent physique. He was the most beautiful man she had ever encountered.

Jodar slowly lowered himself back down onto the bed and started to kiss Sheye slowly, enjoying her tongue as he teased her with his. As they kissed, Jodar explored her with his hands, and then his fingers guided gently inside of her. She was so wet; she was so ready. Jodar moaned, but he knew he had to take this slow. He wanted to enjoy every second and have this never end for them both. She felt so ideal, so right beneath him. Jodar flicked Sheye's swollen flesh between her legs with his fingers as the other explored inside of her, and she bucked. He released her mouth and continued to kiss and lick her neck, and then he moved to her perfect breasts again. He could not get enough of her.

Sheye could feel Jodar's manhood pressing and throbbing against her thigh. She never wanted to have a man penetrate her more than right now. She began to beg him. "Please, Jodar, I need… I need you."

Jodar continued to move his fingers inside of her as she writhed underneath him. "What is it you need, my star?"

Sheye moaned again as his fingers played within her. "I need you. I need you inside of me. I need all of you."

Jodar removed his fingers from inside of her and placed both of his hands on the side of her cheeks and turned her to face him. "Are you sure? I don't need to. I will if only you are ready." This pained Jodar to say this as he was so hard and aroused by the woman beneath him, but he loved her so much it would be okay if she said no. She had been through so much lately, and he would understand if she was not ready for this kind of intimacy. Sheye opened her eyes, and in her response, she grabbed his hard member between her hands and began to stroke him gently. Jodar bent his head back in ecstasy at her touch and did a little moaning of his own. Sheye pushed him back and made him lay with his back on the bed.

"I want you inside me so much, but I want this to last. I need to feel you too. I need to touch all of you."

Jodar closed his eyes as he felt her warm mouth and lips surround his. Now it was his turn to feel the immense pleasure of what his woman could give to him. He felt like a young boy dealing with his first time with a woman. He was so ready and so aroused that he had to calm his body, lest he comes too soon. Her mouth felt like nothing he had experienced before. It was soft and sucking, then hard and warm. She used her teeth to glide up his shaft, and then she was down sucking again. He could not take it anymore. He swung up and flipped her back beneath him. He had to feel her silky sheath surrounding his member. He had to be inside her now. Sheye instinctively spread her legs and lifted her pelvis under him. She would finally know what it was like to experience a man she loved so much to completely love her. Jodar slowly and with all his energy guided his manhood gently to her entrance. He wanted to make this as pleasurable to her as it was to him.

"This may hurt for only a moment, my star."

Sheye snorted and looked him directly in his eyes. "Make love to me, my warrior. I am sturdier than I look."

That was Jodar's undoing. He quickly entered her warmth and then held himself in check for a moment to have her virgin sheath adjust to his size.

Sheye was unleashed; there was a small tearing sensation, but that was nothing compared to the urgency and of the amazing sensations of having him inside her. She looked up at Jodar and could see the beads of sweat on his brow as he held himself back for her sake.

"I won't break my sweet, Jodar. Give me all of you."

Jodar grit his teeth but then obeyed and began to rhythmically move in and out of her. They both melted into cries of pleasure. Jodar pumped in and out; the heat in her entire body built up to a point that she felt like she had begun to float. She began to see stars as his shaft pulsated inside her again and again. Jodar began to pick up the pace, and Sheye received all of him as she raised her hips and joined him in the rhythm of two bodies connected. Sheye was taken to a place she never knew existed. It was warm. It was exploding. It was gripping her into a frenzy. She did not realize that her nails were digging deep into Jodar's shoulder, but neither did he. Suddenly, a loud moan escaped Sheye's throat. "Harder, oh god, Jodar, harder," and Jodar slammed his hardness into her, her explosion came. Her insides throbbed and spasmed in the most glorious release, and her breath was taken away. Jodar was right behind her as he could feel her orgasm pulse around his shaft, and that was it; he exploded in bliss, and they came together, clinging to each other as if their lives depended on it.

Both their orgasms were so powerful and shocking that they lay together without moving, trying to catch their breath. Jodar began to pull out, but Sheye stopped him.

"No, don't move. Let me feel you inside me for a little while longer."

Jodar obeyed without objection as she felt so wonderful with him still inside her. He had no difficulties in the least leaving part of him inside of her as if they were connected, and they fell asleep together still as one.

Sheye awoke first, and Jodar was still half atop her person, and it felt glorious. The weight of him was not heavy as she would have thought. It was soothing, safe, and made her feel protected. He slept silently and as peaceful as a child. Sheye looked at Jodar's face, and she instantly smiled to herself as reality started to surface. What she had with Jodar was like a dream. It was so surreal, yet he was everything that she had ever desired in her life for a partner.

Jodar was so strong and yet so caring and gentle. Her body had never experienced that kind of pleasure before, but neither had her mind. Thinking about life now without Jodar in it brought hot fat tears to her eyes, and she blinked them away a little shocked. She had been abducted, stolen from her life, tortured, almost raped more than once; she had killed and maimed others, yet she realized that she wanted to be no place else but with this man. Nothing else mattered anymore except staying with Jodar. The feeling was overwhelming for her. These feelings were all so new. She wanted and needed Jodar. How had she managed so well before without him was a concept she could not figure out. She had been so strong and so able for herself after her father died; she had come to accept that maybe she would be one of those women who did not need a man to be happy. All that was gone now as she knew with all her heart if Jodar was not in her life now, she would not want to live.

Just as she was thinking how much she loved Jodar, he stirred and opened his eyes. The smile that spread on his face when he noticed her beneath him melted her heart again. How could a man so handsome become even more so by just a smile? Sheye felt him harden against her thigh, and she laughed.

"My, my, do I feel a little love coming my way?"

Jodar growled and scooped her up in his arms, and they made love passionately again. Sheye had never felt so happy and satisfied in her life. This was where she belonged. After another explosive orgasm, Sheye was straddled atop Jodar, and they just looked at each other. He was still blown away with her beauty as she sat above him with her legs on either side of his hips in all her naked glory. Jodar sighed in complete satisfaction; he did not want to leave this bed ever again if Sheye was with him, but he knew they had a particularly important day ahead of them. This was the day she would be bonded to him forever. Sheye would be forever his, but as he tried to remove Sheye from him, she giggled and stated, "I am not done with you yet, my warrior," and proceeded to wiggle seductively above him.

Jodar was hard and ready again in moments as he watched his woman straddling his midsection. She raised herself up a little and softly guided his hard shaft inside her. Sheye groaned in pleasure as her weight came down onto his body, and he impaled her. Jodar groaned but refused to close his eyes; he wanted to watch. She was mesmerizing as she rhythmically moved her perfect body up and down above him. He watched the pleasure on Sheye's face as she rode him. His pleasure built at an intense speed as his eyes focused on hers. They watched each other as she traversed her body on his hard, hot, shaft in ways he had never experienced before. Her breasts bounced lightly up and down, and her nipples were hard and erect. The pure ecstasy of watching her ride him made him feel overwhelming pleasure. Again, they climaxed together, and Sheye collapsed on top him, breathless. By the fifth star of Prantus, he never wanted to leave this bed.

Eventually, Jodar removed himself from their entwined bodies reluctantly. "We have a very important day ahead of us, my star." Jodar sat on the edge of the bed, and Sheye wrapped her arms around him as she kneeled on the bed behind him. Jodar held her hands as they wrapped around his torso. He found that he was nervous, extremely nervous, for the first time in his life, but he had to ask. "Sheye, today is important to me as we will be bonded. This means the same as marriage is on your planet, but even more so to me. I would never ask this of you if I did not want you to be with me for the rest of my life." Jodar turned to Sheye and looked her right in her eyes. "Is this something that is agreeable to you? Will you do me the honor of bonding your life with mine for the entirety of our lives? Sheye, I have never wanted nor loved a woman so much as I do for you, even before we experienced the knowing. I have always wanted the knowing with the woman whom I fell in love with, but when I saw you, that did not even matter anymore. I wanted you. I craved you with my entire being. I must apologize for ripping you away from your life and your world in my selfishness to have you, but I must ask you now. I need to know if this is what you want too. Sheye, will you be my life mate?"

Sheye never averted her eyes from him as she listened to his heartfelt confession. She became lost in his lion eyes as he spoke to her about his desire to be bonded to her for life. She had been contemplating her feelings for Jodar since her second abduction, and she had already concluded that she could not be without Jodar for even a single day. Sheye shifted her position, so she was able to crawl onto his lap. His embrace was intoxicating to her. Sheye let a few tears escape as she responded, "Jodar, I hated everything that had happened to me and Mandy at first. I was confused and scared, but every time I saw you, I felt something that connected us even with all my fear and hatred about what was happening to me. Then in the cell when you stepped forward to stop me from falling and I looked into your eyes, the knowing happened. I want you to say if circumstances had been different and I saw you on Earth, I would have fallen in love with you at first sight even without the knowing. Jodar, the feelings I have for you are so intense that I can't even describe them nor understand them. When I thought you were dead, I was devastated! My feelings are so powerful for you that I can't deny them anymore. I can't live without you, my warrior man. You are now part of me, and I am willing to stay here with you. I am eager to be yours and yours alone. Jodar, I love you, yes! I will be honored to be your life mate. Forever and for always, Jodar, I am yours."

Chapter 25

Sheye and Jodar entered Sryzon and left their hover craft at the main terminal, and they walked hand in hand, both smiling from ear to ear into Chanlon's palace. Sheye and Jodar walked through the main lobby, and everyone within the building congratulated Jodar or welcomed him back all the while staring at Sheye. Jodar knew they were all dying to ask who she was but held their curiosity to themselves because of Jodar's status as the head guard of their supreme commander. Jodar directed Sheye to what looked like a medical room. When Sheye looked around not understanding why they were in a medical bay, Jodar only said, "You must have your best friend at our joining ceremony."

Sheye was ecstatic and hugged Jodar, followed by a bunch of kisses for what he had just said. Mandy would finally be reunited with her. Suddenly, Sheye became terrified at what Mandy would say or feel when she was released from the hibernation pod. The experience of coming out of hibernation was excruciating. Jodar felt Sheye's apprehension and explained. "The normal process of releasing one out from a hibernation pod is quite a euphoric experience when done properly. Your friend will feel like she had the best sleep of her entire life. You were released under duress, and it was not conducted properly. Mandy won't suffer any discomfort with the correct hibernation release process."

Just as Mandy's pod was escorted into the bay, Tannor burst in through the door breathless.

"Did I miss it?"

Jodar and Sheye were startled, and then Tannor looked around the room.

"Oh, good, I haven't missed her release. Thank the fifth star of Prantus."

Sheye glared at the man who had just entered the room. She still harbored bad thoughts about Tannor even though she had found out that her horses had not been killed by him. Tannor lit up when he saw Sheye though and immediately came over to her and gave her a huge bear hug.

"Thank you for saving my life, Sheye. I am indebted to you for eternity. Anything you need, I will be there for you."

Sheye just went limp in his arms and did not return the hug for a few moments. Then she realized that this man was Jodar's best friend, and she had to let go of her hatred for him as he did not deserve her wrath, so she hugged him gently back. When he pulled away from the embrace, Sheye looked at him with slight embarrassment and then stated, "I must apologize for breaking your nose. I had thought at the time that you had killed my horses. They meant the world to me, and I fully intended to eventually kill you. I thought they were dead, and I blamed you for it all. I guess I can't kill you anymore. I found out they are still alive, but they are all alone in the wild, and I still harbor some anger for that, but for now, you are forgiven."

Tannor just smiled a huge smile from ear to ear at her and answered, "It was worth every break from such as you, my lady. No harm done. I was immediately fixed up as good as new being right by the medbay. I am sorry for causing you such stress about your beasts. All I can do is prove to you that you are as much a friend to me now as Jodar has ever been in my life. I will die for you as I would Jodar."

Sheye laughed at the enthusiastic Tannor. He was extremely likable now that she had let go of all her hatred. He was a true friend of Jodar. "Well, there will be no death and destruction anymore if I can help it." Tannor hugged Sheye again and only let her go when Jodar growled low in his throat as a warning to Tannor that he was holding his woman for far too long for his liking.

Tannor let Sheye go and then turned to the Blue Cloaks that were hooking up Mandy's pod for her release.

"Can we get this moving, gentlemen? I have a woman to claim here."

Sheye frowned at Tannor's comment, and Jodar pulled her aside a little and whispered in her ear, "Tannor set his eye on Mandy as I had set my eyes on you. He wants nothing more than for them both to experience the knowing together."

Sheye was stunned for a moment; she turned back to Tannor and the Blue Cloaks thinking that if Mandy liked Tannor, they would possibly make a great match. They were both a little off the mark, and both had very enthusiastic personalities, so maybe this would work. Maybe, just maybe, Mandy would be happy with her new and altered life. Sheye began hoping that the knowing would happen for them both together as well. If only so Mandy would be as happy as she was with their new situation.

Sheye did not realize that she was holding her breath as they released Mandy from the pod. Jodar was holding her hand as they all watched the Blue Cloaks work on her. Tannor was right up at the pod, and the Blue Cloaks were becoming annoyed with his proximity while they worked. Several times, Tannor had to be asked to back up. He would at first, but then he would find himself right back up to the pod waiting for Mandy to awaken. The Blue Cloaks finally gave up and worked around Tannor as he bent over the pod.

Mandy suddenly sat up and stretched with a large yawn, and she almost punched Tannor in the face. Sheye's heart was pounding in her chest as she watched Mandy wake up. Mandy opened her eyes while she stretched, but then she paused in midstretch as she took in her surrounding. Her eyes focused on Tannor, who was hovering so close to her face focusing on her eyes. Mandy looked at Tannor for a moment with much appreciation in her eyes at what she saw but did not comprehend.

"Well, hello, handsome. Oh dear, how much did I drink last night? I sure hope I did not disappoint you, but I don't remember a thing."

Tannor just kept looking in Mandy's eyes, waiting for something to happen.

"Well, does a cat have your tongue, honey, because—" Suddenly Mandy looked around, and her memory started to kick in.

"What in tarnation? You there"—Mandy pointed at Tannor—"I don't care how darn good-looking you may be but stop staring at me like you want to eat me alive no matter how flattering it may be. Where in the dickens am I?"

Sheye stepped forward at this point and pushed Tannor aside, who was still trying to stare in her eyes. "Tannor, back off. It is my turn," Sheye mentioned.

Tannor reluctantly gave way. Mandy's eyes brightened when she saw her best friend. "Oh golly, it wasn't a dream, was it?"

Sheye just shook her head and that told Mandy everything she really needed to know.

"Well, shit doodles" was all Mandy said as she began to try to remove herself from the pod that she was sitting in.

The Blue Cloaks rushed over to help her out, and Mandy bulked. "Back off, little boys, I got this."

They listened to her immediately, and Mandy, with her aerobics dexterity, jumped out of the pod and landed on the floor in front of Sheye only slipping a little. Jodar laughed a little when he remembered Mandy's size difference compared to Sheye. Mandy was indeed the tiniest woman he had ever seen, but he instinctively knew that she was so much more than her tiny stature.

Tannor tried to press himself in between Sheye and Mandy trying to look in her eyes again, but Jodar stepped in and made him back off. "My brother, let us leave the ladies to get reacquainted. Shall we go and get ourselves ready for the ceremony and my day of being bonded for life with my woman?"

Tannor looked disappointed but eventually nodded. This was Jodar's day, not his; he could wait a little while longer, and then the two men left the room. Jodar laid a kiss on Sheye's forehead before he exited. "I will see you soon, my star."

Sheye grabbed his hand and squeezed it before the two men left. "I will see you soon too, my warrior."

Mandy looked on with the most perplexed look on her face as Sheye grabbed Mandy's hand in hers. "We have so much to discuss and so little time to do it. Let us go somewhere that we can be comfortable while I explain everything as fast as I can. We only have a little bit of time."

Mandy hesitated and looked down at her nakedness. Sheye laughed. "Oops, I guess we need to address this situation" and waved her hand toward Mandy's naked body. Before she even had to ask, one of the Blue Cloaks brought over a robe, and Mandy put it on. The Blue Cloaks turned their backs in respect as Mandy donned the clothing. Then the two women were shown to a private sitting room, and they were left alone.

When the ladies sat down a medibot immediately came up to them with one glass of liquid and sat there. Mandy looked at it with interest but had no idea what it meant for her to do. Sheye picked up the glass and handed it to Mandy. "This will help you. It tastes good and is quite refreshing."

Mandy automatically took it and drank it down realizing that she was extremely thirsty. "How the heck did that machine know that I was dying of thirst?"

Sheye shrugged. "I am still getting used to everything here as well. I am still amazed with all I see and experience."

Mandy's eyes widened, and she looked at Sheye. "I was in such a panic a moment ago, and now I feel calm. Sheye, whatever was in that drink calmed me down. I am not terrified anymore." Sheye nodded. "Like I said, everything here is so different from what we are used to back home, and it is mostly a good, amazing thing once you get used to it."

Mandy turned to Sheye. "Everything I remember is true then, right, Sheye? We were taken. You got me out of that pod in that big ol' cold room. We tried to escape. We fought off some men who looked like the ones that just gave me this robe. Then everything just goes blank. Sheye, you must fill me in on everything. What in the heavens is happening? Where the dickens are we?"

Sheye proceeded in the next half hour to explain as much as she could about everything that had happened. Mandy stared wide-eyed and opened-mouthed as she hung on to every word that Sheye was saying and explaining. "Darlin', you have just explained the best science-fiction movie to me, that I would pay to go see in a theater.

The fact that I believe you because of my small experience with what I remember happening is saying a lot." Mandy looked around when Sheye felt she had explained all that she could. Mandy stood up and walked around the room looking and touching everything. "It isn't that much different if you weren't looking for it to be different, am I right?" Sheye watched as Mandy picked up several things in the room and examined them. "Mandy, you realize that everything had changed for us. We will never be able to go back to Earth. Our lives have been altered in every way imaginable. Are you okay with what I have told you?"

Mandy stopped exploring and looked out of the large window taking in the alien view of the city. "Darlin', this is a lot to take in, considering!"

Sheye held her breath as she waited for Mandy to collect her thoughts and continue. "All I have to say is, I have really not lost anything from Earth. I have no family left. The only thing that mattered anymore was my job and you."

Mandy stopped for a moment and then turned to Sheye with a huge smile on her face.

"Well, hot damn girl, this is the most exciting thing that could ever happen to me. This is so exhilarating. It is all new and refreshing. Oh my! Can I dare ask you? Who was that hunk of a man who kept staring at me earlier? If all the men are like that one on this planet, girl, I think I just died and gone to heaven."

Sheye laughed out loud and was so relieved that Mandy was not angry nor in denial. "That man that you called a hunk is extremely interested in you. He really likes you, and he is Jodar's best friend. So…you seem to be taking this rather well. I must ask you though, Mandy, if you are not still in shock. Are you willing to be with me and stay on this planet? If so, I would love you to be my maid of honor, for when I marry, or should I say, life bond with Jodar today."

Mandy squealed and ran back over to Sheye. "Isn't this the best thing ever? My god, Sheye, we are in a completely different space thingy, planet, alien world, and such! There are all these gorgeous men around us. We hit the jackpot, girl! I have never been so excited about something in my life. It is all new, different, foreign but in a good way. Of course, I will be honored to stand beside you on this most fabulous day. My best friend has found the love of her life, even though he is an alien. We are on a completely different world. There is already a handsome alien after me! You have told me that sleeping around is not taboo here, and lord lady, if it were not for you inviting me to your cabin, I would still be leading my mundane, boring existence on Earth, trying to get my ex to leave me alone. I would still be going day-to-day with living but not actually living. Do you know what I mean?" Mandy was rambling, but Sheye was so relieved. She thought that this would have gone the exact opposite of what was happening right now. Sheye just assumed that Mandy would be devastated. Here before her was an entirely different person receiving all this information like she was living in a movie that was a best seller. Sheye could not be more relieved.

Two Blue Cloaks arrived and asked the ladies if they could accompany them to get ready for the ceremony. Sheye grabbed Mandy and just said, "Wait till you experience the dresser and the beauty enhancer. They are the coolest things ever, once you get used to them."

Mandy smiled from ear to ear. "Lead on, Sheye, I want to experience everything." Mandy was like a little kid in a candy store that was told she could have everything that her heart desired. When she met the White Cloaks for the very first time, instead of being frightened, she was walking in between them and touching their hands and their arms. She even grabbed a chair and stood on her tiptoes to touch the hair and the face of the leader of the White Cloaks that Sheye had the privilege of being introduced to on the ship when she first needed to be dolled up for meeting Chanlon for the first time.

Mandy was like a two-year-old child with no fear; she was so full of intense curiosity and did not hold back. The White cloaks entertained her and let her examine them. Turned out, they were just as interested in her because of her tiny stature and exuberant personality. Mandy suddenly grabbed the head White Cloak's face in between her hands and stared at him. "You have the most beautiful blue eyes, darlin'. Are they real?"

The tall, slender man chuckled slightly, then leaned over to Sheye with a slight smile before he became serious again. "Ladies, I must insist that we get ready for the ceremony. You won't be disappointed in what I have picked out for you both. You will turn the heads of everyone in the palace."

Mandy just squealed in delight. "Well, you tall, beautiful man. Bring it on!"

Again, the main White Cloak smiled just a little and then ushered the machines into the room and began his work on the two women.

Mandy could not get enough of the dresser. She freaked out just a little bit when she first felt the strange material grow on her skin, but she was soon calmed down by Sheye who told her to just enjoy the experience. Mandy listened and then asked the tall slender man to keep changing her outfits so she could experience the dresser more. She laughed the whole while, but then the White Cloak insisted on the outfit he had chosen for her. Then he asserted that they move on to the beauty enhancer. Mandy pouted for a bit but then agreed, only after she was promised a private session with the head White Cloak to develop a wardrobe for her another day. The White Cloak seemed to be as enamored with Mandy as she was with him. Sheye just smiled as she watched her friend having the time of her life. Mandy's enthusiasm was infectious for everyone who met her. She understood the White Cloaks' attraction to her. It was quite humorous watching the two of them together. Mandy was so darn tiny compared to the white-cloaked alien who stood even taller than Sheye was.

While Mandy was now fascinated with the beauty enhancer, Sheye was able to get into the dresser. Soon, she was standing in front of a mirror. She was stunned at how beautiful the garment was that the White Cloak had designed for her. It was spectacular. It was not only elegant and all translucent white, but when you turned, it shimmered as if covered by a million diamonds. It was sexy too as the bodice and long skirt were tightly molded onto her entire body from the neck down to her toes. She could walk in the dress without any difficulty as the material was easy to move in as it flowed with her as she walked. The dress was like a second skin. It had a long train that started from her shoulder blades and floated behind her as if it were alive. The sides of the bodice were open in an oval form under the edge of her breasts down to her hips. The neckline went around her neck, like a choker.

Just below the choker around the neck, it plunged deeply down to her belly button. The plunging neckline had two crystals dangling down the center of her chest bone in between her breasts. The plunge only showed the center of her chest and not her breast; they were completely covered, with only the sides of her cleavage showing. Her shoulders were also bare with the material snaking around and down her arms. It looked like silk-painted strips that molded to her arms. When she spread her arms, the material was attached in a way that made it look like she had wings. The back of the dress was completely open as well and only held together by the neckline and the train at the shoulders. The open back plunged down to just above the start of her buttocks without showing the crease or cheeks. Sheye felt like a new updated version of an elegant, sexy Cinderella. Mandy's dress was similar but a little more of a cream color, minus the train. It was cut just above the knee in an angle shape as one side floated past her calf like a wispy scarf.

Mandy's hair was slicked back to her scalp, and it accentuated her big blue eyes and tiny face. Her makeup was flawless, and it seemed like she did not have any on. She glowed magnificently, and Sheye thought how beautiful she was. She was breathtaking to look at. Mandy had never looked so happy and elegant as she fluttered in front of the mirror with immense joy at her own reflection. "Well, I never. Who knew that I was this darn gorgeous?"

Sheye laughed aloud and turned to Mandy. "I always knew."

Mandy giggled and turned back to the mirror to fawn over her reflection again. Sheye's glorious burgundy hair was piled high on her head with a jeweled crystal chain placed around the pile of a perfectly messy quiff updo. She had tendrils of hair hanging around her perfect face. Her makeup was also flawless and seemed like she was fresh faced and yet gleaming. When Sheye was finished, everyone stood back and just stared at her in awe, including Mandy who was finally able to tear herself away from the mirror.

"You look like an angel." Mandy gasped out.

The White Cloaks all nodded, and the head White Cloak clapped his hands together in appreciation. "I have outdone myself on you both. People will be talking about you two for many eons to come. Sometimes I amaze myself."

Mandy ran to him and jumped in his arms in a great big hug. He caught her as he stumbled back a little startled by the show of her affection. "Thank you for making us look so blasted fabulous, blue eyes. You are number 1 in my books."

When Mandy slid down, the White Cloak was blushing, and then he cleared his long, elegant throat. "Well, it is time, ladies. The ceremony is about to start, and we don't want to be late now, do we?"

Chapter 26

Sheye did not know what to expect as the White Cloaks directed them to the large hall that the ceremony was going to take place in. As they entered the front, behind a large room separator, the White Cloaks told them to have a seat and to not enter the conference hall until they were summoned. The White Cloaks left them there and exited. The ladies sat down and waited. They could hear Chanlon addressing the throng of individuals who had gathered. They were in the middle of Adrya's trial, and she could hear the vote that the council of the planets all agreed that Adrya would be assigned to spend the rest of her living days in the custody of the Black Cloaks. The crowd clapped, cheered, and yelled out comments as the screaming Adrya was taken away to start her sentence. Chanlon addressed the room again. "Now that we have dealt with the traitor, I have a special ceremony planned for you all today. I must thank you all for coming on such short notice to this grandiose of days. All our collections to rebuild our world are now complete. The Blue Cloaks are hard at work establishing new breeds of beast, fowl, plant life as we speak.

"All the women are being comforted and educated to their new lives and will soon be open to meeting and accepting offers and claims to be life-bonded to the men of our world."

The crowd cheered again, and then Chanlon continued, saying, "My longtime personal guard, who has saved my life on numerous occasions that I have lost count, has been not only the best personal supreme commanding guard to myself, but he has also been the son that I have always longed for. I am proud to announce that Jodar has been graced with the knowing to the most amazing woman named Sheye. This spectacular lady is one of the women we collected from the planet called Earth within the Milky Way galaxy."

The crowd could be heard gasping, clapping, whispering, and then they began to cheer Jodar's and Sheye's name. The room became silent again as Chanlon continued his speech. "The woman you are privy to witness bonding with Jodar is also the woman who saved my life and Tannor, head of securities life also. To add to all this, she is also the one responsible for eliminating our nemesis, Dorian of Bionas, from existence and enabled us to capture and sentence the traitor Adrya."

The crowd erupted into amazing applause, cheers, whistles, and loud comments of joy and awe. Sheye was blushing profusely behind the wall as her heart pounded in her chest. Chanlon was talking as if she were a hero. She did not feel that way as she only wanted to help the people she had come to care about.

Mandy was patting her on the back. "Wow, sweetie, you never explained all that to me. You have to fill me in on everything after, and I mean everything, darlin'."

Chanlon quieted the amazed hall of people and then asked Jodar and Tannor to join him up on the stage. The crowd cheered and clapped again as the men stepped up to Chanlon. "Jodar, today is the day that not only do you bond your life with Sheye from Earth, but today is the day that I announce, from this moment forward, you are to be considered of my blood. You are now honored with my lineage and be known as my true bonded son."

Jodar gasped, and then the crowd again erupted in true delight and ovations.

The honor that Chanlon had just bestowed onto Jodar was exceedingly rare and incredibly special. It had only happened a few times in history on the planet Sarbus. Chanlon turned the stunned Jodar around and personally took off Jodar's cloak and replaced it with a new purple one that was of Chanlon's family color. Then Chanlon addressed the crowd again. "I am losing my personal guard, but I am gaining a son to be proud of. Tannor, will you grace me with the honor of stepping into the role as my new personal guard?"

Now it was Tannor's turn to gasp. The role of being Chanlon's personal guard was one of honor and respect. Chanlon turned Tannor around and took his cloak off and gave him a new cloak that was the color of his new authority. The room was again on its feet cheering.

The two men bowed to Chanlon, and he returned the gesture. Then he raised his hands in the air to have the room's attention again. "This has already been a day to be written in the history books of Sarbus, but we are not finished with the events of this day yet." Chanlon turned to Jodar and had him come beside him. "Jodar of Sarbus, son of the supreme commander, you are here to be bonded with a life mate, Sheye from Earth. Who is here to step forward as witness to have it written that the knowing happened between Jodar and Sheye so it can be recorded in the books?"

Several soldiers and White Cloaks stood up and raised their hands above their heads and then kneeled before the three men. In unison, they stated, "We are all witnesses of the knowing between those of which you speak."

A Blue Cloak entered with a large book on a floating tray and went to each of the witnesses. He poked each of the men's finger to draw blood. "Are you all willing to sign in blood that this event is true and binding? They all nodded, and then they each placed their blood print onto a page within the massive book. The men stood and returned to their seats. The Blue Cloak and the floating tray moved off to the side of the stage.

Chanlon spoke again. "Tannor, will you be the second witness to bind your blood to the book for Jodar and Sheye's bonding?"

Tannor stepped slightly forward. "I will and accept the bonding with my blood."

The Blue Cloak brought the floating tray over to Chanlon and Tannor and pricked their fingers, and then they marked the book with their prints also. Before the Blue Cloak exited, he addressed the audience. "Now will everyone stand to witness and invite Sheye from Earth to enter for her joining to be bonded with Jodar of Sarbus upon this stage?"

This was the women's cue to enter the hall as a dozen or so Blue Cloaks came in from behind them and placed Sheye in the front of the line, with Mandy behind her. They explained that they were to walk up the center of the room with the Blue Cloaks behind in a line.

Sheye was a pile of nerves. She was about to be bonded with Jodar. She could explode with happiness at this moment. Never could she have imagined that she would be abducted by aliens and then end up marrying one of them in her wildest dreams, but here she was about to do just that, and she was overjoyed about it.

Sheye took in a deep breath and stepped out from behind the wall. The crowed gasped at the vision before them. They all leaned forward to get a better view of Sheye from Earth. She was a vision to behold. Sheye was astounded at how many people were in the hall. There must be well over four hundred people standing and gaping at her. The minute her eyes settle on Jodar at the front of the room, her panic subsided. He was dressed in the finest of outfits. His hair was tied back, and he looked so very handsome with the purple cloak flowing behind him. Sheye focused on Jodar and walked slowly up the center of the hall. Gasps and whispers could be heard from every direction. Sheye smiled wide as she walked toward Jodar. Jodar was astounded as he watched Sheye walk up the isle. She had never looked so beautiful, so elegant, and she was to be his forever. Jodar was smiling from ear to ear; he even felt like he was choking up with tears from his emotions as he watched her come toward him. Tannor was also smiling from ear to ear as he watched Mandy enter the room. He was thinking the same thing about Mandy and hoped by the end of the day she would agree to be his life mate.

As they approached the stage, Jodar could not help himself; he stepped down and met Sheye just before she reached the stage. He held her hand the last few feet toward Chanlon and the Blue Cloak up onto the stage. Sheye was turned around, and Jodar stood behind her with his hands placed upon her shoulders. Mandy was placed beside Tannor, and Tannor stood as close as he could to Mandy without making it to obvious that he was claiming to the room that she would be his.

Sheye could feel the heat coming from Jodar's large warm hands resting on her shoulders. She could feel his joy oozing into her own. Jodar could also sense Sheye's emotions of joy as well. He was the happiest man in the universe right now. Chanlon was speaking, but Sheye did not hear a word of what he was saying. Suddenly, the Blue

Cloak was standing in front of her pricking her finger and placing it on the book. He did so to Jodar as well and then to Mandy. Chanlon threw his arms up in the air and entered center stage.

"Jodar of Sarbus, son of Chanlon the supreme commander; and Sheye of Earth, daughter of Joseph DuMontte, you are now bonded to be life mates until your lives have ended."

The hall stood up and exploded in praises and more rounds of applause. Jodar turned his new life mate to him and planted the greatest kiss onto her lips, which made the crowd cheer even more. Chanlon stepped forward and bowed to them both, then Mandy pushed in and gave Sheye and Jodar a huge hug. Tannor stepped forward and raised his arms in the air so that the crowd understood there would be another surprise awaiting. Everyone became silent.

Tannor addressed the crowd. He began the story about how they had come upon Sheye and Mandy and explained what had happened when they captured them both. He then explained the beasts that the women were riding. The crowd was enamored with Tannor's story, and you could hear a pin drop as Tannor spoke. He then explained how Sheye was in the belief that her beloved beasts had been killed. He turned to Sheye then and knelt before her as he grabbed her hands in his.

"I am sorry for the anguish I had caused you. Even though you had assumed I had damaged your beasts, you still chose to save my life. I arranged with the collectors of Earth beasts to collect a surprise for you, and I would like to present my bonding present to you both, Sheye and Jodar now." Tannor stood up and signalled toward a Green Cloak. Everyone in the room turned to look in the direction the Green Cloak had exited from. Then they all could hear stomping and animal noises. Suddenly, a magnificent black beast entered behind the Green Cloak, followed by another, a large red beast. Sheye screamed in delight and flew down the steps as tears flooded down her cheeks.

"Onyx, Big Red!" Both horses neighed and pranced as Sheye ran toward them in response. Sheye grabbed Onyx's head and placed her forehead against his as she whispered to him. She then treated Big Red the same way. The crowd was so impressed by the beasts that Tannor continued. "I have the Brown Cloaks busy building a large stable and fenced-in yards to look exactly like your stables back on your planet Earth to make you feel more at home. I had the Brown Cloaks start right after you and Jodar left his home this very sun rising. We would love you to train our men how to ride these beasts as well as the children who are sure to come from the many new bondings that will be happening in the next while. We have also brought the rest of your beasts here for you from your stables you had back on Earth as well."

Sheye ran up the stairs and jumped into Tannor's arms in tears. "Thank you, Tannor. Thank you so much. You will never know what this means to me."

Tannor whispered back in her ear, "As long as you don't try to kill me anymore, you are very welcome."

Jodar came over and slapped his best friend on his shoulder with a huge smile of appreciation on his face. "How did you keep this from me, Tannor?"

Tannor responded, "It was one of the hardest things I have ever had to do, my brother, as you know, I can't keep secrets from you, but it was well worth my immense effort for the last several months."

Chanlon held up his hands to silence the room again.

"I have one more announcement to make before we all depart to the food hall that has been set up with a magnificent feast for all on this joyous day. I, Chanlon, the supreme commander of Sarbus am withdrawing some of my leadership over to Jodar. We will rule Sarbus together until he is fully capable of taking over my reign. The time has come to start the transition of supreme commander for the good of Sarbus, and there is no one I trust more than my son, Jodar."

The audience again burst into cheers and applause. Even the council of the planets were nodding in appreciated acknowledgment and relief that it was Jodar who would eventually rule Sarbus and not Broud. Jodar was taken aback. This was never even in his wildest dreams to become Chanlon's official son, and now he was given the honor of ruling Sarbus in a conjoined effort with Chanlon, and he had the woman of his dreams now bonded to him officially. This day could not get any better. He felt like he should pinch himself for he felt as if he were dreaming.

Chapter 27

The party that was going on in the halls of the palace was like none had the privilege and honor of attending in many years. Everyone was enjoying themselves and congratulating the group, right and left. They were bombarded for most of the night. Sheye was in a wonder world as she met so many different races of humanoids with Jodar by her side. She was overjoyed about her bonding with Jodar and having her horses and her best friend with her on the best day of her life. She could not stop smiling, and she felt like she was floating. Mind you, she had downed quite a few glasses of their magnificent wine throughout the day. Mandy was also having the time of her life as many of the soldiers and other men were fawning over her to Tannor's disappointment. He was wanting to have Mandy all to himself, but she had many admirers. Tiny little Mandy was in seventh heaven. Jodar sat down in a one-person lounger finally and pulled Sheye onto his lap so they could watch all the festivities together for a moment in silence.

They were enjoying themselves but also were anticipating their wedding night together. Jodar was whispering naughtiness into Sheye's ear and was touching her everywhere that others could not see. Sheye was so hot and bothered by her husband's touch that she just wanted to escape and have him all to herself, but she knew the time would come soon, and there were still many people coming up and congratulating them on all that had occurred. Sheye was watching Mandy and then spotted Chanlon chatting with some of the council of the planet members not too far from where Mandy was flirting with several soldiers. Tannor was hovering beside her and kept trying to catch her eye. Poor Tannor. Jodar was disappointed for his friend. The knowing was not something that could be forced, and it seemed that Tannor was desperate to get Mandy to experience it with him. It was not to be though.

It was evident that no matter how long he captured her direct gaze, nothing was happening. Sheye realized that she had not introduced Chanlon to her best friend and noticed that Chanlon was getting very bored with the conversation with the council of the planets constant chatter of what was to come with their decision with Bionas now that Dorian was gone. Sheye turned to Jodar even though she did not want to leave his lap.

"I think it is time we rescue Chanlon. This is a party, and he looks like he needs a little entertainment. Let us introduce him to my spitfire Mandy. Nothing can brighten a bored man more than Mandy can."

Jodar smiled at his woman and agreed. He looked over to his leader and saw that he was desperately in need of being rescued.

They both stood up and excused themselves from the people around them and headed their way over to Mandy. Sheye entered Mandy's circle of admirers and grabbed her hand. "Sorry, gentlemen, but I must insist on stealing her away for a while. I will return her to you soon."

Mandy giggled and waved goodbye to the soldiers as Sheye led her over to Chanlon. "I love it here, darlin'. There are so many good-looking men, and believe it or not, they are all interested in me. Who knew?"

Sheye laughed with Mandy and stated, "I want to introduce you to the supreme commander of Sarbus. The poor man is utterly bored and needs your exuberance."

Mandy giggled again but then stopped Sheye when she realized who she was bringing her to meet. "Oh lord, do I look decent? Oh my, he is so attractive. I have been trying to catch his eye all day, but the man has constantly been surrounded by so many people. Do you think he will like me?"

Jodar bent way down to reach Mandy's face and looked her straight in the eye. "He will adore you."

Tannor was like Mandy's puppy dog, so he trailed along as well as Sheye and Jodar entered the group surrounding Chanlon. When

Chanlon turned, the relief that came to his face was almost laughable. Jodar cleared his throat as he addressed the group surrounding Chanlon. "Excuse me, gentlemen, we must talk to Chanlon about an urgent matter."

The group around Chanlon dispersed, and Chanlon turned to Jodar. "Thank you, my son. I was drowning in boredom with their constant banter about what we are now to do with Bionas."

Sheye stepped up and led Mandy behind her. "I want to finally introduce you to my best friend, Chanlon. Chanlon this is Mandy, my best friend. Mandy, this is Chanlon, the supreme commander of Sarbus."

Chanlon had to almost get on his knees to meet Mandy. Mandy was ecstatic to finally meet the extremely handsome man whom she was trying to catch his eye for the last several hours. Chanlon was very intrigued to meet this tiny, beautiful lady who was such a good friend of Sheye's.

"We finally meet, my tiny beauty." Chanlon reached for her tiny hand and gave it a kiss as he looked into her eyes to show his appreciation at who he was being introduced to.

Mandy bowed slightly and then looked into his eyes. "Your Eminence."

Suddenly, all the lights began to flicker, and Mandy and Chanlon were stunned into utter stillness as they looked into each other's eyes. The tables began to shake around them, and the room vibrated with a loud humming sound. Even the pillars of the room were quacking. Everyone turned in their direction to find out what was happening. An immense hot light exploded from Mandy and Chanlon. The intensity of the light had everyone blinded for a moment. The light turned into a soft glow as Mandy and Chanlon had to grab onto each other as their entirety of their memories entered each other's minds. Chanlon picked Mandy up in his arms subconsciously to protect her, but they never broke eye contact. The room shook, and the light vibrated around the two. They seemed to meld together like their minds were joining as well as their bodies. They lifted off the floor and began to float a few centimeters above it.

Then Mandy and Chanlon both began to spin in midair. The wind escaladed as the two swirled together. Everyone viewing had to shield their eyes as they watched the scene before them. Some people were screaming, and others just gaped in awe at what they were witnessing. Experiencing this situation of seeing an actual knowing happen was a sight to behold. A beam of light exited both Mandy and Chanlon up into the ceiling, and they were enveloped into the light and disappeared for a few moments. The room began to shake violently. Food and drink toppled off the tables onto the floor. The light diminished, and then Chanlon still holding tiny Mandy in his arms were placed gently back onto the floor before they both collapsed.

When it all ended, everyone was stunned at what they had just witnessed. Mandy and Chanlon were clinging to each other breathless and sweating. Suddenly, as if it were planned, everyone roared with amazement and surrounded Mandy and Chanlon. Sheye, Jodar, and Tannor were forced out of the area as everyone pressed in to congratulate the two on their knowing. Jodar grabbed Sheye and backed off so they would not be trampled. Tannor quietly exited the room. In the center of the throng of people, Mandy and Chanlon still stared at each other, and then Mandy threw her arms around the giant Chanlon in tears. "Oh my, so that is what it is all about. Kiss me, you big lug."

Chanlon immediately swooped down to claim Mandy's lips. The kiss that they all witnessed brought many blushes and gasps from the on-lookers. When Chanlon pulled away from kissing Mandy, he kept staring into her eyes and never broke contact. The smile that was on both their faces was an experience to behold. Without hesitation or care about who was around, Chanlon stood and carried Mandy out of the room toward his personal chamber without any apology or any embarrassment. All who were in the room did not even try to stop them. They understood. This was a day that would be written in the history books for all that had happened. Everyone was cheering and toasting and demanding more wine. What a day this had been. What stories and gossip would be spread around the worlds about what had all transpired on this magnificent day!

Sheye and Jodar were as much in shock as the rest of them. They now understood what everyone had seen with their knowing. Now they were able to see what had happened to themselves through Chanlon and Mandy. It truly had been a sight to behold. Jodar did not apologize either and scooped Sheye up in his arms and exited the hall heading toward their private chambers as well. What he had witnessed and in his happiness for himself and Chanlon aroused him so much that he had to have Sheye at that very moment. They entered their private chambers, and without any concern for their beautiful outfits, they tore them off and proceeded to ravage each other and enjoy skin on skin, lips on lips, body to body. After a few times at lovemaking that could be entered in the book of exceptional sex, they lay in each other's arms just stroking each other on their backs as they stayed entwined.

Sheye spoke first. "Poor Tannor. He wanted Mandy to have the knowing with him so terribly. I hope he is okay."

Jodar lifted his head up and looked into Sheye's eyes. "I have been thinking about that. Would you mind greatly if I went and looked for him to see if he is okay?"

Sheye traced her hand down Jodar's jaw and gave him a kiss. "I don't mind, my love. I am so very tired anyways, and he is your brother. Go take care of Tannor."

Jodar gave Sheye a mind-blowing kiss. "Sleep, my star. I will be back soon. Don't be surprised if I wake you up to enjoy your body more when I return. I can't seem to get enough of you." Jodar hesitated and then said, "Thank you."

Sheye smiled at the love of her life. "I look forward to your return, my warrior. Now go. Find Tannor and make sure he is okay."

Jodar placed a gentle but intensive kiss on her lips with the promise he would not be long. Sheye was asleep before Jodar even managed to leave their chambers.

Jodar thought he would find Tannor in a drunken stupor in his chambers, but he eventually found him talking with some members of the council of the planets. Jodar had never seen his friend so serious as he approached the group.

"Do you mind if I speak with Tannor a moment?"

The council members nodded and removed themselves from the presence of Jodar and Tannor. Jodar turned to his best friend. "Tannor, I am sorry for what has transpired. I know that you really wanted to experience the knowing with Mandy. Are you okay?"

Tannor scoffed and waved his hand. "Don't worry, my brother. I am to be sent on a mission to Bionas to understand how the people of the planet really view the demise of their leader. I will be too busy to care about Mandy. I may be gone for quite some time, so this was for the best."

Jodar stopped Tannor and frowned. Tannor was never a serious person as he was now, and he was never so focused. He worried for his friend as he spoke so callously about what had just happened.

"My brother, you are not okay with this. I feel your pain as if it were my own. It is understandable why you are hurting. Speak to me, my brother."

Tannor backed away from Jodar. "I am leaving tonight with a team. I understand that I am supposed to be Chanlon's personal guard, but that is impossible now. Explain to the supreme commander that he will need to find someone else to protect him. I will keep you updated with my progress, but I am going, Jodar. I can't stay here now." Tannor was damaged.

Jodar never realized how much his friend had wanted to have Mandy fall in love with him. He had never seen Tannor so destroyed.

Tannor left Jodar standing there after he slapped him on the shoulder and then walked away as Jodar watched him leave. Jodar could not stop him. Somewhere deep inside, he knew that this was what Tannor needed and did not step in to talk any sense into his best friend about leaving. When Jodar entered his chambers once more, he was saddened for his friend. He sat on the edge of the bed and reflected on what all had come about the last year of their lives. Here he was sitting on the edge of his bed with the woman of his dreams, who was now his life mate. He was now Chanlon's adopted son with all the power and responsibilities of running Sarbus with Chanlon.

Dorian, Broud, and Adrya had been taken care of and were no longer a danger to his planet. Now he had just lost his best friend to his sorrow for Prantus's star knows how long. Jodar sighed. Almost everything he dreamed for his life to be had come to pass. If only Tannor had been able to experience the knowing with Mandy, then absolutely everything would have been pretty damn perfect.

Jodar prayed to the fifth star of Prantus that his brother would be safe. He looked down at Sheye, who slept peacefully. Jodar smiled as he thought how blessed he was to have a woman who he loved with his entire being, love him back as much. Life could only go up from here. Jodar lay down and gathered Sheye to him. She cuddled in and moaned a little as she snuggled into his warm, strong embrace.

"I love you, my warrior."

Jodar sighed and pushed Tannor out of his thoughts. Tannor was a grown man after all. He would be able to accept what had happened and work it out someday for himself. Jodar brought himself back to the moment with this beautiful woman in his arms. He sighed again and thought about his present happiness. He snuggled his face into Sheye's neck as he whispered, "I love you more than you will ever comprehend, my star. All I can do is prove this to you every day forward from this moment on."

Epilogue

As Tannor left Jodar standing in the bay, watching him leave, he made sure his head was held high, his back was straight, and his gait was strong. Jodar had found his calling and his love. Tannor could not show Jodar how devastated he really was over what had transpired with Mandy and the commander. Jodar did not need to feel like he now had to look after him as well. Tannor's heart was shattered. He desperately wanted what Jodar had found. He never realized this until he saw how truly happy his best friend had become. Tannor realized that he was green with envy. He was so jealous that he knew if he stayed, it would cause a terrible rift between himself and his life brother. Tannor knew the only way he could cope with his feelings was to leave and busy himself in matters that did not have him around Jodar, Sheye, Mandy, and the commander. He would find his calling in life away from the pain that was now here on Sarbus.

Without waiting for his entourage, Tannor boarded a small craft that could take a modest group to Bionas. He did not wait for anyone as he entered coordinates for his intended flight path. Tannor then sat at the pilot's seat and lifted off. As the craft shot out of the landing bay, he took one look back at Sarbus as he left the planet's atmosphere. With a sigh, he turned back to the captain's chair and entered his ship into autopilot. He was bone tired and decided to lay down as the ship directed itself to its programmed destination. Tannor turned down all intercoms and alarms that might disturb him while he slept. He did not want to have Jodar try to contact him and talk him out of leaving. What Tannor did not realize, in his haste to leave and his mental condition not being at its best, he had entered a few miscalculations with the coordinates to Bionas. As he fell asleep, almost immediately, his ship shot off toward the asteroid belt that surrounded what remained of the two destroyed planets from eons past. As Tannor slept like the dead, he did not see or hear the red warning lights flashing throughout the ship's cabin as it closed in on imminent danger.

About the Author

J. T. Conners resides in a small close-knit community within Southern Alberta with her partner, two sons, her mother, and a small brood of animals. J. T. has been able to keep her sanity throughout the COVID-19 pandemic by releasing her energy through her writing, her work, and being with her family. She leads a simple life and dreams that her passion for writing fiction will be simply enjoyed as an escape for a few hours by many readers for years to come.

CPSIA information can be obtained
at www.ICGtesting.com
Printed in the USA
BVHW082057010522
635411BV00001BA/5